MANIFEST

ALSO BY BRITTANY CAVALLARO

A Study in Charlotte
The Last of August
The Case for Jamie
A Question of Holmes
Muse

with Emily Henry
Hello Girls

MANIFEST

BRITTANY CAVALLARO

KATHERINE TEGEN BOOKS
An Imprint of HarperCollins Publishers

Katherine Tegen Books is an imprint of HarperCollins Publishers.

Manifest

www.epicreads.com

Library of Congress Cataloging-in-Publication Data

Names: Cavallaro, Brittany, author. | Cavallaro, Brittany. Muse.

Title: Manifest / Brittany Cavallaro.

Description: First edition. | New York: Katherine Tegen Books, [2023] | Audience: Ages 14 up. | Audience: Grades 10–12. | Summary: Set in reimagined American monarchy, twelve-year-old Claire Emerson fights for her own freedom while also setting out to change the government from within, or burn it all down.

Identifiers: LCCN 2022031728 | ISBN 978-0-06-284029-5 (hardcover)

Subjects: CYAC: Government, Resistance to—Fiction. | Kings, queens, rulers, etc.—Fiction. | LCGFT: Alternative histories (Fiction) | Novels.

Classification: LCC PZ7.1.C464 Man 2023 | DDC [Fic]—dc23

LC record available at https://lccn.loc.gov/2022031728

Typography by David Curtis

Map by Daniel Hasenbos

22 23 24 25 26 LBC 5 4 3 2 1

First Edition

For Andrew, today and every day

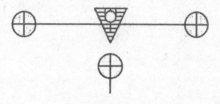

Why do gentlemen's voices carry so clearly, when women's are so easily stifled?

—Sarah Waters, *Affinity*

We are defined by the lines we choose to cross or be confined by.

—A. S. Byatt, *Possession*

ONE

From her window, Claire Emerson watched the carriage as it wound up toward Wardenclyffe Tower.

It moved slowly, more slowly even than the others she'd seen make this approach. To those visitors it must have looked like magic: the tower in the distance, cables and wires spiraling up its sides into the sky. And below it, light, like the constellations had all fallen to earth. A thousand light bulbs pushed into the black ground and burning bright.

If you plucked one, held it in your hand, you'd find there was no cord to feed it. The earth itself was crackling with power.

What better place from which to rule?

"Ten minutes, then," Claire was saying over her shoulder. "Five to see them the rest of the way here, and then five to have them cool their heels in the parlor. It's long enough for me to finish my meeting."

"But Mrs. Duchamp . . ." Helplessly the young maid held

up Claire's slippers again. "And your hair—there's to be a photographer, and pardon my saying, ma'am, but you look fit for the stables—"

Claire smiled as kindly as her patience allowed. "Georgiana, you're doing a lovely job, this being your first day, but if I want to be a horse, I'll be a horse. I need you to find me Margarete, and then you can see if they need any help . . ." *What on earth do maids do, and why do I have one again?* "Polishing furniture."

Georgiana hesitated. "Begging your pardon, ma'am, but this is the only room *with* nice furniture. Well, other than the Governor's sickroom, but everywhere else in this place is still all concrete and awful *laboratories* filled with God knows what—machines with wires running everywhere, making black magic, and I—"

"No polishing, then," Claire said. She eased the slippers from the girl's hands. "Why don't you, ah . . . go help in the kitchen? Go peel some leeks. Just find me Margarete first?"

"No need," Margarete said, stepping into the stateroom as Georgiana rushed out past her. "Oh no. Are you terrorizing the help again?"

Two weeks ago those words would've been as barbed as a fishing lure. But quite a bit had changed since then. Margarete wasn't the urchin that Jeremiah Emerson plucked from an orphanage and brought home to wash his floors for free. Now she was the private secretary to the lady wife of the

Governor of St. Cloud, and Claire saw to it personally that Margarete was paid a small fortune.

"Tell me where we're at with provisioning for the dinner tonight," Claire said, taking a seat at her desk. She put her feet into the embroidered slippers and wiggled her toes. Ten dollars for a pair like these, far too much for something that disappeared under your dress. They looked ridiculous against the poured-concrete floor, but she'd lost the only other pair of shoes she had sailing off the roof of the Palace of Fine Arts during her and Remy's escape from the General, in a glider made mostly from wishes and dreams.

These shoes had arrived in a little ribboned box. The enclosed note had read *Thank you for walking with us*. It was signed *The Daughters of the American Crown*.

If Claire's life this last month had been bound up like a story, she'd have thrown the book across the room by now.

Margarete was taking out a notebook and a nub of a pencil. "I must say, I thought it was rather brave to send the maid to the kitchens. It still looks a bit medieval down there. I don't think Augusta has two leeks to rub together."

Claire closed her eyes. "I almost told the girl to go lawn bowling. I still don't know why I need a lady's maid when I eat all my meals off this desk."

"Propriety," Margarete said, flipping a page. "The papers would have a field day."

"We have *mice.* I'm fairly sure I have small biting things living in my stockings. The papers aren't interested in that?"

"We've informed them that our court in exile is rather . . . rustic."

"That's of course why we have a pony living in the parlor," Claire said. "You know, when Georgiana told me I looked like a horse just now, I realized she might have thought that Smokey was my sister."

"The stable needs a new roof. Poor Smokey kept getting rained on."

"Poor Smokey keeps *pissing* on the *rug—*"

"This attitude, you know, is how you scared off the last one."

"The last horse?"

"The last *maid*, Claire."

"All *she* wanted to do was paint my face and"—Claire's face twisted—"ask questions about my whirlwind romance."

At that, Margarete finally met her eyes. There was pity there; well-meant, but it curled Claire's stomach. *No one wants to talk about Remy,* she thought, *least of all me.* How to explain a "romance" that had begun by being kidnapped by her province's Governor because he thought her able to grant his wishes with the touch of her hand, to make him a better leader? A romance that ended in a sham marriage, a marriage of convenience, as he lay dying on a boat in the middle of the lake?

Remy hadn't died—not yet, at least. But his feelings for

her had. Claire didn't know what was worse, that the two of them had fallen in love somewhere along the way, or that they had just as quickly fallen out.

Claire's own feelings were a stew of betrayal and longing that she had neither the time nor the inclination to sort out.

"Fine," Claire said to Margarete, after a moment. "We'll keep Georgiana, even though she told me I look like I need a feed bag. Provisions. What were you able to find today? Just an overview, the first of them will be here any moment."

"Do you think it's terrible," her secretary said, "that we're organizing a feast when our soldiers are toe to toe with the enemy at the border?"

"This is a biblical feast. This is a feast that's meant to save our lives."

Margarete sighed.

While the few hundred men who were loyal to their Governor stood guard at the border, watching the Livingston-Monroe guard towers and fingering the triggers of their lightning rifles, Claire had asked Margarete to take the youngest and greenest of them for a "special mission." They'd been tasked to scour the countryside for staff and supplies. They put out the word that if Duchamp was to properly govern from his temporary exile, he would need their help. Word was that his gratitude, when he was restored to his rightful home, would be immense. And fulfilled in gold.

The folk along St. Cloud's western border were, historically, not the most ardent supports of their Governor. At the best of times, they felt abandoned out here, so far from Monticello and its sprawling lake that brought so much of the trade to their narrow province—and now was not the best of times. Abigail Monroe, the wife of Livingston-Monroe's Governor and the real architect of their province's conflict with St. Cloud, had disappeared into a dungeon, and her province's fragile alliance with the General had held. The Livmonian soldiers would support the General's bid to overthrow Governor Duchamp, and even now their redcoat soldiers were swarming the border they shared with St. Cloud, waiting for a chance to invade. And the first fields they'd burn and pillage would be those here, around Wardenclyffe Tower.

St. Cloud's western citizens didn't like this, not one bit. "When is that whelp Duchamp going to grow up and throw some punches?" a farmer had furiously asked Margarete. When Claire arrived and took stock of their surroundings, she realized she didn't know who the citizenry hated more—the Duchamps, or Livingston-Monroe.

That was a problem.

So Margarete's handpicked squadron of soldiers went into the countryside to make nice. The farmers out here weren't used to this kind of personal attention from their Governor, and the response had been, at first, grudging interest. Some out-of-work locals were paid to convert Tesla's wireless laboratory into a working manor, laying wooden floors, assembling furniture, glazing windows. Coin began to flow into the local coffers. After they overcame their initial hesitation, St. Cloud's westernmost farmers realized they were happy to sell their produce to Wardenclyffe—why wouldn't they be, when Duchamp paid three times what they would get at market? But given the region and the season, what they had to sell was . . . corn.

So much corn. I'm going to grow an extra pair of ears if this keeps up.

Corn cakes. Corn fritters. Corn risotto and corn fricassee and a pork loin festooned with bright streamers of corn. Corn biscuits slathered with a sweet corn jam (you *could*, Claire had learned, make jam from corn), and some sort of hot corn stew that Augusta the housekeeper dreamed up. It was absurdly delicious, for all that it looked like slop.

Amid all this bartering, the soldiers on the western border kept to their orders: hold the line. Claire received reports from their commanders each day, studied her maps, moved counters, felt increasingly out of her depth. At night, she fell asleep reading the book on military strategy that one of her corporals had loaned her out of pity. She was uneasy wielding this much power—a consequence of having been so long powerless—and she wanted to get it right. To keep them all alive. Claire was doing her damndest, and still it was nowhere near enough, not with the King's visit so quickly approaching. She knew that the Duchamp court in exile reeked of weakness.

And then yesterday, she had awakened at dawn with a spark of an idea.

"Two milk cows and another for beefsteak," Margarete was saying, moving her pencil down the page. "A calf for tonight's fete. Got a fair price for those. A butter churn that Private Henderson bought off some old lady's porch. From the mayor of Tarrytown two miles south, a gift of lumber, clay for making bricks, lots of windows left from a church renovation—"

Claire sat up. "Enough materials to begin building housing for the soldiers?"

"I'd say so," Margarete said, "though we'll consult with the local builders to be sure. Our men will be happy. They've been sleeping on straw pallets on the floor."

"And Tesla?"

"Do you need him to design a better . . . straw pallet?"

"Has he," Claire said patiently, "eaten yet today?"

"Well, we've learned that he's allergic to corn."

"Dear God. He survived the General and the coup and the flight from Monticello and now we're going to kill him with corn. Do we have anything else he can eat?"

The day after Claire and Remy arrived at Tesla's hideaway, the inventor himself had arrived in a wig and cap, driving a smart little team of horses. He'd laden his cart down with barrels; though passersby might assume he was hauling sugar and flour and tea, those barrels had in fact been stuffed with cables and copper wire and glass.

("Did you enjoy pretending to be a cooper?" Claire had asked him.

Tesla had clasped his hands together. "Yes. It was *wonderful*.")

On the seat beside him had been Beatrix, rosy-cheeked as a farm girl, his "apprentice cooper." She'd been delighted by their days together on the road; she'd had endless access to Tesla's brain, and him with no distractions. He, in turn, had been impressed by her engineering chops, and upon their arrival the two of them had sequestered themselves in the largest of Tesla's workshops on the east side of the building to do whatever two strange geniuses did with their days. They emerged only for meals, dusty and sooty and perpetually pleased, heads close together over their meal as they sketched their next advancement on blueprint paper.

Claire hadn't quite forgiven Beatrix for abandoning their friendship for the Daughters of the American Crown's set of half-baked ideals, their "grab what you can and damn the cost" approach to women's liberation; she hadn't quite forgiven Tesla for keeping her in the dark about his sham alliance with the Livmonians, and then disappearing just as Claire's life was on the line.

And even though she didn't want to see either of them,

Claire was still the mess of contradictions she'd always been. Because she also couldn't quite forgive Beatrix for replacing her as Nikola Tesla's assistant.

Still, Claire woke up most mornings in the haze of a half dream. She'd been back in her grand escape, the glider dive from the top of the Palace of Fine Arts, the wind snapping the ends of her hair. She remembered Beatrix's hands stretching the canvas over the glider's bones, Tesla's lightning rifles in the hands of the soldiers guarding her back. Despite her fear, despite their betrayals, she couldn't shake the magic of those moments in the sky.

I have enough enemies. I should try, at least, to forgive my friends.

"I'll send away for some figs," Margarete was saying. "And what does Beatrix eat?"

"Anything and everything."

"And the preparations for tonight . . ." Again Margarete consulted her notes. "They're complete. More or less."

"More or less?"

"Tesla ran the experiment again this afternoon. He was quoting Shakespeare. 'When shall we three meet again? In thunder, lightning, or in rain?' And cackling, a bit. Have you heard that man cackle?"

"Do you think the show will have the desired effect?"

"I certainly hope so," Margarete said stoutly. "You've spent enough of our goddamn money on this exhibition."

Claire stood. "And you'll be the unseen hand ensuring all goes to plan. Meet with Augusta. Direct the soldiers. Make whatever decisions seem right, spend whatever coin you need."

"Remind me again why you're putting me in charge."

"Because I can't," Claire said, "be seen to be in charge."

"I don't understand."

"Tonight, I need to begin acting like an utter fool," Claire told Margarete, "so that the King trusts my husband to govern."

The reporter was a woman, and she had dark skin. A white man trailed behind her, laden down with bags and a camera on a stand.

"John Mackenzie, from the *St. Cloud Star*," the girl said, extending a hand.

Claire suppressed a smile. "Remy Duchamp, in exile," she said, and shook it.

The reporter laughed. "Point taken. John Mackenzie is my byline; my real name is Lizzie Cochrane. But the *Star* has me put on a man's mask so I can write the stories I want to."

"That's progressive of them."

"More like the opposite," Lizzie said, as the man behind her hung back. "They want plausible deniability in case anyone picks a bone with a story written by a girl. It's like that woman Eliza Blackwell. Have you heard of her? So determined to become a doctor that she did the whole course in trousers. They thought she was a boy. She got top marks all the way through. After she had earned her license, she gave her real name, and they tried to take it away."

Claire winced. "I'm . . . not surprised."

"Me neither. She held on to it, though, with her teeth. Practices here in Monticello. Every now and then she gets held up by the preachers as an example of the degradation of society. We have tea sometimes, her and me."

"That sounds like a good time," Claire said.

"It is." Lizzie waved her assistant over. "That's Bill, by the way. He's my Trojan horse. He gets us in the door, pretends to be both writer and photographer."

Bill nodded to them, and then busied himself with his tripod.

"And what do you pretend to be? His secretary?"

"Most times. But I figured we didn't need to put on the show for you."

"Yes," Claire said. "We have our own show here, running day and night. Nosebleed seats only."

Lizzie guffawed. "All right then. Let's get down to brass tacks, Mrs. Duchamp. Tell me about the government of St.-Cloud-in-Exile."

After the General's attempted coup, Claire and Remy had fled from Monticello-by-the-Lake on a boat that Rosa Morgenstern had chartered for their escape. They had gone north, and then west. After a short overland journey, they had arrived at Wardenclyffe Tower with five loyal soldiers, a physician, and the clothes on their backs.

Remy, more than half dead, was immediately installed in a makeshift sickroom.

He insisted that he did not want to see Claire, and so Claire saw him not at all. Not that it was a hardship. She didn't care about him, about his delicate constitution, about his delicate little moral compass. Remy kidnapped her, and then found a way to blame her for spying on him? *No*, Claire thought, the acid rising in her throat even now, the hundredth time she'd turned it over in her head. *It's even more unfair than that.* Remy *kidnapped* her, then the Daughters of the American Crown *blackmailed* her into spying on him, and still she did everything she could to keep the young Governor in power.

Remy, the boy king who had no desire to rule. No, he deserved *nothing* from her, especially not a visit to his sickbed.

(*I thought you were on my side*, a little voice inside her cried out. *I thought I finally had someone on my team.* What little faith he had had in her, this man who said he was in love.)

But Claire didn't wander the halls in black, mourning her sham of a marriage. Instead, she did something Remy had never done, not really: she took charge.

"Tell me," the reporter said, "about your fortress here. It looks impressive."

Wardenclyffe Tower had concrete floors, concrete walls, windows that refused to fully close. It had messes of wires and sparking fuses and light that came from nowhere, connected to nothing. It was staffed by a small group of men who worked tirelessly to send and receive messages from what they called "the dish," the gargantuan bowl on the top of the tower that traded information with every last corner of the First American Kingdom.

("Tell no one we're here," Claire had instructed them. At that, one of the men had ducked his head and said, "Ma'am, we've spent the last month workin' on sendin' a picture of an Irish setter to a station in Alta California using nothing but the air and these wires. We work magic here. Nobody much cares about you and your secrets.")

What Claire feared most was the General. His men were foaming like rabid dogs at the border, waiting for God knows what signal to come and overwhelm them at Wardenclyffe. Each night, Claire worried over a string of *what-ifs* as though they were rosary beads. What would happen to her if the Livmonians overtook St. Cloud? What would happen if the General was still alive? If he was, what if he still had the loyalty of enough Monticellan troops to shore up his position in the city? If he had their support, what if he made himself St. Cloud's figurehead, if he moved into the mansion and fortified it—if the King decided it was easiest to crown a military man who'd already taken over, rather than the sickly boy no one had ever much liked anyway?

And the moment he was crowned, to solidify his position, the General would find and kill that sickly boy, and his young wife with him.

"What do you know of the mess you left behind you, in Monticello?" Lizzie Cochrane asked, flipping through her steno pad. "Do you care to comment?"

Claire didn't.

There were too many unknowns, not enough spies loyal to the Duchamps. On no fixed schedule, messages came in from Captain Miller, who refused to disclose his location. On Monday, his report said that the General had reportedly died from his injuries; on Tuesday, that no, the General was reportedly alive and kicking and sleeping in Remy Duchamp's abandoned bed. Captain Miller went silent for two days and then cabled them from Alta California; three days later, he was laying low in Orleans.

Recently the messages had all been from Monticello. They appeared to be coming from one of the General's own signal towers. Claire didn't know what that meant, whether Miller had gone over to the General's side—even though she'd last seen him with his hands around the General's throat, she could believe Miller to be a turncoat. The General was his father, after all. Had he turned double agent? Was he feeding the Duchamps misinformation? Or was he simply a more skilled spy than they'd thought?

And then, three days ago, his messages had stopped altogether.

Despite her worries over Miller's loyalty, she'd read and reread his last report, looking for a reason for his disappearance. But his last message had only echoed what she'd read in the papers. In St. Cloud's capital, soldiers drew guns and lightning rifles on each other in the streets; preachers and teetotalers clashed with lightskirts; tourists, amazingly, still poured out of their trains to come visit the Fair. It was as though the rough-and-tumble Levee district had grown and spread overnight until its boundaries were the same as the city's. The Levee, where you could find a drink, a kiss, and a fistfight on every corner.

For all intents and purposes, Monticello had no ruler. St. Cloud had no ruler. At least not until King Augustus Washington arrived tonight at the Wardenclyffe Station on his Royal Limited train, then waved his scepter (at least, Claire imagined there would be a scepter) and put someone in charge of this godforsaken territory.

And it had better be Remy Duchamp. Not because she still loved him or thought she did. Not because she thought he'd make a good ruler.

Because he was her only chance of escaping this mess alive.

If Remy was restored to power, they'd have the protection of the King's military. She might persuade him that, if they could get past their mutual enmity, the two of them could forge some kind of alliance. She could help him strategize. She might, God forbid, be able to persuade Remy to take a passing interest in his citizens. To do a little good.

It was better than spending the rest of her life on the run

from the General's men, hunting down every loose end that might come back to wrap itself around his neck.

And as Lady Duchamp, wife of the Governor, all she'd have to contend with would be the desperately corrupt Daughters of the American Crown pulling her strings and her madman of a father off proselytizing in the streets.

In comparison, that would be a holiday.

Besides, it was in the interest of St. Cloud to have an uninterested ruler rather than a downright evil one. The General, if he managed to wrest power from the Duchamps, would immediately ramp up his campaign of "insurance" payments from local businesses, diverting money from education and infrastructure to beef up St. Cloud's military. Then he'd throw away those soldiers' lives in war.

For the General only knew *more* and *bigger*. His thirst for power could not be slaked; it would invade every corner of St. Cloud, from its military barracks and livery stables to the bedrooms and bank accounts of its citizens.

Once, in a council meeting, she'd heard him throw his support behind a bill that would let men commit their wives to insane asylums and take possession of their money.

"It shouldn't just be wives. Fathers should have the right to do that too," the General had said at the council table, casually, as Claire tried very hard not to vomit.

No, she had one choice, and one choice only. She had to

persuade King Washington to keep Remy Duchamp in power, and she had to do it tonight.

Claire revealed exactly none of this to Lizzie Cochrane.

Instead, she folded her hands and smiled a practiced smile. "We are looking to the needs of the people on our western border as they suffer the consequences of this war of western aggression. Once we've been assured that our defenses are strong—and it's important to note that they *are* strong, shored up by the fearsome technology that Nikola Tesla has granted us—we have a plan to consolidate our power, one that will be revealed in time. I promise you that Livingston-Monroe will be drummed out of our province, then *kept* out, and that Governor Duchamp will again rule from the mansion. We look forward to the confirmation of King Washington's support."

She had practiced that little speech in the mirror all day. She liked it; it sounded like a story that should be true.

At the very least, it was better than the truth. *We have a few dozen soldiers, a bunch of magic lightning rifles, a half-dead pouting Governor who refuses to take charge and instead does math equations from his bed for fun, two cows for milk and one for beefsteak and a pony in the parlor—and oh, by the by, a brilliant tactical plan that I came up with after yelling into my pillow until I was hoarse.* Her voice still hadn't entirely recovered.

Not that the reporter seemed to notice; she was scribbling

notes on her steno pad. "And Governor Duchamp is in agreement with these plans?"

"These plans came from his brilliant tactical mind," Claire said. "I'm just his helpmeet."

"You know," said Lizzie, holding up her pen, "there could be a story to be told here about a woman rising far above her station. A woman who sees a rare opportunity in a man's world to take charge—and takes it."

What happened to that fellow feeling, us two girls against the world? "Charge? I take no charge. I have no authority here."

"You *are* the one talking to me."

Claire smiled grimly. "I am only a man's mouthpiece, nothing more."

How sad, the truth in that statement.

"No, follow my thinking here. An inventor's daughter, a surprise engagement, after which the most powerful man for a hundred miles is *immediately* shot in the chest—then a wedding that takes place on open waters, in secret. . . ." She spread her hands like she was putting up a name on a marquee. "'Claire Duchamp: Meet the Real Power Behind the Crown.' Why, our readership would double overnight."

And our male citizens, who think a cat would be a better ruler than a woman, would desert Governor Duchamp once and for all. Even if the General really is dead—knock on wood—they'd dig him up and stick his bones on the throne.

Lizzie Cochrane clearly knew that as well as Claire did. After a beat, Lizzie said, "Of course, I won't write that story if I have a more interesting angle. Like an exclusive interview with Governor Duchamp."

"Governor Duchamp is still convalescing from the injuries he suffered at the hands of the Livmonian soldiers," Claire intoned. She knew she sounded like a history book, one translated badly from another language. "My husband is feeling strong and hale, but out of an abundance of caution, he is conserving his energy for his summit with King Washington tonight."

"So, no visitors."

"No *questions*," Claire said. "Though he'll be happy to sit for a photograph for your excellent newspaper."

They eyed each other.

Unexpectedly, Lizzie grinned. "What fun you are. I could do this all day, Mrs. Duchamp. What if I told you that, unless I walk away with photographic evidence that our Governor is sound and well, my headline tomorrow will announce him dead? Or at least dead until proven alive."

Claire folded her hands. She felt horribly exposed. *Someone in that room with him alone—someone who would ask him how he feels about me.* "You seem to have invented quite a few possible stories," she said to Lizzie, stalling for time. "Is this how the news is made? You toss around different versions of the truth until you find one that will sell papers?"

"You must be unfamiliar with my work. I've set up shop in the worst parts of Monticello to write about the rights of garment workers. For months I did their daily labor. I won their trust. I advocated for reforms in my series on their plight. Why, I've even lived among the elizabeths—yes, of course I know that word—to write about women working toward the right to rule. Good women, selfless women—"

Clearly she hasn't met Rosa Morgenstern.

"—and for them, for victims, for the disenfranchised, for the people who need my help, I always find a way to help them tell their stories. I'll go to *war* for someone who needs my help. But you clearly don't need it, Mrs. Duchamp. You're doing just fine."

Claire stood. Her feet were crammed into the too-small slippers that Rosa Morgenstern had sent her, shoes meant for small delicate steps around a sitting room, shoes that would never let a woman run. She toed one off, then the other, and the concrete below was hard and cold.

Really, it was an odd sort of relief to be seen for what she was. An opportunist. A strategist. If you were generous, perhaps you'd call her a survivor. But that was all she'd ever been. In her father's house, and in Remy Duchamp's, she'd lived underneath a man's hard hand.

Like she was picking a scab, Claire let her thoughts return again to her father. Her father on that fishing trawler, ridiculous in his priest's robes, so certain of his right to hurt her however and whenever he wanted.

No, Claire would never let a man hurt her again.

"Yes," she echoed. "I'm doing just fine. Why don't you come and meet my husband? And then you might as well stay for dinner with the King. I do hope you like corn chowder."

TWO

The first day they'd arrived at Wardenclyffe Tower, Remy Duchamp had been hallucinating that he was the god of rain. No, the god of thunder. "Let the heavens open!" he had shouted. "Smite the heathens!" He had hollered all the way down the concrete halls, this wasting-away man kicking his legs in too-expensive trousers. The three radio operators escorting him had to tie him to his bedpost to keep him from doing them harm.

None of it was his fault. His gunshot wound had begun to fester, and he was in the grip of a mighty fever.

Claire had trailed behind them, calm. She was no stranger to men trumpeting their manic displeasure. (Though she found, when she looked down, that she was worrying a handkerchief between her hands like some soothsaying crone.) She watched as the radio operators secured the Governor with rope and gave them a nickel each for their silence before they left. She didn't know where anyone's loyalties were anymore, and she wasn't taking any chances.

When Remy had finally quieted, when he finally looked at her, his eyes were merciless and unseeing. "You pity me."

Claire had no reason to lie to him. "Of course I pity you."

"Get *out*," he had roared, and when she didn't, he kicked his bedpan across the room. It smashed into the wall beside her; she was lucky it had been empty.

She left. She didn't have to be told twice. And in the days that followed, all Claire had to do was pass his sickroom door for there to be a commotion. He would yell, throw his things; nurses would rush in and out; a doctor would shout for help, for calm.

I have no idea how he knows I'm there, she thought, *he can't see me through the walls. . . .*

I hate him. I hate him for this.

For now Remy sincerely believed that Claire had never loved him at all. That she'd playacted her affection in the interest of saving her own neck. How rich it was. This, from the man who had kidnapped her—he had the temerity to be *offended* by what she might have done to survive.

But that wasn't the worst of it. No, the worst part was that Claire had come to love him. It had come over her suddenly, like a fever, and driven her deeper and deeper into a conflict she wanted no part of, all to save her life and his. And then, in the moment of their escape, Remy had learned that the D.A.C. had been blackmailing Claire into passing on information about his actions, and he accused her of betrayal.

She had frozen over with the shock of it.

Why was everything inside her always all wrong? Some small part of her loved her father despite what she'd suffered at his hands. She loved her best friend, Beatrix, despite her betrayal, loved Tesla despite his disregard for her life. But this man in the sickroom, this boy king who wanted no part in securing the welfare of his own people, or even, it seemed, in safeguarding his own—this man who had lingered on the edge of death for days now, never quite stepping over the line, waiting for something, and what, she didn't know—all she could do was *hate* him.

It was as though Remy's poor health required her to forgive him for the terrible things he had done to her, and that guilt only made her angrier, and all that ended up happening was that she stewed in the feeling like she was a very meager chicken and her frustration was a very large pot.

Today, she did her best to keep her face clean of any real emotion. "This way," she said, and Lizzie Cochrane and Bill the photographer trailed her all the way to the sickroom door. The halls, thankfully, were empty—all hands were on deck in the kitchen, preparing for King Washington's fete. Those who weren't cooking were sweeping the floors of their ever-present dirt and dust, or beating clean the curtains they'd made from sailcloth someone had found in the yard, or, Claire fervently hoped, off somewhere hiding the pony.

"Would you give me a moment?" she asked, her hand on the knob. "I'd like to see if he's awake."

"Of course," the photographer said, perhaps taken with her wifely devotion. Lizzie narrowed her eyes and nodded.

In the sickroom, Claire found herself squinting in the low light. Like so many of the neglected corners of Wardenclyffe Tower, this room had a lingering smell of dark, loamy earth. In here it felt like twilight even at full noon. At least it stayed cool when the heavy, humid St. Cloud air outside left you as wet as a fish in a pond.

But the day had ended, the temperature fallen. Without quite looking at the Governor, she passed his bed to open the window.

"I don't want you here," he said.

The night air spilled in like a secret.

"That's unfortunate," Claire said, keeping her voice light, "because here I am."

"Get out."

This man, with his dandy's vocabulary, his European turns of phrase, reduced again to two of the most guttural words in the English language.

She took a step toward him. Someone had brought in a

rug, she saw now, a little threadbare number beside his bed so that he could stand at his shaving table without catching a chill. An armchair, an armoire, a chair for his caretaker angled next to his bed. His mattress had been remade with different sheets, worn but soft looking, and a pile of quilts waited at his ankles for him to grow cold.

Claire felt another familiar rush of guilt: she hadn't asked for any of these small comforts. His night nurse must have seen to it.

On the floor beside the bed, an ewer filled with cool water. Claire took it and perched on the mattress.

Finally she allowed herself to look at him.

Her husband: a wax doll with chapped and darkened lips, his chest wrapped round in bandages. He'd closed his eyes so he didn't have to look at her.

"We have guests." She kept the hesitance out of her voice, worked to shape each word to sound as though she spoke to a dear friend. It was an impossible task. (*How am I this hurt?* she wondered. *How has he hurt me this much?*) "They're just outside."

He winced. "Tell them to leave."

"Remy," she said, "it's a reporter and photographer from the *St. Cloud Star*, and if we don't present a united front, if we can't convince them you aren't seriously ill—"

"Dying," he said.

"—seriously ill, King Washington's support of your cause

will mean nothing. And who knows if we can even drum up his support?"

"I don't care."

Claire didn't know what Lizzie Cochrane could and couldn't hear through the door. She leaned forward and whispered, dark and low, "If you are deposed, the General will hang you by a rope in front of your own people while they *cheer*. Do you want to give him that pleasure?"

He opened his eyes.

For a moment—for just that moment—he was the boy she remembered from the day of the Barrage, the two of them before the cheering Fair crowds, tall and strong and true. She knew that Remy had never been considered handsome by his citizens. Beatrix, a connoisseur of beautiful people, had gone so far as to say she'd never let a librarian-looking fellow like the Governor put his hands on her.

But Claire's first impression of Remy had been of a kind of appealing slimness, an angularity—long fingers, long legs. Ardent eyes in a long and thoughtful face. She'd been surprised by it, the rush of feeling she'd had when she first saw him, the desire to fling her arms around him like he was some long-lost companion of her youth, found again at her door.

For that moment, he was beautiful again, and then an eyeblink later he wasn't.

Yes, Remy had wasted away during his long and painful

recovery from his gunshot wound; yes, he had all the terrifying signs of blood infection. Dark and spidering veins radiated out from below his bandages.

But that wasn't why Claire was so unnerved. This Remy Duchamp had a weedy look in his eyes. He looked craven. He looked hateful.

He's ugly in a way he never was before.

"What do you . . . require of me?" he asked, and coughed. There was an empty glass on his shaving table. She filled it from the ewer and offered it to him.

He hesitated, then accepted it with shaking hands. When he sat forward to drink, she stacked pillows behind him to support his back. "I need you to pretend to be two things," she told him. "Healthy, and in love."

"In love?"

"I'm not locking you into a cellar full of scorpions. I'm not asking you to tap-dance in the nude in front of Nikola Tesla. I'm asking you to pretend that you don't hate me."

"There's a difference between indifference and love," he said, and took a careful sip. His shirt was unbuttoned at the throat; she watched the cords of his neck as he swallowed. "I don't know if I'm well enough to pretend."

"If you're well enough to point out that distinction, you'll be just fine." It was so hard to keep her voice light, unaffected. It was so hard not to want to howl about the unfairness of it all: how he had thrown her to the wolves and then blamed her when she didn't let them eat her up. "As for pretending to be healthy—we'll just pass your current appearance off as, say, recovering from a slight complication. Perhaps the flu. And anyway, you'll be well enough in no time, so it's not a lie, is it?"

"Claire," he said.

She couldn't make herself look at him.

"Do not pretend," he said, "that you desire for me to get better. You're waiting on me to die so that you may consolidate your power."

She stood. Instead of boxing his ears, she used her hands to fluff his pillows, to pull up the sheet to his chest. "I could have left you on that boat with my father. I could have thrown you overboard. I could have simply not called for a doctor, and watched you bleed to death in the cabin! I could—" Shaking with rage, she did up the neck of his shirt. "I could have smothered you *with this pillow* at any point in the last week! But no. You're right. My patience has untold depths. I am, in fact, planning to wait the forty or fifty years it will take for you to die happily, in your bed, surrounded by fat grandchildren."

Outside the door, a low rustle. Claire bit her lip, hard—she had been shouting.

"If you die—" She fought to keep quiet. "If you die, we'll be annexed by Livingston-Monroe. The General will take power, or the D.A.C. will. And what will that look like?

Worse than you, somehow! *You* don't have any policies of your own, other than a vague interest in science and invention and perhaps some sympathy for European immigrants. You don't care about your farmers. You don't care about your poor. You don't arm your borders. You let the General shake down businesses for his 'protection' and you look the other way. You're bad enough, but—"

"Thank you?"

"—but the General will be worse." She set her jaw. "You might not know what you're doing, but he does. I guarantee it. And I'm serious about the hanging. Or maybe he'll just shove you out of a very high window, if I don't do it first."

Remy seemed taken aback at the vehemence of her argument. "It is good," he said, "to finally know your true feelings about me."

"I have *always* been honest about my feelings," she said. "You fool."

He shut his eyes, took a breath. "Do you have a plan, then, other than threatening my already tenuous existence? What is it that you want from me?"

"I want you to stay alive. So that I can stay alive. I want you to *want to stay alive*, and to do that, you have to be madly in love with me, you utter pea brain."

Before he could protest again, she was flinging open the door.

"May I present Miss Cochrane," Claire said, ushering in the reporters, "and her photographer, Mister, ah—"

"His name isn't important," Lizzie said. Claire saw her take it all in: the threadbare room, the stale, sweet smell of illness, the hollow-eyed Governor. "Good to meet you, sir."

Remy managed a small, self-deprecating smile. "Forgive me if I don't stand to greet you," he said. "I'm suffering the indignities of a flu. Though I am blessed, of course, with the very best caretaker one could ever wish for."

He extended a hand to Claire, and she took it fast, before they could see how much he was shaking. His palm was hot and dry, and she could feel the sudden jump of his pulse, as though she had the power to bring him back to life.

Maybe she did.

"It must be difficult to marshal your forces from a sickbed," Lizzie said, watching the two of them.

Claire fluttered her eyelashes a bit. "Oh," she said, "my husband has such a sharp mind that he could be at *death's door* and still solve quadratic equations. Isn't that right, dear?"

"You flatter me, *darling*," he said, with the slightest edge.

If that's how you're going to play it . . .

"*I* do no such thing. Why, you could be in the throes of—of cholera, and I imagine you'd still fling yourself up on the horse and lead our troops to victory! Metaphorically, of course. The horse being your campaign desk."

If he were any stronger, his grip would have broken several of her fingers. "She's quite the enthusiast," Remy said to Lizzie Cochrane.

"Really, the love we share, it lights me up like—like a Ferris wheel," she said, beaming.

Remy looked like he was either about to laugh, or vomit.

"Speaking of electric lights, where *is* Mr. Tesla?" Lizzie asked, pulling out her notepad again. "I expected to see him. Governor Duchamp?"

Claire stiffened. Questions like these, about logistics, were dangerous. One misstep, one contradiction of something she'd already told the reporter, and the world would know that Remy wasn't in charge of his own province.

To her surprise, Remy gave the reporter a knowing look. "Miss Cochrane, you couldn't possibly expect for me to provide you with the location of my secret weapon."

Her gaze sharpened. "Do you refer to Tesla himself? Or one of his inventions?"

"Darling, you've said too much already." Claire made a show of pulling his hand to her chest. "Haven't you?"

"Ah," he said, "Miss Cochrane here is such a disarming figure, I'd nearly wanted to give up the whole game to her."

"You'll have enough time to do that later. They're staying for dinner with the King tonight."

This time, he managed to squeeze Claire's fingers hard enough that she yelped. She turned it into a horrible sort of feminine squeal. "Oh," she gasped, tears in her eyes, "I'm just so excited to host my first state dinner!"

Lizzie Cochrane was looking at Claire like Claire had

cut off her own head and offered it to her on a platter. "I see," she said.

"My wife is a woman of many passions." Remy dropped her hand. "I imagine there is to be a photograph now, yes?"

Before Lizzie Cochrane could reply, Bill the photographer stepped forward, his camera held up to his chest. "Begging your pardon, Governor," he said, "but I'd be fine with you having a chance to clean yourself up first, seeing as we know we surprised you a bit with our coming. Specially since this will be front page, above the fold, and all. Want it to be a good one."

"Why, thank you," Remy said, sounding genuinely touched.

For her part Lizzie looked murderous. *It would have been a much better photo*, Claire thought, *the Governor ill and languishing, his idiotic, shoeless young wife beside him—*

But Lizzie didn't contradict the photographer. Perhaps she didn't have the authority she thought she did.

Well, that makes two of us.

"You're so kind," Claire told Bill, rushing over to take his arm. *He likes a devoted wife, right? I'll give him one.* She covered her mouth, seemingly overcome by her own boldness. "Really. We'll send for his valet, we'll have a lovely dinner with the King—why, I still can't believe our luck!—and then perhaps we can, the three of us, pose for you after. We'll be in our very best, so it'll make for a *beautiful* photo. I even have a new dress for the occasion!"

Claire did not have a new dress for the occasion. She had two dresses, full stop, and the other had a scorch mark on the back from standing too close to the fire. *At least that's the one they haven't seen.*

Over the photographer's shoulder, she met Lizzie Cochrane's gaze.

Claire deliberately let her smile drop. The two of them studied each other like a pair of bare-knuckle boxers.

Go on, test me, Claire thought at her. *I spent my whole life acting a feminine fool in front of my father to keep myself alive. I don't give up. I don't get tired. I can go on like this for years.*

"Dinner, then," Lizzie said curtly. Bill nodded and followed her out.

And though she knew she shouldn't, Claire called after them, "I hope you like corn chowder!"

After the door shut, Remy cleared his throat. "You were—"

"Vapid?" she said, scrubbing her face with her hands. "Disgusting?"

"I was going to say marvelous," he said. When she looked at him, he was studying his nails. "But I could revise my answer, if you'd like. You were . . . heroically insipid."

A week ago it would have made her laugh. Today, it made her want to stake him through the heart. "Remy."

"Yes?"

"Do you realize your hands have stopped shaking?" She

took a step toward him. "And the veins in your neck—I don't see them anymore."

Wincing, he sat up a bit straighter. "Are you saying that your very presence has cured me?"

Claire thought of her father, holding out his hands for her blessing. She thought about her fingers fastening Remy's collar, her fingers intertwined with his. "Did you even *want* to recover? Do you now?" she asked, and when, outraged, he began to counter her, she put a finger to his lips. "Remy. Tell me. Do you want to . . . to, well, *live*?"

His skin was cooler than it had been even minutes ago, his blue eyes clearer. She fought the urge to slip her palm against his cheek.

A wall of ice had formed between the two of them when Remy discovered that she'd passed along information about him to the D.A.C. Claire couldn't quite believe his anger at her. She'd been his prisoner. She'd had no loyalty to him.

She couldn't forgive his lack of forgiveness.

And that wall between them grew thicker and colder with every passing day they did not speak, did not touch. Did not lock eyes with that fiery recognition she felt now.

What was this thing between them, that turned and twisted, grew and diminished? It would be the end of her.

"There has been . . . so much uncertainty," he said, low, and with a sound of despair he pulled her hand away from his face. "I never wanted the throne, Claire. And perhaps

I was too naive to know it before this, but I'd never before thought that . . . my dethroning would likely also mean my death. But I became used to the idea. And more and more, it seemed easier to . . . to let myself sleep, to let the bullet wound take me where it would. . . ."

In the Palace of Fine Arts they had held each other in the dark, they had made vows. They had told each other to be strong. Claire had thought they'd been planning their future.

But Remy had been saying goodbye.

Had it been love or desperation that had led her to leave her heart in his hands? They had known each other for days; he had sequestered her away in his palace; they had spoken only a handful of times, but candidly. He had asked her questions, believed in her intelligence. He had been beautiful, if he wasn't now.

But wait. Was it just the angle from which she regarded him, or was his brow higher, suddenly, his eyebrows bold, his jawline square and strong?

"If I died, I knew you would . . . you would die as well. I could not care. I cannot care. What I have lost—my father, my sister, I have no allies, and you have every reason to run—" His eyes were glassy, wet. "And you should have run, Claire. We were strangers. We *are* strangers. Perhaps we each just needed a friend and saw more than what was there. For no matter that I feel as though I know you, I do not."

"I don't understand, Remy. What are you trying to say?"

"I don't know." To her surprise, he laughed. "I have felt too many things and all of them hold knives to the others."

"Remy," she said again. "Do you want to live?"

"I do not . . ." He looked away, tracing the stitching of his quilt. "I do not want you—I do not want my people to suffer."

"Then help me. Help me."

"How? I am still useless. I am weak. It would take strange magic to make me what I was. I—"

His head snapped up. "Your father believed your touch could grant his wishes."

"Yes," Claire said, not following.

"Never mind *your* wishes."

"Yes."

"Then grant mine," he said, fumbling her hands into his. "Make me well. Make me Governor, earn me King Washington's support. Make me a good man, a leader of men. And from my throne I'll grant you the freedom you so desire. You will have the protection of being my wife, and as long as I live, I will ensure you will live your life as you choose. Your power will help me keep mine. And you won't be forced to pretend that you love me, or that we love each other. This I promise."

She swallowed hard. *He does not love me,* a small voice inside her said, and she squashed it.

Claire had begun as his prisoner, and she was his prisoner now. A captive who would die without his protection. And he was prisoner to her, as well: without her intelligence and her will, Remy would have died weeks ago.

They were bound together by circumstance. Love could not grow from such cold concrete.

"We would be friends, then," she said.

"Yes. We would be friends."

One final time it rolled over her, a dark wave of resentment, and she saw then how things had broken between them. It was too easy to hate him for what the world made them do. "What if I say no?" she asked, just to see what he would say.

To her great surprise, Remy pulled away from her touch, climbed up from his bed. At the shaving table he braced himself, looking down at the brush and razors and cream. His legs were unsteady, but his voice was sure. "You won't say no," he said.

"I won't?"

"Neither of us can say no." He lifted the longest razor from the table and tilted it to and fro, looking at his reflection. "This—these scraps are all this world has left us. We must make a meal of it."

Claire forced herself to nod her assent.

"Should you call for a valet?" he asked her. "I should like to be presentable to meet the King."

THREE

Wardenclyffe Tower was not a palace, and it had no interest in being one.

This posed certain . . . problems when one needed to host a king for dinner.

Tesla's personal laboratory had been a place for transatlantic communiqués received at midnight, for thirty-foot towers playing games of lightning tag. It had been a place where monocled investors roamed its grounds, wondering aloud how much power their money could buy. And now that the Duchamps had moved in, it was a place for soldiers and builders and servants and advisers milling about in its vast, echoing vaults. Its smaller laboratories had been made bedrooms, its spartan kitchen made to turn out small, simple meals for its people.

Not *feasts*.

When Claire Duchamp had ordered Wardenclyffe Tower's largest chamber made into a ballroom, she'd understood its limitations. In the past, in this space with a ceiling as high as a cathedral's, Tesla had undertaken his most dangerous experiments, and he had done so on a grand scale.

Here he had tested the generators that were later installed at Niagara Falls by the province of New Columbia; no one had known, before Tesla, that a waterfall could power an entire city.

No one except Remy Duchamp. He had paid for the endeavor.

It was the story Claire instructed the attendants to tell to the King and his men as they were ushered into Wardenclyffe's halls. They were to do so in hushed tones, as though they were speaking of a great, terrible secret.

When they threw open the double doors, their guests were meant to cower at what they saw.

Rumors of the King's love for pleasure and comfort and splendor—indeed, some called it debauchery—were well known throughout his kingdom. When Claire learned the precise date that the King's train and his entourage would be pulling into Wardenclyffe Station, she knew that there was no way she could marshal the money and resources she needed to meet his expectations. The King had danced in a thousand ballrooms, supped at far finer tables than hers. Even if she emptied all the Governor's coffers, she could only produce the palest imitation of the King's usual weekday meals.

Claire had to take a different approach.

She'd spun out her plan to Augusta the housekeeper and to Georgiana, her new maid, and while they'd shaken their heads at her to begin with, they'd come around in the end.

The housekeeper had enlisted the tower operators to lift and haul and arrange the room. They grumbled about being taken from their duties, but Claire knew they were just spending their days waiting for messages to Wardenclyffe that rarely came. As long as one man was there to receive them, the rest could do some labor.

Claire had sent a request down to Tesla, their elusive landlord, and he and Beatrix had spent a merry afternoon devising a design for their set. ("Conductors," Tesla had said, "we'll need conductors," and Beatrix had made a joke about hiring an orchestra.) In consultation with Georgiana, Margarete brought in a team of farm girls from the surrounding area—half of them to assist with dressing the room, and the other half to sew costumes to kit out the staff.

Livery, Claire thought. *Not costumes.* Even though it rather felt as though they were staging an elaborate play.

It certainly wouldn't be what the King was accustomed to. Rather than long, gracious tables set with elegant linen and silver, rather than massive epergnes crafted from massive odiferous flowers that blocked one's view of their neighbors, rather than the courses brought out and served from platters by the very finest English butlers (for here, in the First American Kingdom, one's butler must always be British), the King would find himself instead dining in a veritable museum of invention and industry.

The Duchamps greeted the King, not outside Wardenclyffe as was exactly proper, but within the building's sad excuse for a foyer. She hoped that Remy's health was a good enough reason for them not waiting out in the night air; it was an excuse that had the added benefit of being true.

She'd half expected the King to sweep inside in his full robes of office, the long ermine-trimmed cape, the coronet on his head. While the monarchies of Spain and England and the Netherlands had all stepped quietly away from the trappings of royalty, the Americans had instead embraced them. This was a land of plenty; why shouldn't the King express his country's boundless capacity for luxury? He should, and he did.

But no, tonight the King wore a suit of clothes—the finest serge and wool, with a beautiful silk lining on his overcoat—and he wore them carelessly, like a rogue. She was surprised by how young he looked. The King was nearing thirty, but his face didn't have the same floridness that other men of power had, that which came with living off the fat of the land, off cream and wine and sugar. He looked as though he went riding every morning before breakfast and then ate a dozen eggs standing up, and really Claire knew that she shouldn't be surprised at his appearance of health. This was a man who traveled with not just his servants and his advisers and even an amusing courtier or two; this was a man who traveled with an entire sports team.

Which, of course, brought an additional complication.

After she had exchanged the official greetings with the King, Remy's hand on the small of her back, she begged an excuse (prettily, she hoped) not to follow the King to the dining room immediately. His baseball team was waiting outside for their cue to enter, and wouldn't it be lovely if she could say a small private hello to her brother?

Her brother, Ambrose, who had abandoned her to the whims of their good-for-nothing father so he could play for the King's touring team.

The boys on the team wore a dress version of their uniforms, a beloved eccentricity of the King's. Their jerseys were a smart navy and had their names and numbers embroidered on the back in silver thread. On their heads they wore their dress caps, piped in silk. Claire had known from Ambrose's letters that the team had initially despised these uniforms, but they'd come to understand the benefits of wearing them. Any young man in Washington ball club kit could walk into a bar, and within a minute, he'd have a girl on his arm and a drink on the house. There was no mistaking a man dressed like that for anyone else.

She nodded to the teammates as they entered, and the boys pulled off their caps and inclined their heads in turn. Surprisingly, some of them had well-dressed women on their arms. She hadn't thought the team traveled with wives and girlfriends.

Any moment she'd see Ambrose. Any moment she'd have to come to terms with his loud and forceful indignation.

Beside her, Remy had settled into what she'd once considered his standard expression, the one he'd often worn in front of his court: an elegant boredom that was somehow deeply French. Tesla had produced for him a cane, a fine one with a brass handle, and he leaned on it with both hands, and perhaps that was the reason he was still standing, but his health still seemed a marvel. Perhaps his well-being was an act. It was easy to forget he had been raised in a household that had assumed he'd one day come to power, and taught him at least a few skills to help him keep it.

Just as she gave in to the urge to whisper in Remy's ear, "Can you stand a little longer?"—it wouldn't do for him to faint in front of their guests—she saw him. Ambrose. He was bringing up the rear, and despite everything, her heart turned over to see him. Her shining brother, with his broad shoulders and his dark curly hair and his six-foot frame, walking toward her. What she would have given to see him only months ago.

Tonight Claire lifted her chin, extended her hands to him in greeting. "Brother," she said. It was the most formal of receptions.

The last time she'd seen him, she'd been drugged and dragged out to a baseball diamond in the dark and cold, on her brother's orders. When she'd awakened on the ground, Ambrose had lectured her on how unwomanly her behavior was.

Tonight, her brother had the good grace to appear abashed. (*He gets no credit for that small mercy,* Claire thought ferociously, *and I will give out no half marks.*) "Hello, penguin," he said, taking her hands and kissing her cheek. "I suppose I should call you brother," he said to Remy, in a voice that was only this side of polite.

"Yes," Remy said. "Can you even imagine." He smiled lazily, the smile of a young lord of the manor. With his bejeweled cane, he looked like the very worst of roués, the kind that slept until supper before going about a busy evening of seducing all the maids.

Ambrose's eyebrows flicked up. He looked to Claire, but she only inclined her head. "We must see to our guests," she said.

"Go on," Remy told him, as though Ambrose was a toddler with a toy hoop.

Claire's brother cleared his throat, then jogged to catch up with the rest of his team.

"Thank you," she murmured as the King's servants filed by them, laden down with luggage.

"For what?" Remy was looking straight ahead, but she saw his lips twitch. "I was just incredibly rude to your brother."

"I know," she said, and turned to take the shortcut to the dining room.

"Miss Emerson!"

Claire halted. No one had called her that in weeks.

"Ah, I think you are addressing my wife—the lady Duchamp?"

"My mistake," the voice said smoothly. "I knew her before, in another life."

"And now here we are, in that brave new world." Claire turned. "Rosa. You will forgive me if I don't shake hands."

For all the world, Rosa Morgenstern gave the impression of wanting to make no impression at all. Her dress was a neat navy silk, her hair was a tidy low bun. She held a little navy silk reticule still in her hands. Her face, pleasant and even, bore no sign of cosmetics, and though she was not beautiful, she also was not plain. Clear skin, small mouth, her chin a touch too pointed; Rosa stood an inch or two taller than Claire, but she certainly wasn't of a height to threaten any man. She could be twenty-five or she could be fifty. She could be sitting on any piano bench in any fine parlor in Monticello-by-the-Lake, playing music to quietly manipulate the mood.

"How odd," Claire said. "I don't remember sending you an invitation. Perhaps I addressed it in my sleep."

For all her bravado, Claire was not unaware of the threat that Rosa Morgenstern posed. Rosa, and the D.A.C., had engineered Claire and Remy's escape from the Palace of Fine Arts. In return, she had demanded the two of them marry.

Remy had been at death's door, then. With him gone, the D.A.C. thought they could control St. Cloud through his widow.

Claire had had enough of being puppeteered. She'd called Rosa's bluff then, and she would call it again now. But she would never make the mistake of underestimating the D.A.C.

"Our mutual friend Beatrix Lovell made sure I wasn't left off the guest list."

I will kill her, Claire thought. *I'll kill both of them.*

Rosa's eyes flickered down to the hem of Claire's skirts. "I see you're wearing my little present! How charming."

Claire extended the toe of one embroidered slipper from under her hem. "Yes," she said, "I suppose I am. I didn't think to bring any formal footwear when I was fleeing for my life."

"What do you want, Miss Morgenstern?" Remy asked coolly.

"Five minutes with the King."

"And what will you give us in return?" Claire asked.

"In return?" Rosa smiled. "I've already given you a province, dear."

Remy snapped a finger. "Guard!" he called. "I need an uninvited guest removed—"

"I will do nothing to endanger your rule," Rosa said, "you fools. You're doing a fine job of that on your own. I am trying to protect the interests of the women in this kingdom. Do you think if I had any other way to achieve my goals, I would be standing here in front of the two of *you*?"

"No," Remy said, his French accent noticeably thicker. A pair of guards came up to loom over his shoulder. "I doubt you'd sully your hands with a frog like me if you had another choice."

Rosa smiled thinly. "I have nothing against your people. They're just not *my* people. You understand."

She tried to step around them, but Claire held out an arm. "Funny, I don't remember you saying what we'll get in return for this little audience."

"Twenty Daughters of the American Crown are already inside your party," Rosa said, "and if I don't walk inside in the next few minutes, they've been instructed to light the tablecloths on fire."

Remy said, "You are joking."

"I wish I was," Rosa said, and swept past them without another word.

Claire shook her head. "After you," Remy said drily, and they followed Rosa down the hall.

As they'd intended, the King and his men had been led to their seats and found, to their delight, that ice buckets of champagne had been laid out six to a table. One of the King's advisers stood and took the ceremonial sword from his belt and sabered the cork off his bottle, to a loud round of cheers. Claire chose that as her moment to slip inside; she needed to take her seat before anyone could get a good look at the scorched back of her dress.

Her maid had done her best, but Claire had to face the unfortunate truth that she was, in fact, dressed for the stables.

Half the men were already busily drinking, while the others held their full glasses in their hands as they gazed around them, agog. Those were the intelligent half, and Claire tried to note their faces so that she could avoid them later. Thinking men were a danger she could no longer court. Beatrix had been placed at her table, several seats down, and she waved to Claire before turning back to her tablemate. Ambrose. They'd known each other as children, and if there was anyone who had the good spirits needed to chat with someone she couldn't stand, it was Claire's best friend. Lizzie Cochrane and her photographer had been seated with the soldiers, with Lizzie given warm and explicit permission to talk to whomever she pleased. (She thanked Claire with a wariness Claire knew she had earned.)

And Tesla had been placed next to the King. Claire felt badly about this; she knew she was deploying the inventor as a kind of curiosity. An amuse-bouche to the main course.

"Your Majesty. Your Majesty, a word?"

Rosa had appeared at Claire's elbow. As always, Claire was begrudgingly impressed by the woman's dignity, even while begging a boon.

"Who is this woman?" the King asked Claire.

"I think that's the head of the Daughters of the American Crown," she responded. "Isn't that right? We like to invite the local women's organizations. Throw them a bone."

Rosa didn't bat an eye. "I'm Rosa Morgenstern," she said to the King. "I only need a moment. A particular friend of mine has gone missing—the wife of the Governor of Livingston-Monroe. Mrs. Abigail Monroe herself. I was hoping there might be an investigation into her disappearance."

Claire knew exactly where Abigail Monroe was: in the dungeons somewhere under the Governor's Mansion, where Captain Miller had stowed her during the General's coup.

She kept her face still as the King sipped his champagne, thinking. "Ah, Abigail Monroe," he said. "I heard talk that she was the real leader of that province, that her husband lived to do her bidding. She's a real rabble-rouser."

"In her role as the Governor's helpmeet, she often spoke forthrightly on his behalf—"

"Save it, girl," the King said. "If that man Monroe has any sense, he's sent his wife to a country house so she'll stop nannying him. Her being gone is a blessing. Let's see if Monroe can stand on his own without her."

For the first time, Claire watched Rosa Morgenstern flinch. "Thank you, Your Majesty," she said, her voice wavering only a little. Claire watched her as she walked away through the dining hall and then directly out the doors into the night. Was this wave of despair she felt for Rosa, or for herself?

You've learned something about what the King thinks of powerful women. You cannot let him see what you really are, she told herself. *Not tonight and not ever.*

As she regarded them, a coy smile installed on her face, she noticed that the King split the difference between observant and oblivious. He was a marvel of motion: refilling his flute, waving for more wine, greeting the inventor beside him with a hearty handshake. But under the bluster was a pair of dark and watchful eyes.

"Tell me, Mrs. Duchamp," the King said. "You lay an interesting table. What will we be dining on tonight?"

"Why, chateaubriand, of course," she said.

Claire Duchamp, née Emerson, born in one of Monticello's tenements, speaking in this familiar way to a king of his well-known preference for beef.

Slowly she began twirling one of her black curls. Her maid had pinned her hair only half up. *Your dress is rustic, so let's make it look that way on purpose,* Georgiana had said. *Pinch your cheeks. Wear no ornaments. We'll make you into a country bloom.*

The King looked to Remy, who was idly rearranging his silverware, and again back to Claire. "All of us?" he said.

The rumors had held that the King loved women. *Beautiful, simple women,* Claire reminded herself. And she needed the King to love her, and by extension, her husband.

"Oh no," she told the King brightly. "I've had a calf slaughtered just for you, sir. I know how you love chateaubriand, and I wanted you to have the most marvelous time. No, I designed the menu to otherwise feature what I've heard described as 'St. Cloud's gold.'"

She didn't need to look at Remy to know what he was thinking. Though his face betrayed no feeling, he radiated an anxiety that you could use to power a thousand light bulbs.

"Gold?" the King asked.

"Corn!" she said. "Isn't it wonderful? Corn chowder, corn fritters, a risotto of corn, and, ah, cornsilk—why, it's a veritable feast of gold."

The King couldn't be allowed to know what desperate straits Governor Duchamp was in. He couldn't know that the General had made off with the bulk of the province's funds and that no rich supporters were stepping up to refill Remy's coffers. Their soldiers had prevented a coup with the support of superior weaponry, not the support of St. Cloud's citizens.

Claire hadn't been lying when she told Duchamp he'd been a terrible governor. The people weren't going to toil to put him back on his throne. To do that, she would have to appeal to their highest power, the King, a man not inclined to like bookish, awkward, uninterested governors.

She needed him to want what she wanted, and then she needed to touch his bare skin.

Claire let her mouth fall open just a little and tilted her head to the side. "I hope to show you the very finest our province can offer." *And to convince you that yes, of course we're flush and successful enough to feed every last man a calf, but I'm just a brainless chit who thought it would be fun to serve them corn instead.*

"I see," the King said. His gaze wandered down to her bosom and up again. "I do love corn."

"Oh, I knew that would be the case," she cried. "More champagne!"

"More champagne!" the table echoed. The doors flung open, and Margarete's army of farm girls fanned out in their neat caps and aprons, their arms laden with chilled bottles of wine. The King's empty bottle was swiftly replaced with a fresh one.

"And this . . . ballroom," the King said. "How did you come to this space?"

Claire knew the self-control it had taken for him to wait this long to ask.

For above their heads, since the moment they'd walked in, two rows of Tesla's coils had been throwing bolts of lightning back and forth.

The room had a palpable charge. It was shocking. Unnerving: the crackle of it crawled into your chest, wormed up and down your spine. The hair on the back of Claire's neck stood straight up, as did the hair on her arms, and she touched her silverware as little as possible.

If the less intelligent men among them were swilling the

champagne simply because it was free, the thinking ones would be swilling it out of fear. Why eat, when you needed to bring a piece of electricity-conducting metal to your mouth to do so? Why eat, when the only food before you was corn, unsophisticated peasant food—and small portions at that? Why do anything but clutch your wineglass in terror and awe as you understood the implications of Remy Duchamp's court wizard, Nikola Tesla, a man whose parlor tricks, whose party decorations, could reduce a man to ash?

Yes, Claire had a very good reason to spend the last of their money on champagne.

"Oh," she said, glancing up at the lightning carelessly. "That. Well, it's not like I understand it—Mr. Tesla, do you mind explaining? I'm just going to tend to my husband."

The platters of corn fritters had arrived, each platter with its own farm girl to serve. Ever the doting wife, she piled Remy's plate high.

Sweat was beginning to bead at his temples. Claire fumbled for his hand under the table. She knew her touch could not possibly grant wishes. She knew too that there was no other earthly reason why her husband, so recently at death's door, could be sitting up so straight.

"Ah," Tesla was saying to the King. "You know, I think, that this station—this Wardenclyffe—is the home of my most important work? Now, this is more true, after the fire in my laboratory and the fire at the Fair." His rueful tone, she knew, was real. Tesla had been haunted by the periodic destruction of his work, as though some god above was punishing his every otherworldly discovery. "Here I send messages, I receive messages. Instantaneous messages, and from countries far and wide. I have, I think, spoken to your advisers about you using my technology?"

"Perhaps," the King said; he clearly knew of no such conversation. "Is that what this—this lightning is doing above us? Is it . . . communicating?"

Tesla managed not to laugh. "Such communication is invisible."

"So you work in both the realms of the seen and the unseen." The King looked again at the lightning above. "A superstitious man might think that your powers are not quite natural."

"I am sorry?" Tesla asked.

"That you have been blessed with some supernatural ability." The King paused. "A superstitious man would not be surprised if you claimed to be able to speak with the dead or raise them from their graves."

He's talking about himself, Claire realized. *He half thinks that Tesla can do it.* The King's brother had died when they were young; perhaps he felt they had unfinished business between them. Perhaps they'd been in conflict before his death.

The King's wish for a final conversation with a dead man was understandable. But resurrection? As a girl, Claire had read too many Gothic novels where ghosts lurked in attics and unnatural beings lumbered out into the night, and she had found them ridiculous even then. No one could bring life out of death. If she didn't know better, she would think the King a fool.

Then Claire remembered the lightning that crackled above them. *A year ago, I would have found this impossible, too.* Why wouldn't this display make the King wonder about the unseen currents around them?

"Thankfully, we are not superstitious men," the scientist said. "We must go to—what do you say? Séances, for that kind of communication. I do not say it is not possible. My own capabilities astound me, at times." Only Nikola Tesla could make such a claim and maintain his modesty.

"And so what is it? The lightning above us?"

"It is simply . . . a prototype. You know of course I build the weaponry for my good friend Governor Duchamp."

The King steepled his fingers. "For St. Cloud."

It seemed a mild clarification, but Claire immediately knew its intent. Where did Tesla's loyalties lie, the King was wondering—to man or to province? Did his cooperation with Duchamp's military come out of patriotism for his adopted homeland, or from his friendship with its governor?

"For Governor Duchamp," Tesla said, raising his glass. "My old friend, my first benefactor. Without you I would have very little."

Claire clinked glasses with him, and after a moment, so did the King.

"All you ever needed," Remy said, with a strained smile, "was money and space and time and for the world to allow you to work."

The friendship between the men was real, but this performance of their friendship had been extensively choreographed by Claire.

In word and deed and atmosphere, Wardenclyffe Tower was crying out the extent of Governor Duchamp's strength. *Don't do it,* Claire thought. *Don't hand our province over to a strongman. Don't give us to the General or to Livingston-Monroe. Let the intelligent stay in power, the gentle; let me take this man who might grow to be a better leader—let me shape him into something worthy. Let me do the only thing this world will let me do.*

"Governor Duchamp," the King said, and Claire realized only now the slight that he'd delivered to Remy, speaking at length to his wife and to his scientific adviser before ever greeting the Governor.

"My King," Remy said, inclining his head.

"Tell me of your rather dramatic flight from the Palace of Fine Arts. I understand it involved rifles that . . . shot out a kind of lightning. . . ."

As Remy detailed their escape from the General and the Livmonian men—a patently untrue version of the story that saw him heroically leaping from the roof in a glider, an unconscious Claire strapped to his back—Claire surveyed the room. Under the crackling light of the coils, the ruddy, drunken faces of the Washington ball club were menacing. The farm girls wove through and around the tables, pouring and pouring champagne; in an hour, there wouldn't be a man standing, or able to.

Not a single soldier would be able to carry out the King's wishes, if the King wished his soldiers to kill the Duchamps.

A slim possibility, yes, but one Claire had nonetheless needed to account for. King Washington wasn't the type to get his hands dirty. He enjoyed playing his provinces off one another from a distance, if he did so at all. No, the King was far more interested in the trappings of power than in wielding that power himself. He liked women, and he smoked expensive cigars, and he had his suits shipped out from London; he loved heavy French cooking and Spanish wines, and he despised cats with a passion.

But more than anything, he loved baseball.

To get the King's attention, to get his signature on a proposal from an adviser, you had to visit the King's Box at the Washington ball club. In that room above the stadium, the King ate deviled crabs—an affectation he had picked up on his state visits to Versailles—while he shouted down at his players to pick up the pace. His current mistress dangled off his arm, drinking manhattans. Every now and then, he'd hold up a finger to silence the politico pleading with him so that he could scrawl orders to his team's manager, which were taken down on a silver tray. And while it was impossible to get time to speak with the King during the first inning, only the very brave or very brainless made an appointment with him during the ninth.

Because if his Washington ball club was losing, the King would deny your petition, even if you were asking him to extinguish his own burning house. But if they were winning, you would have the King's ear, and his undivided interest. For many it was worth the gamble. For years, politicians made the pilgrimage to Philadelphia to see the ball team.

Which was why the King began touring with his ball club on the Royal Limited.

In the last five years, every town, large or small, had constructed a train station; every town had started a team. And if you petitioned the King for a game, he would accept. He honored every invitation, and his touring manager arranged their seasons so they wound through the country one province at a time. When the Washington ball club came to your town, an army of ballplayers rolled in, looking to spend some of their hard-earned coin; the King's advisers and ministers climbed out of their little shoebox homes and stretched their legs on Main Streets everywhere, meeting the common folk and hearing their stories.

King Washington, men would say, shaking their heads in

envy. *Our king knows how to live.* Whether he knew how to rule was beside the point.

Throughout the fete, Claire kept her eyes on the King. After the fritters and the chowder and the cornbread were cleared away, after the King had finished a cut of beef meant for four and a cheesecake besides, after his players and his advisers and even his servants had stumbled out into the night in search of a trough in which to vomit before seeking their carriage-car beds, after Bill the photographer had taken a picture of Claire and Remy flanking the King, the lightning in the background nearly as bright as Claire's smile, after Lizzie Cochrane was introduced to the King (it was her third time meeting him, she'd explained; Claire wondered if she had been a baseball reporter in the past) and took notes on what Claire could see were the final pages of what had been a fresh notebook; after Remy and Tesla had staggered off into the night to "discuss the schematics you spoke of" (really, Claire knew, they were headed back to Remy's sickroom); after Beatrix had winked at the King with her good eye (winked!), it was just the two of them left, Claire and the King, as the liveried farm girls carried out clinking baskets of empty champagne bottles.

Many of those had been drunk by the King himself, while Claire had nursed a single glass of bubbly the entire night.

"And you're saying your father was a great weapons inventor?"

She was praying that the King didn't read the *St. Cloud*

Star, or he would know that her father had been arrested after accosting her on the front steps of the Governor's Mansion. "I adore my father," she said, giggling, "and why yes, thank you, he did happen to be a genius. An absolute genius. Really, just blessed by the hands of God."

"You sound very close." The King sat forward a bit unsteadily. "What was he working on?"

"Oh, some giant gun." Claire waved a hand. "I didn't know anything about it, but apparently my dear Governor Duchamp saw it and knew he just *had* to have it for himself! I was lucky, of course, that my father was in the trade he was. Otherwise I would have never met my Remy, and of course my darling Nikola Tesla."

He frowned. "So you met Tesla also as a child? You sound as though you have been friends for years."

"Friends? More like family!" Had he noticed she hadn't answered a question straightforwardly? Was his an act, like hers, one meant to ingratiate and disarm? "My home produces the most brilliant minds. I know I could never leave St. Cloud, and I'm certain Mr. Tesla and my Remy feel the same."

"Civic pride," he said. "It's a pity. I'd like to steal that Mr. Tesla away from you all."

The maids were nearly done tidying. The night was waning on, and she still saw no way to spur on the next part of her plan. If only she were someone else. If only she knew how to pull off a scheme. She'd always loitered at the back of the

Perpetua Club, too afraid to participate in her own life, while Beatrix did all the living for the both of them.

Wait—what would *Beatrix do?*

"You beast!" Claire exclaimed. Then she leaned forward to swat the King of the First American Kingdom on the arm. Lightly.

After a half second in which she was positive she'd be beheaded, the King roared with laughter. "I wonder if the young Governor knows what he has in you."

"Oh, he's ever so busy, what with the coup and all," she said. *Thread the needle carefully.* "I do love him, but I feel so lucky to have a man's—your attention tonight. And the night is so young still! Do you know what I've always wanted?"

"No. I don't." His expression was inscrutable. *Is he fascinated? Is he growing bored?*

She blushed, fanning herself. "Really I shouldn't say anything. Oh, this champagne has really gone to my head."

"Speak," the King said.

Slowly, Claire brushed a stray curl away from her face. "Do you think you could teach me how to hit a baseball?"

FOUR

There was no baseball diamond at Wardenclyffe Tower.

One of Margarete's many missions over the past few days had been to hunt down a proper white ash bat, a Washingtonian Slugger. The King's touring team only used those made at his own factory, and that made them collectors' items. Margarete complained to Claire that she'd paid as much for the slugger as she had for corn.

Claire had the bat slung over her shoulder as she led the King out behind the tower. The electric bulbs in the ground illuminated his face from the bottom up, as though he held a candle under his chin, and the effect aged him several decades. In his suit, he looked like a vampire from some British novel. All over the field, cicadas were rubbing their wings together in song, and their even, endless hum rose from the grass.

Through the trees Claire could see the two guard towers they'd hastily constructed upon their arrival, from spare scaffolding from Tesla's experiments. Bluecoat soldiers were stationed there every hour of the day. Out there in the darkness, a patrolman raised his lightning rifle in salute.

"Nice bat," the King told her.

"Thank you!" She made a show of examining it. "Oh, I didn't realize! Washingtonian Sluggers—are these yours?"

He smiled at her indulgently. "Mine, in that my factory manufactures them for my players," he said. "They're hard to find outside of New Columbia. Though I suppose your brother has played for my team for several years now."

"Ambrose loves being your shortstop," she said. "I looked forward to his letters every week. He's always been so very proud of his team, and sometimes, when I was younger, I pretended that I too was crossing the country, bringing the joy of baseball to children. Unfortunately I never learned how to play the game."

"Well, women can't play anyway," he said. "But I take your meaning."

She paused in the middle of the field, where the grass was high enough to hide the scorch mark on the back of her dress.

(A memory, unbidden: her father buying the most ridiculous, expensive white lace gown for her to wear about the house, back in those days when she and Margarete had to stretch a penny to feed the three of them for a week, and then him spilling a glass of whiskey onto its skirts, him drunk as always, and the next morning, having blacked out the memory, him insisting she wear it as she served him supper, and to keep from being beaten for ruining the dress she'd worn a shawl of her mother's draped just so and kept her father distracted by asking for stories of his greatest achievements, and how was she back here already?)

"Beautiful," the King said from behind her, and when she turned he was peering into the night sky. Then he grinned and produced a baseball from his pocket. "One of my boys left this on your ballroom floor."

"How do I stand?" she asked, holding the bat out before her like a baton.

He chuckled. "Like this," he said, and circled her to wrap his arms around her. Gently, he eased her into position, the bat up over her left shoulder. His chest was firm and warm against her back, and for a half second she let herself believe it, her just the flibbertigibbet she was pretending to be, a girl hungry for the touch of a powerful man. She let herself pretend that this was all as easy as breathing.

The King said, "Breathe in," and when she did, he swung her arms out in a sweeping arc. "Good," he murmured into her ear. Then he dipped his nose into her hair.

Claire shut her eyes. She thought of Remy beside her at dinner, willing to go along with her plan to save their lives, willing himself to be well enough to see it through. What had been the worst of it, for him—that his intelligent wife was acting like some brainless girl, or that she was doing so to capture another man's attention?

Had he felt even the slightest touch of jealousy?

"Oh," she said, "I can't . . . I don't—it's been so hard for me to think with everything going on." And with that she dropped the bat and broke into a half sob.

A pretty sob. *Don't let your face go blotchy.*

"What's the matter?" the King asked, leaning in. "Not to put too fine a point on it, but if you're worried about your husband's reaction, there is such a thing as the lord's privileges—"

Claire couldn't take the time she needed to wrestle with that idea. Did the King expect to have his way with any woman, anywhere he went, without consequence? One of the D.A.C. delegates from Alta California had spoken about her governor's appetites, and it had been horrifying. Claire hadn't realized that that behavior was perhaps one learned at his King's knee.

"No," she said, "my husband and I are very modern, we have an understanding—of course I'll need to give birth to an heir before I take any . . . lovers. . . ." She knew this was too complicated for a tearful chit like her to be saying. "I'm so afraid that we're going to die, that's all."

"To die?" He laughed. "Do you think something is going to fall out of the sky and kill us?"

"The General doesn't want us alive, that's for sure."

The King tucked his hands in his pockets. "Come now. Don't be dramatic. We see all kinds of these intraprovincial squabbles—everything ends up all right in the end. Most of the time it does. And no one ever blames the wife for these things." He was speaking to her off the cuff, in a way he hadn't at the beginning of the night, and Claire was grateful again for the second bottle of champagne he'd drunk at dinner.

"But isn't it the wife's job to cleave to her husband?" She lowered her voice. "I really don't know what Mr. Tesla would do if Remy is . . . is . . . disposed? Does that mean removed from office?"

"Deposed," he said gently. She beamed at him. If she'd learned anything from her father, it was that men loved any chance to correct you. "What *do* you think Mr. Tesla would do?"

"Well, you know he's a bit mad," Claire said, lowering her voice. "You've seen Wardenclyffe now. You understand what he is capable of. And I know he and Remy have weapons stored away in Monticello that I couldn't even imagine! Terrible, powerful things that Mr. Tesla has invented, and if he lost his very dearest friend to that horrid General's angry mob . . ."

The King produced a handkerchief, which she took with a watery smile. Dabbing at her eyes, she said, "I know my little worries don't concern you. Really, I know I'm being a silly woman."

But the machinery had come whirring to life behind the

King's eyes. He was still holding the bat, and he juggled it now from hand to hand. "We were to have a game in Monticello this past week."

"Oh?" she asked, sniffling, as if she didn't know that full well.

"To celebrate the opening of the Fair. Of course, given the unrest in your province, it didn't seem prudent for us to go on with it. But now that things are quieter, perhaps . . ." He glanced down at her with real sympathy. "Poor girl. A flower like you doesn't belong in a place like this. What if you climbed aboard my train? You could ride with me until this is all over. I promise to feed you a real meal. None of this . . . corn."

This wasn't what she wanted. Not at all. The King was supposed to like her, to pity her; he wasn't supposed to whisk her away.

"My liege, I apologize if my hospitality was not—"

"Pssh." He swung the bat in the air, slowly; his form was beautiful, but Claire saw that he was a touch unsteady on his feet. "You're doing the best you can, anyone can see that. This damned war, turning everything upside down. Livingston-Monroe doesn't deserve to run this province. And that so-called General of yours—is he an ambitious man?"

"My husband says the General has been shaking down businesses for . . . protection money? Is that what he called it? I admit I don't know what that is."

"Why, he's a thug, just like those damned Italians." Scowling, the King swung the bat again. "You know, my great-great-grandfather gave St. Cloud to the French—bless him, I suppose he had his reasons. And while I admit I'm not very fond of them, they do make a very good beef dish. That chateaubriand tonight! Beautiful. Like you." He burped. "Pardon me. Ah, girl . . . Clara—"

"Claire," she corrected him, then remembered to sniffle.

"Clara," he said again, confidently. "As much as I'd like to, I can't give you and your husband my support. I just don't involve myself in these petty little squabbles. And I'm fairly certain you won't lose your head over this one. You're a lot more fun than Marie Antoinette! But come with me—come with me to Monticello. We'll have that game. I'll put you in the King's Box next to me. It's the best protection I can offer you. Nobody would dare to hurt a favorite of the King."

Despair.

Utter despair.

It was the last thing she wanted, to leave Wardenclyffe, to go back to Monticello, and on the King's arm. To leave Remy here on his own, vulnerable. But if accompanying the King would give her even another day or two to persuade him to support the Duchamps—

Claire clasped her hands to her chest. "Oh, you are so wonderful," she said. "I would gladly go! Just . . ." She faltered.

Because the King took what he wanted, and what he

wanted was pleasure, and Claire had never slept with a man, not even the "husband" she had married before no priest and no witnesses. And no matter the peril her province was in, there was only so much she was willing to sacrifice.

Especially to a man who thought it appropriate to talk about himself in the third person.

"You really don't think my husband will mind?" she said, drawing toward him.

"I'm not in the business of asking permission," the King said, and before he could lean in wobbily to kiss her, she began again to sob. "Dammit," he said, under his breath, as he patted her shoulder.

Eventually, when she did not stop, he walked her back to the tower, and Claire, clinging to his arm, told him that she was crying happy tears. For the first time that night, she wasn't lying.

Though was she imagining it—the light on in the kitchen whose windows overlooked the lawn behind Wardenclyffe, a woman in silhouette writing furiously in her notepad?

FIVE

Claire knocked on Beatrix's door at midnight.

Her friend answered in her nightdress, a shawl thrown around her shoulders. "No," she groaned, when she saw Claire standing there. "Tell me tonight wasn't a disaster."

"It wasn't a disaster. Well. It was partially a disaster."

"It was?"

"Perhaps." Claire considered. "Also partially a triumph."

"Thank God. So I can go back to—"

"Also, I think I might now be a courtesan."

Beatrix blinked at her. "I suppose you should come in."

There wasn't much in the room, just a pallet and a threadbare rug and some day dresses hanging from pegs. These days, as before, Beatrix did most of her living in her laboratory. Claire sat down heavily on the floor, her back against the bed, and after a minute Beatrix joined her.

"Haven't seen you much," Beatrix said.

"Been a bit busy saving our necks."

At that, she looked at Claire sidelong. "Are you going to forgive me anytime soon?"

"I thought I already had."

"You had." Beatrix folded her arms. "Really. Because you've said two words to me since we made it to Wardenclyffe. This last scheme had you good and mad, admit it."

Claire sighed. "You scheme. That's what you do. Schemes just bubble up from you like—like you're some kind of magnificent geyser. Do I get mad at geysers? I don't."

"'Not mad' isn't forgiven."

"Bea," Claire said, her resolve breaking, "you do what you want, and damn the consequences. You left me dangling on the D.A.C.'s fishing line at the Governor's Mansion. And don't—no, I can see you about to say 'Well, you survived!' Yes, I survived, and with no help from you. You went ahead and invited Rosa here tonight!"

A pause. "You don't understand what it's like to sacrifice for a cause."

"Don't tell me," Claire said, "that I don't know anything about *sacrifice*. Do you know what Rosa wanted? She wanted to track down Abigail Monroe!"

Beatrix scowled. "She wanted no such thing. She said she was trying to free female political prisoners that the General had taken in St. Cloud!"

Claire leveled her with a look.

Beatrix had the good grace to look ashamed. "Oh."

"Oh," Claire echoed. "Well, at least she didn't lie to you."

The two of them stared straight ahead.

"Why are you here?" Beatrix asked. "I was sleeping and then I wasn't, you were announcing your new aspiration to be a woman of the night, and then you started berating me—"

"You haven't been around to talk to! For months now, Bea. This last month, it was like . . . it was like I realized how little I knew you. The *elizabeths* knew you better, and me your best friend."

Beatrix rubbed the back of her neck. She wasn't wearing her eyepatch—she'd been asleep—and without its glint of gold, she looked younger. "I didn't know them. Abigail Monroe set me pretty straight on that," she said. "As . . . as I guess Rosa has, as well."

Claire sighed.

"Nobody was *talking* about it," Beatrix exploded. "The horrible things women have to do to survive in this country. And yes, it's worse for the immigrants, it's worse for so many others, but I kept thinking that if we could just get a woman in power, someone who understood what it was like to be seen as a child or a threat or a plaything—a white American woman, someone who was a little easier to appoint—with that kind of leader, we could lift everyone's boats at once, and I know it was naive, but I was just—"

"You were wrong," Claire said.

"Well, and you were doing nothing at all, Mrs. *Duchamp*, so don't think you can judge me."

"I was," Claire said. "I was doing nothing for a long time. My life was a misery and it meant I couldn't look beyond it. But here I am now, looking."

Outside, the cicadas crooned and crooned.

"What are you and Tesla building?" she asked, to break the silence. "Off in your little hideaway?"

"Instruments of flight, and instruments of war," Beatrix said, biting a hangnail. "Big ones. Frightening ones. Nothing you should know about until you have to."

"Fine by me."

The disagreement hung between them like a vapor. Claire knew that to dispel it, she'd have to apologize. She had no intention of apologizing.

Was there a way to sit with this tension? To talk to her oldest friend without acknowledging fault she didn't feel?

It seemed that Beatrix felt the same way. "Tell me," she said, "how did tonight go? Do you have the King eating from your pretty little palm?"

"Course I do."

"Tell me *everything*."

Claire grinned, despite herself. "All I did was tilt my head and then ask myself, 'What would Beatrix do?'"

"Did it work?"

"Course it worked."

Beatrix bumped her shoulder against Claire's. "What's this about you being a concubine?"

"A *courtesan*," Claire said, then paused. "Is there a difference?"

"And how did you come about this job offer?"

Claire told Beatrix about how she had garnered the King's sympathy, about his offer to take her to Monticello for a ballgame at the Fairgrounds.

"I thought that had been called off," Beatrix said.

"I think when the King decides a game is back on—"

"—it's back on. Of course. Well, are you here to just say goodbye, or do you want something from me? Because I spent all afternoon tweaking a formula for thermal conduction, and then I drank a *disgusting* amount of champagne, so if it's all the same to you—"

"Bea," Claire said, laughing a little. A headache was forming behind her eyes. "Did you know the Royal Limited has so many cars that the King gets lost in it sometimes?"

"Claire . . ."

"I have an idea."

A month ago, Claire would never have dragged her best friend into a plot that could cost her her life. And then Beatrix had done that very thing to her, and without the courtesy of the slightest warning.

She had loved Bea, but perhaps that was all in the past now. Could you love someone who would throw you bodily into the lion's den?

"Tell me!" Beatrix was saying.

"I'm not sure I—" Claire coughed. "Bea, how afraid are you of, say, being executed for treason?"

Back in her room, Claire packed her valise. She left a note for Tesla, one for Margarete, one for Georgiana. She counted again their small coffer of coins, then decided she didn't need to take them. The King's household traveled on his train, and she would want for nothing under his protection; besides, Wardenclyffe was on a tight enough budget. She paced the length of her room, ran a hand over the surface of her campaign desk.

She wondered again if Lizzie Cochrane had watched the King wrap his arms around her body.

If Remy had.

Just go, she thought, and bag over her shoulder, she went. Wardenclyffe's railway station was a short walk down the hill from where they stayed in Tesla's tower, and if she rode Smokey the pony, she could take the supplies she needed without waking any of the soldiers.

Her feet took her to Remy's sickroom door instead.

All was still. Enough that she thought she could hear him breathing through the walls, in and out, in and out. But perhaps it was the whir of generators in the dark, or the churn of her heart.

Before she could question herself further, she pushed the door open.

He was sleeping, limbs akimbo, sheets kicked off to one side. She could see the soft hair on his chest, the cords of his throat. A curl had settled on his forehead, as though he'd just run his hands through his hair.

Evenly he breathed, like a man sleeping in a hammock on a sunny afternoon. Like a man who had never been ill a day in his life. And while Claire had suffered for years under the fear that her touch could grant men's wishes, she'd never seen such evidence as this.

Watching the wave of his breath ebb and flow, ebb and flow, she thought again of the King's arms around her, his face buried in her neck.

Skin on skin.

Granting Remy Duchamp's wishes was enough to scare her sleepless. But if the King of the First American Kingdom knew that he could use her this way, she'd spend the rest of her days chained to his wall.

Remy stirred. "Claire?"

"Yes," she said from the door. "I just came to say goodbye."

"Loved you." Is that what he said? His voice was so thick she thought he might still be sleeping.

Compelled, she drew closer. "Who loved me?"

"He loved you," he said again, more clearly this time. "He loved you the way I knew he would."

Had she been wrong? Was he still ill? She laid a hand on his forehead. It was cool. "I'm accompanying him to a baseball game in Monticello. I think he might throw his support behind our cause."

"You don't need to do this."

"I do," she said. "It's a trifle, Remy."

"It's not. It's dangerous." Awake now, he pushed himself up onto his elbows. "Claire," he said, tousled hair, insistent eyes, more forceful than any version of him she remembered. "You don't need to do this for m—for St. Cloud."

"If you hang, they'll hang me beside you. I'm no martyr. I have to do *something*."

His brows knitted together as she picked up her valise and turned to go.

"How did you make it through dinner?" she asked, her back to him. "You were too weak to stand this morning."

"I am done hiding," he murmured, and he spoke as though his will—her will—could rearrange the world, throw open all its doors to the morning.

There was nothing she could say to that. Nothing at all.

He looked so much as though he wanted to tell her something, something just there, behind his lips—*don't go*, or worse, that he did in fact love her, had all this time, and what would she do with that now that she had to throw herself into another man's arms—

"I have to leave," she said, and fled before she told him anything more.

It took two hours and Beatrix's clever hands and a winch

and much walking on tiptoes, and then a birdbath in her quarters to get the grease off her hands.

But by dawn, when the Royal Limited rolled eastward out of Wardenclyffe Station, Claire's plan was in motion. She watched from the window of her sleeper car as the bulbs in the ground went out, one by one, in the rising light.

SIX

The Royal Limited was a full mile long, and when it stretched out along the landscape, streaming onward to its next destination, Claire imagined it looked like the world's longest blue ribbon winding through a girl's hair.

On the King's train, you wanted for nothing. It boasted eight dining cars, one for each of the Kingdom's provinces; the New Columbia restaurant was widely considered to be the best, as it served the King's favorites and so, usually, the King. Bone china atop crisp white tablecloths that rattled ever so slightly as the train rounded a bend; gold cutlery that matched the trim of the train car; an English butler for every table. In the bar car, the King could sample a merlot that was two hundred years old, a scotch distilled on the Isle of Skye. There was a tailor who fitted and refitted the King's suits, and a barber who trimmed his hair and beard, and in the library car where he took his meetings, the bookshelves lined with little velvet ropes to keep its volumes from spilling out around a turn.

Rumor had it that the train's best-kept secret was a sauna like the Scandinavians had, hot rocks and steam and cedar-wood, in the car just before the caboose that no one else was allowed inside.

And all of that was reserved for the King and his guests. The players had their own amenities, housing for their coaches and trainers, traveling rooms for them to run and stretch and build their bodies. On days when they weren't playing, the team often successfully petitioned the King to allow them to stop in a town overnight to carouse.

It was, in short, a boy's dream come true, and in a way Claire hadn't expected. There were very few women on board to break up the men's festivities.

"Just one or two gals here at a time," said the cheerful second baseman across from her.

She'd been buttering a piece of toast in the dining car closest to her when the ballplayer plopped down across from her. He had to be fifteen or sixteen, younger than her; he declared himself "in training" as he demolished the pile of bacon before him. "You know, sometimes we're put up in a hotel for a while, and then we can send for our sweethearts if we like, but the King doesn't like for us to have distractions while we're working." He shrugged good-humoredly. In the morning sun his brown skin shone, and he had a charming patch of freckles on his nose. Clare liked him quite a bit. "Can't say I'm complaining! Better pay than I could find doing just about anything in Santa Fe. And in a lot of other ways, there wasn't much there for a boy like me."

"What did you want to be?"

"Well, I've always loved to dance," he said. "Thought I'd join up with one of the big ballets in Philadelphia or Monterey. Might still, someday! But this job lets me save my pennies, see the world. Maybe fall in love."

"With some girl in port?"

"Oh, sure, someone like that," the boy said, shoveling eggs into his mouth. "No one here. No, I'd never get too friendly with one of the King's guests. He's a jealous one."

Claire took a tiny bite of toast, her stomach turning. For some reason she hadn't considered the optics: St. Cloud's lady leaving her governor to take up with the King. "The King is kind enough to give me a lift back to Monticello," she said. "I'm eager to see your team play, of course, but then I must attend to some urgent business at the Governor's Mansion. Where I'll be staying. Alone. In my own bed."

The boy shrugged again. "Easy come, easy go," he said. "Lots of fellows don't like to chat with the girls that come on board. They say it breaks their hearts when they disembark. Your face is likely to do some of that, Mrs. Duchamp."

She hadn't been called a heartbreaker before, and she probably wouldn't be again. Claire was pretty enough for "everyday purposes," as her mother had once put it, but when you were the only girl these men had seen in weeks . . .

"Thank you, ah—"

"Jonas." He pulled his cap back onto his head as he stood. "Won't be much longer till we get to Monticello. I'll tell you, I appreciate the days when we get a short ride like this. Prob'ly have you to thank, seeing as the King was visiting you folks last night."

Where we fed you all spectacular amounts of wine. No wonder all the men I've seen this morning look like they're infants; the young ones bounce back faster. All the older players must still be sleeping it off. "You all play well tonight," she said instead. "Though I'm sure you will."

The King didn't call for her before late afternoon. But rather than leave her idle, he sent her several ladies' magazines, a dime novel (a potboiler, nothing she would read on her own), and a selection of lemon ices. She spent the morning nervously shredding one of the magazines to pieces before panicking and tossing the evidence out the window. The lemon ices she let melt.

By noon she was convinced she'd made a terrible mistake. Last night she'd felt like a spymaster; in daylight, her schemes looked like a child's. Her clumsy attempts at flirtation. The secret she and Beatrix had smuggled aboard. All she wanted to do now was escape. But thanks to her mother's lessons, Claire knew enough of railways and practical mathematics to be able to estimate that if she flung herself from the train in a bid to save her life, she'd more likely just die.

Her only choice was to stay put.

By one o'clock she'd read the potboiler in full, chewing her nails to the quick, and at two she was surprised by a knock at the door of her berth.

"I thought you might enjoy that novel," the King said, stepping inside before she could answer.

"Oh!" Claire clutched the book to her chest. Her surprise wasn't feigned, and she watched as the King's smile grew. He wanted her wrong-footed.

A sober King in daylight, with a home-field advantage. This was another kind of King entirely.

What had she been thinking, agreeing to this journey?

Claire dropped into a shaky curtsy. "My lord."

He strode to her, put a confident hand under her chin. "Rise," he said. "I see you were not prepared for my arrival."

Not in the least prepared. She tried to gather her wits. "I would have dressed for the occasion," she said. "I've just been . . . whiling away the hours until I saw you."

"You didn't bring a girl to assist with your toilette?" he asked.

I was too busy planning an act of treason to think to bring Georgiana. "We decided to leave so late," she said, scrambling, "and in our rather rustic country . . . ah, estate . . . I do share the services of my maid with others—"

"Poor child," the King said, and seemed to mean it, as though the worst any woman had faced was dressing for the day on her own. "I'll send someone to you. The last girl we hosted . . ." He paused, smiled. His beard framed his teeth like a tangle of Tesla's wires. "Suffice it to say, on the Royal Limited, we have many lady servants in search of work."

Claire saw immediately through it. It was an old trick of her father's, the thrown-away comment meant to unsettle. She was meant to ask, *Who was she?* in jealousy, or *What happened to the last girl?* in fear.

"Oh," she said instead, with a luxurious sigh. "A girl to do my hair properly. You know, I haven't had the pleasure since Monticello."

The King's smile didn't falter. His eyes seemed to twinkle. "I only came to be sure that you are prepared," he said.

"Prepared?"

"It's a very big game tonight," he said. Without another word, he showed himself out.

He clearly meant to catch her wrong-footed. Fat chance of that. *En garde, you bastard,* she thought. *I've been training my whole life for this.*

When another knock on the door came not five minutes later, she squared her chin. "Enter," she said promptly. *If it's the King again, let him see I'm not afraid—*

It wasn't the King. It was the King's dressmaker, an odd

employee for a King who had no Queen to clothe. But if what Jonas had told her was true about the King's companions, she imagined Mrs. Daly kept very busy.

Mrs. Daly bustled in with a bevy of assistants, who set up a standing mirror and a stool and then cleared away the soupy remains of the lemon ices, laying out vivid bolts of fabric in their place. Delicate flowers were printed against the bright rippling satins and silks, and Claire couldn't resist running a hand down her favorite, a royal blue patterned with tiny honeybees.

In short order, Claire was measured for a short-sleeved afternoon dress to wear to the King's Box at the game, cream silk trimmed here and there with a rose-colored chiffon, and an evening gown "for if you'll be entertaining the King later," extravagantly cut from the honeybee cloth she had admired. She liked it less, now.

Mrs. Daly's assistants did up her hair and painted her face; they snipped and pinned and sewed.

Claire felt a bit as though she was being fattened up for slaughter.

Then again, that wasn't precisely a new feeling.

"The King loves beautiful things," Mrs. Daly said. She had rejected outright Claire's offer to pay for the dresses. "When he is happy, I am happy. We will deliver these to you before you disembark."

You'll break hearts when you disembark, Jonas had said, as though she were harmless so long as she was on the train. On the train, and under the King's command.

But wasn't all the First American Kingdom, then, an extension of its ruler—a carnival designed for a single kind of man, and all those who weren't male or white or moneyed enough made to swallow swords for his pleasure?

As they neared Monticello-by-the-Lake, all Claire could think of was how, just weeks earlier, she had never before left the city of her birth. And now she returned as the wife of its Governor, on the arm of her country's King, in a scheme to secure her place that was so wild it could have been stolen from the dime novel she'd just read.

She was too afraid to wander far from her sleeping car for fear she'd run into the King. And as much as she wanted to check again on the cargo she'd smuggled on board, she knew too that her presence that far back on the train would raise too much suspicion.

Claire had to stay penned up.

She paced a tight circle, watching the landscape out her window. The cornfields turned into a patchwork of family farms, and those turned into towns, and factories. Her dresses had been delivered, and a reticule, a hat, and a fresh pair of slippers. As the Royal Limited pulled into Unity Station, mere blocks from the sparkling lake, a note was delivered that instructed her to ride in the King's carriage to the baseball field beyond the Fair.

Claire donned the dress, the hat. She stuffed the dime novel into her bag. She gathered her wits about her, and when she stepped into Monticello's fading daylight, she was again a simpering, simple girl—the only kind of girl she could be, if she wanted to survive.

SEVEN

Claire had been dreading the ride to the Fair in the King's carriage, afraid that he would ask her to fulfill the half promises she'd made him the night before. But when she took her seat, she remembered that, though the King's mood was foremost on her mind, she was to all appearances *his* very last priority. The King lounged between his team's manager and his assistant coaches, and the three of them spoke a fast-paced version of baseball English that she'd never heard before. Claire leaned instinctively against the door, her bonbon of a dress crushed in around her as the men made their plans.

She was hardly the most ridiculously dressed person in the carriage. The King wore his coronet with his jersey. *No wonder the rest of the world says that the First American Kingdom is a flea-bitten carnival, not a country. I think I agree with them.*

The shutters were drawn inside the carriage, and so she couldn't get even a glimpse of the Gold Coast district between Unity Station and the Fair. She'd walked these streets as a girl, running errands for her father; she and Beatrix had once even been treated to a fancy dinner here by a pair of oil barons they'd met at Perpetua's dance hall. But she knew that even if she could have seen them from the windows, the streets would be empty. All roads were cleared when the King's entourage drove by.

When they arrived just west of Jackson Park, the King and his coaches got out first. Then the King turned to offer her his hand to help her down, and she had to stifle a horrified laugh, remembering the way Captain Miller had stuffed her into a carriage on the way to the Fair, the first time she was to speak to Remy alone.

How much things had changed, and how little.

For Miller was AWOL now, just when she most needed him to guard her back, and the King was raising an impatient eyebrow, and as Claire alighted and took his arm, glancing up to see the ballpark at dusk, she was blinded by the sudden crush of flashbulbs.

Newspaper reporters.

What would they make of her being on the King's arm while blocks away, her province burned?

The King smiled and waved, and Claire smiled and waved, and he said nothing to her. He remained silent as he led her up to the boathouse on stilts that they'd constructed for the King's Box.

Claire's unease only deepened. When she'd first seen this field, she had thought of it as a temple to baseball, to chalk and geometry and fresh-cut grass, to ingenuity itself. The diamond was surrounded by fields of electrical lights, designed in cooperation with Tesla, and this place, here, where they were all standing, was the first where you could play a ball game after dark.

(Her brother, Ambrose, had told her that there had been a proposal to stage something called a "Wild West show" on this spot, but that Governor Duchamp had rejected it on account of it being too violent. In this country, baseball was always the safer option.)

So why did the King look so dissatisfied? As a Monticello Whale threw practice pitches into the batter's box, the King leaned so close to his observation window that his nose was pressed against the glass. "Wrong," he was muttering, or something that sounded like "wrong."

Claire had been placed beside him on a very elegant backless stool; she'd been handed a pair of opera glasses. "What is?" she asked. From what she could see of the field, every adult and every child in the three surrounding provinces had turned out for the game. Even with the unrest in St. Cloud, Americans would take whatever glimpse of their King that they could get. "Wash-ing-ton," they chanted. "Wash-ing-ton."

From what she could see of the players' dugouts, the Monticello Whales looked resigned to their coming defeat. Not that they won all that often, anyway. Ambrose hadn't even considered playing for them; he'd said that they were cursed. Something to do with a billy goat.

"It's all wrong!" the King was saying. "The distance between the mound and the batter's box. It's not regulation. It's a good foot and a half too short."

She put a hand to her chest. "That's horrible. Didn't they consult the experts?"

"Fat chance of that," he raged. "The bases aren't the right size either! All it would've taken to get it right was a letter to my household! Everyone knows we keep the official measurements, and my steward responds within the day. Really, the thoughtlessness of it all astounds me."

As he ranted, Claire felt her nerves begin to settle. *The irony of that.* But this was familiar: an angry man who needed soothing. She might not be a practiced schemer, but she certainly knew how to navigate someone's temper.

"You must know that Governor Duchamp is baseball mad," she reassured him. "He insisted on a diamond for you. Some man wanted to stage fake wars out here for people to watch, men dressed up like cowboys and Indians. That, instead of baseball."

The King shook his head. "That's a shameful part of our history. We need cleaner contests. Healthy male athleticism. My brother—my brother was a real specimen. You should have seen him round the bases. We need more men like my brother. We need peanuts!" he roared suddenly, and a servant ran up to him with a tray of cardboard boxes.

Claire snapped open her fan. "My," she said, "isn't it hot?"

"Wash-ing-ton!" the crowd chanted. "Wash-ing-ton!"

The servant, red-faced, was saying, "I can fetch you peanuts, sir, or Cracker Jacks, the snack specially commissioned for the Fair."

"Both," the King said, "and quickly. I don't eat once the game's begun, you know that. Bad luck." He touched his lips with two fingers. "Avert," he murmured.

Another servant scurried up with a tray of boxes, and warily, the King took one of each. He opened a box of the Cracker Jacks and chewed. Then chewed some more. Mollified, he turned back to the field.

The room, which had gone silent at his explosion, burst back into life. Claire turned at the sound, surprised at the extent to which the King's Box had filled up behind them. She spotted one of the industrialists who'd haunted the court at the Governor's Mansion, chomping now on a cigar while he read the newspaper. A few nervous-looking men in suits waited by the door. One she recognized from Duchamp's war council, but he was avoiding her gaze, studiously pretending they'd never met. These, she knew, were the petitioners who were waiting to speak to the King the moment his team began to win.

And in the corner, taking notes, was Lizzie Cochrane.

Beside her, Bill the photographer was cleaning a camera lens with a cloth.

Lizzie grinned at Claire with all her teeth. She wasn't even ten feet away; she could hear every word Claire said to the King.

And then it would end up in her paper for everyone to read.

"Stand," the King barked, following Claire's gaze. "You. With the camera. Stand. No men can be sitting in the King's Box once the game's begun, and we're just about to have the anthem."

Bill the photographer leaped to his feet.

"Bad luck," the King was murmuring. "Bad luck to have a sitting man. Enough that we sat through a lightning storm last night. I don't like these omens."

Claire fixed a smile on her face. She hadn't known him to be so deeply superstitious, but then so many sporting men were.

"Let's have the other one in here!" the King was calling behind him.

"The other one?" Claire asked.

"Come to the window," the King said, "so they can see you. This is why they buy their tickets. For this. They're here to see their leaders. Wave at them. Wave, girl. Where," he yelled again, "is the other one?"

She pinned a smile on her face and lifted her arm. As she tilted it back and forth, she wondered at what it was like to love something this much. Some*thing*, too. Not a person, but a game. Her mother had told her she'd know she was in love when the world shrank down to just her and her man. But what if the great love of your life couldn't love you back? What did it do to you?

King Washington, who had been a subtle, intelligent man the night before, was today a monomaniacal fool. And she was smiling her approval beside him.

So much for "their leaders." We're all madmen.

Wait.

Their leaders, the King had said. *Meaning me?* Was this it? Had she persuaded the King? Did she and Remy finally have his support to rule St. Cloud?

"Ah, there he is," the King was saying. He wheeled Claire around, his arm around her shoulders. "I think you've already been acquainted, yes? Mrs. Duchamp, have you met General Montgomery?"

EIGHT

The General was supposed to be dead.

The General was supposed to be sleeping in Remy Duchamp's vacated bed.

The General should be living on the moon, for all they knew; really, the last she'd heard of his whereabouts had been in one of the daily messages from Captain Miller—until those messages had abruptly stopped. When had she last received one? Three days ago? He'd been keeping tabs on the General's communications with Livingston-Monroe. Miller was certain that, even given Abigail Monroe's disappearance, the General was still colluding with their military to shore up his support in Monticello.

"It's good to see you looking so well, Mrs. Duchamp," said the General smoothly, from a face that was mottled purple and yellow and green from bruises.

"You too," she lied.

The anthem ended.

"Ah, so you do know each other." The first of the King's batters was stepping up to the plate. He appeared to have only half an ear on their conversation, but Claire knew now that that appearance was wrong.

He loves the game, she realized with a sudden clarity. *He loves the game of it all.*

Behind them, a pair of redcoats stood at deliberate inattention. "Are those men necessary?" Claire asked quietly.

Before the General could speak, the King said, "Too many people in here. Too loud, too much." He pressed two fingers to his lips. "Avert," he said again.

"Sir," Bill the photographer piped up, "I was hoping to finish writing a piece about the Washington ball club's winning strategy this year—"

"He can stay," the King said. He winced as his batter swung and missed. "No bodyguards or petitioners. Everyone else out."

As the King's Box emptied, Claire sat back down on her embroidered stool and once again pulled out her fan. It wasn't an affectation. She needed air, or she was going to vomit her lunch all over the General's uniform.

She'd known him since she was a girl. The General had come to their Lordview house at least once a fortnight to check up on her father's current contract with the Crown. Were his guns sufficiently deadly? Was his explosive powder exploding? Each time he'd left her father's office, he'd eyed Claire up like a cut of meat he'd put out in the smokehouse to age. *Any day now,* his gaze had said. *Any day now, and I'll have you how I want you.*

Remy had known him too, since the General had served as his father's adviser, and when Remy had come to power—young, untested, uninterested, and, worst of all, *French*—the General had seized his opportunity to wrest away power. With the help of Livingston-Monroe, he could finally step out from behind the curtain and run St. Cloud the way he wanted to. All he needed was Remy dead.

Too bad Remy hadn't died.

Tonight the General stood beside the King, his gloved hands crossed behind him in the artlessly formal manner of military officers. But he was favoring a leg, he was holding his shoulders too stiffly. She'd never considered him an old man, not particularly, but his injuries had aged him. He looked as frail as a mended teacup.

Good, she thought. *I'll be the strong wind to knock him over.*

The crack of bat hitting ball; the crowd roaring to their feet; the electric lights flashing off and on in celebration. The King made a fist and slammed it in the air. "That's my boys!" he yelled. "That's my *team!*"

"Well done, sir!" Claire cried, snapping her fan shut.

The King was ebullient. "Tell me more of what you've

seen in Monticello." He clapped the General on the back. The General winced. "And gimlets! Gimlets for the men!"

"No gains, sir." The General spoke with the clipped delivery of a man delivering a field report. "No gains at all. The bluecoats hold the mansion and the Gold Coast and the Fair—you should have seen the abuse shouted at my guards as they escorted me here—and the redcoats have the Levee, some of the foreign districts of town, the wealthy addresses up north and west. Support up those ways for a ruler who knows his way around a sword."

There was no mistaking the ambition in those words, or the disdain.

It wasn't lost on the King. "You're referring, I take it, to me," the King said. "As I—*run*, Halverson! *Run!*—am the ruler of this great nation, and the leaders of its province merely govern. There is a difference, you know, between power and stewardship. We cannot have one without the other. So let's mind our words, shall we?"

He knows that the General won't be satisfied with ruling St. Cloud, Claire realized. *After taking our province, he'll want the whole damn country.*

But the King showed no fear. He accepted the gimlet from a servant carelessly. "Ah, thank you. Delicious. Claire, would you like to try this?"

"I'd love to," she said, taking a sip. *The General just struck out, and now I'm up to bat.*

"Drink quickly," he said. "We're at two outs, and it's bad luck to imbibe while our team is fielding."

She handed him back the cocktail. "Oh, that's lovely! I've never had one of those before."

"You haven't seen much of the world, have you?" the King asked.

"No, sir," she said. "There's so much I'd like to see, and do. There's so much still to explore."

"And you'd rather stay in stuffy old Monticello rather than ride around seeing the world with me?"

The General's eyes were a pair of burn holes in his face.

Claire swallowed. "May I have a gimlet of my own?" she asked the servant, who fetched her one. "I'll only drink it at the appropriate time."

"Good," the King said. He watched her bring her drink to her lips. Somehow, her hands weren't shaking.

"Oh," she said, "I imagine that after Governor Duchamp returns tomorrow from reviewing his troops, within a week or so, our lives will be back to normal! And I'm certain that then I'd be free to ride the Royal Limited as long as you would like."

Claire didn't turn to look at Lizzie Cochrane, but she could hear the frantic scratching of her pen.

Steady, she thought, *steady . . .*

The King said, "I asked around about you a little today."

"Did you?" She put a hand to her mouth. "I hope you only heard wonderful things."

"*Interesting* things, for sure. I read a few weeks' worth of newspapers. Talked to your brother, Ambrose, some." Unexpectedly, he touched the chiffon at her neck. "While you were having those pretty dresses made."

Claire fought to keep her panic off her face. *There's so much he could have learned, true and untrue, from my brother.* "Thanks ever so much for them. I've never had anything quite this nice."

"That's a pity." The Whales were trotting in from the outfield, and the King's team was taking their places. There was a hearty debate happening in the Whales' dugout; it wasn't clear who was batting next. Still, the King's focus remained entirely on her. "I heard that you've been making little trips into the countryside around Wardenclyffe, spending your husband's money on crops and trade goods and fripperies, hiring servants from the locals."

"Yes, sir," Claire said, confused as to where this all was headed. "I'd never been to our western border before. I thought, if I were to help *govern* these people"—the General winced at her use of the King's preferred word—"I should speak to them at least a little. And besides, my husband didn't think to bring along a girl who could dress my hair." She pouted for effect. "We needed servants. Might as well use the help that's available."

The General looked very much like he wanted to interrupt.

"And how have you dealt," the King was asking, "with the continued rumors that Mr. Duchamp has, in fact, died?"

She laughed. To her own ears, she sounded metallic. "Oh, people are so *silly* sometimes. Yes, my husband was shot, and while it was a minor wound, that sort of thing is always very scary. But you saw for yourself at dinner last night. My husband is well, and strong, and eager to return home."

"I heard you tended him with a single-minded devotion. I heard, too, that you defied your father on the steps of the Governor's Mansion when he tried to bring you back to the family home. That you were a girl in love."

"I did." It came out as a whisper. "I was. I—I mean, I *am*." She almost meant it.

"Dear God," the General said, disgusted.

"Really, it's a romantic image. The devoted, beautiful young wife, defying her family for love," the King said. "You do know then, of course, that you are far more popular with the people of St. Cloud than your very unpopular husband? Who chose to abandon his city in a time of great need to see to armed conflicts on the border that are . . . imaginary? Forgive me, General, but am I correct in my assumption that the bulk of Livingston-Monroe's army is in Monticello right now?"

"Aye, sir."

"Why aren't they playing?" Claire asked, in a desperate bid for diversion. "Sir?"

"Our pitcher's ailing," he said. "They're sending for relief. Any reason you didn't bring your husband along with you today, girl?"

She hadn't been "girl" to him before. "To the game, sir? I wasn't aware that he was invited."

At that, the King guffawed. "This one's good, isn't she? Her brother told me that this morning. Said the last time he saw her, she was in a man's suit, sneaking out of the Governor's Mansion at night. Said she had a mouth like a sailor on her. I said, that can't be the pretty flower I met the night before, and he said that you were a cunning little chameleon, you. That you'd do whatever it took to get your way."

Her heart hammered in her chest.

"I've known her since she was a child," the General said. "That behavior is damn well in keeping with what I've seen."

The game still hadn't started back up. The King had turned away from it entirely now, turned himself toward Claire. His dark eyes were fixed on her mouth.

She stood up straighter, stared him down.

Behind her, she could hear Lizzie Cochrane flipping pages.

"Excuse me, sir," the butler said again, at the King's elbow. "A laborer asking to clean the box's windows for you during this short break—"

"Fine," the King said, and to Claire he said, choosing his words carefully, "I am not unsympathetic to your position. I think, also, there are many things I'd do to make sure my head is not the one on the chopping block at the end of this little game. Staying in power takes . . . sacrifice. My older brother always said so. And I understand the Governor's fascination with you, as well, though I wouldn't go so far as to marry some girl that came up from nowhere." He squinted a little. "You have a quality. You make a man feel—good. Capable. Hale."

Claire's fingers twitched. *Of course,* she thought, *of course I do.*

Another awful man who saw her as his muse.

"Yes, my offer still stands. Keep traveling with me, and I will see to your protection."

It was an exit out a side door, one she'd never anticipated.

She'd thought he'd wanted her for one night—which was unsettling enough—but this sounded like he wanted Claire to be his mistress. The King didn't always keep one, but when he did, the girls rode with him to games, gave interviews to the press about their favorite players, hosted glamorous fetes in each new city they visited. Katarina Sokoloff, the Russian ballet dancer, wore only canary yellow. Aislinn Kelly's ginger hair was always exquisitely styled, and her charming freckles convinced society maidens they should spend more time in the sun. They were breathlessly discussed for six months, a year, and then without fanfare, they disappeared.

If she said yes, Claire would once again be subject to a man's whims and caprices. She would hang on his words.

She would sleep in his bed. All the while, she'd be digging her own grave.

"What if I tell you," she said, dissembling as quickly as she could, "that I've never wanted power. I've never wanted anything but to live a quiet life. That I'm just a girl in love with her handsome French husband, and that I couldn't betray him like that?"

"I'm not sure if I would believe you," the King said.

Over his shoulder, she watched the window washer in their harness. Their squeegee went up. Their squeegee went down.

"Sir," the General said, in a diffident tone she'd never heard from him, "given that girl's refusal of your very generous offer, might I make another one instead?"

"I'm listening," the King said, but a roar below from the crowd took his attention back to the field.

"Sir," the General said again, "the girl is young. The boy too. I may have been a little hasty in my conversations with Livingston-Monroe—"

"Your attempted coup, you mean," Claire said. The time to play the fool was over.

Behind her, Lizzie took furious, audible notes.

The General coughed. "Forgive me. I only wanted St. Cloud to have a strong leader. But how about a compromise? Remy Duchamp never completed his education in America. He was thrust into this position, grieving his father, and he was young and untried. What if I served as his Regent? Kept the province for him until we'd determined he'd come of age?"

"Emerson's up to bat," the King said. "Someone get that window washer out of here. That 'boy' is twenty-one, or thereabouts. If he's not a man by now, he won't ever be one."

When the King was distracted by the game, his logic was nearly impossible to follow. The General frowned. "Duchamp, you mean?"

"Swing! *Swing*, Emerson! Of course I mean Duchamp." He snapped his fingers for the servant. "Make sure the men in the box stay standing, dammit, and fetch cocktails for the top of the next inning. General Montgomery, you know I respect the military. You know too that these little lawn games our provinces play with each other are amusing only until someone loses an eye. The boy has the bloodline, but no backbone. You have too much backbone and no bloodline. Too bad the girl can't do it, she's got the subtlety of mind, and—"

He paused.

Ambrose Emerson had hit a home run, and the roar from the crowd was enough to lift her off her feet.

But the King was entirely unmoved.

"Really," he said, "it would be ideal if we could just give this girl to you to wive, General—"

Again.

Again she was being offered up on a platter.

Why was she still standing here, in the same situation she

had stared down just weeks ago? What would happen if she walked out of the King's Box and disappeared into the streets of the Levee, cut her hair, and changed her name? She could take the train to Alta California, set up in a mining town and tend bar, learn to ride rough terrain, how to run off men with a shotgun. Anyone who tried to *purchase* her again, she would blow his head clean off.

The King was still talking, but she couldn't hear him. A crowd was still roaring in her head.

"Yes, you're right," the King was saying, "she's more trouble than it's worth. And there's no real way for me to dispose of Duchamp. Inheritance, and all that. Too bad. Pretty girl like that, you want to *do* something with her."

You could leave her be. You could let her live her life.

"But you know what I say, Monty." The King clapped the General on the shoulder. "Winner makes the rules. If you want her, go out and fight for her. Let's watch this play out."

NINE

It was an invitation to the General to win the civil war.

"Seventh-inning stretch," the King said, rubbing the back of his neck. "Don't look so sad, girl. I'm sure that man of yours will keep you safe. Or he'll try, anyway."

The General murmured something and withdrew. Claire was left standing beside the King.

As the players below them trotted back to their dugouts, the electric lights shivered. Unease rippled through the crowd, but the spectators settled again as the concessions vendors trotted up and down the steps of the bleachers, hawking their wares.

Just weeks ago, she and Remy had wandered the Fair arm in arm, sampling the prizewinning drinks and confections. In the exhibition hall they had marveled at a previous incarnation of the King's Royal Limited train, presented for the public's supposed edification. Really, people had come just to gawk at the King's excesses.

It *was* excess they were seeking, all of them, the King and the General and even Remy Duchamp. The pursuit of mindless pleasure, of total control, of knowledge for knowledge's sake.

"My team is going to win," the King said to Claire, almost idly. He was tracing a finger over the window. "My team always wins, you know. Even when we lose. Losing means only that someone else has been scouting talent for me. Your hitter gets a grand slam? I purchase him that night, put him in my own Washington blue. I look around my Kingdom, at all these provinces that run themselves, that pay the Crown taxes and do what they please, and do you know what I see? I see teams that don't know how to win. Who don't even realize there's a game on. Do they realize their own power? Do they realize how little they need a monarchy?"

"Why are you telling me this?" she asked. *Is it treason if your own King says it?*

He smiled. "Look at West and East Florida. Brothers locked in an endless struggle for five hundred miles of land. Look at St. Cloud—you control this country's major thoroughfare, the mighty Mississippi. You control all the ports on our great lake. What *money* can be made there in trade! How you could line your pockets—line the *Crown's* pockets! But no. Instead of finding a way to pad your General's coffers, to bring him back over to your side, you instead wage war against him. You, and your weakling husband. You hire a madman to build you fantastical weapons, weapons out of my wildest dreams; a madman loyal to you, who would never think to arm your enemy for profit. *Still* you lose. You end up in a backwater warehouse, friendless and alone, and when your King comes to evaluate your worthiness, you serve his ballplayers *corn soup*. Have you no alliances? Have you no *sense*?

"Claire Duchamp, can I tell you the thing I want most?"

She stood, transfixed, as all her plans came howling down around her. "What's that?"

"I want a worthy adversary," he said. "I am so very bored."

She felt, rather than heard, the General's men coming up from behind her.

The electric lights shivered again.

It was the signal she and Beatrix had agreed on.

"Look," she said weakly. Then again, louder: "Look!"

It was a glider. A glider with a magnificent wingspan, some great canvas bird shot through with light. Its pilot wore a helmet and trousers and big men's boots, and though Claire couldn't see for sure, she was positive she also wore a glorious smile. It was twice again the size of the craft that Claire and Remy had used to make their escape, and sturdier. Beatrix had asked for Tesla's expert eye on her design.

"I asked him too for some bells and whistles," she'd told

Claire last night as they'd sat on her bedroom floor. "He was very happy to help."

"What kinds of bells and whistles?"

"Oh," Beatrix had said. "You know. The new model folds up so small you can fit it in a steamer trunk. One you could hide away in, say, a train car of other steamer trunks, and you would never know the difference."

Two such trunks had ridden the Royal Limited from Wardenclyffe to Monticello: one for Beatrix's glider and the tools to maintain it, and one for Beatrix herself, the latter drilled through with breathing holes so the girl didn't suffocate on the journey. When the train arrived at Unity Station, Beatrix had disembarked in a flash. Her trunks in hand, she'd summoned a hack on the street and made it to the King's Box before the Washington ball club had even stood up from their supper in the dining car.

At the Fair, she had dressed as a laborer and, in the harness and ropes she also used as a pilot, she'd washed the windows of the King's Box. Then she levered herself to its roof and unpacked her glider.

The glider in which she was now sailing across the length of the field, a banner streaming behind her.

It had been a brilliant plan. Claire had seen the old conspiratorial gleam in Beatrix's eyes as they had hashed it out—and with the two of them working together, they had never not been a success. Even with the bad blood that lingered between them, Claire hadn't doubted their scheme. Why, she had just come from a midnight rendezvous with the King, she had just been invited as his special guest to the Fair; why wouldn't she be a smashing success the next day? Why wouldn't she be able to convince him to grant her and her husband the continued governance of St. Cloud?

Tonight Claire watched miserably as the banner flying behind Beatrix's glider snapped and straightened again in the wind. WE THANK GOVERNOR DUCHAMP FOR HIS HOSPITALITY, it read.

They had debated over the "we." Claire had wanted it to say "the King," but Beatrix had made a case for plausible deniability. *He'll be charmed by it either way,* Claire had said, supremely confident. *He seems like a man who loves a bold gesture.*

It *was* a bold gesture. The crowd was shouting. Here was a message flung from the seat of power itself: the King supported the Duchamps' claim to St. Cloud.

Someone put a hand on Claire's shoulder. She didn't need to turn around to know it was a redcoat. Beside her, the King was mouthing the banner's words as he read.

"I didn't send for that, did I," he said quietly.

"No." She swallowed. "Perhaps it's from the Monticello Whales, grateful to be playing again."

Last night, she had imagined she already had the King's support. That she would turn to him with an impish smile and say, *I just wanted to announce your approval to the world. Don't I work fast?* That he would call for another bottle of champagne.

"Is that your opening gambit?" the King asked her. He drained his cocktail.

Claire forced herself to smile. "What gambit, sir? I only see words on a banner."

He smiled at her, and then he sighed. "But words are so easily erased. Send for the General," he told the redcoat behind her. "Have him send that girl back to her husband. And someone grab that pilot when he lands."

When no one moved, the King snapped, "Clear the box. Now."

She had, once again, bored him.

She kept her head up, her expression even, but her confection of a hat bobbled ridiculously as the redcoats muscled her out of the box.

Briefly, she locked eyes with Lizzie Cochrane, who had the good grace to look horrified.

"The pilot's escaped, sir," someone was saying behind her. "He's gone." And the door behind her shut before she heard anything more about Beatrix.

The carriage waiting at the bottom of the stairs was plush and luxurious, the King's coat of arms painted on its door. For a moment she let herself believe that it would, in fact, take her to Unity Station. That she could travel back to Wardenclyffe unharmed.

The redcoats didn't put her into the carriage.

They dragged her to the thing waiting behind it.

It was a prison wagon, with wooden doors and a padlock on the outside, and when Claire saw it she began to yell. At first she yelled orders, "Don't touch me!" and "I am the Governor's wife!" and then she yelled "Stop!" and then she yelled wordlessly, scratching and biting, going for the redcoats' eyes until the soldier who took her by the hair shoved her into the wagon headfirst.

When the bluecoats who had been dicing in the shadow of the box, glorying in their easy duty, finally looked up at the noise, they rushed to her defense.

At least that was what Claire imagined, later, in the scene she would replay over and over again in her captivity. The bluecoats hadn't had Tesla's lightning rifles, but they had guns and their fists and they had fought for her bravely. They had battled the Livmonian soldiers out of their love of their Governor and his wife; they had cried out in defeat as the prison wagon sped away.

They hadn't just sat in the shade, playing whist, unblinking as she screamed and wrestled and was finally overcome.

In the wagon, when they pinned her arms behind her and the smallest one, a redcoat no older than fifteen, took out a pair of rusty shears to saw off her hair at the roots, she told herself that she must have been mistaken.

Her face was pushed into the wooden floor of the wagon. *Soon*, she thought, *they will overtake the wagon. They will rescue me.*

Soon.

Any moment now.

TEN

Why did she still think that manners would protect her? That her gender would? Why did she believe that anything about her conferred the privilege of safety? Why, despite everything she had experienced, did she think she was entitled to the smallest bit of happiness?

"What can I give you?" Claire asked the redcoats, on the ride to whatever dungeon they had in mind. "What can I give you in exchange for my life?"

The little one snickered. "Nothing we don't already have. 'Sides, they ain't gonna kill you. Just put you in a little cage somewhere, wildcat that you are."

The wooden floor of the cart was hot against her cheek. She said, "How much is the General paying you?"

More snickers.

"I am the Governor's *wife*," she said, "and you are fools if you think my coffers are not deeper than General Montgomery's."

A creak behind her, a whisper. "Lawrence, don't you think—"

"The General pays us more'n enough," the pipsqueak soldier said loudly. "It ain't money we're after. We're after puttin' a real man on the throne."

She forced herself to relax, one muscle at a time. There was a straightforward way out of this; she just had to make herself think clearly. "Everyone has a price," she told them. "You know that, right? If it isn't money, it's something else. It's safety. Or it's your family's safety."

"We're loyal men of the General's," the soldier said, and the other voices agreed.

This is a good sign, she thought. They were still responding to her. That meant that they were still listening.

She banished all her despair, her helplessness. She cloaked herself instead in her rage.

"You know that your General wants me alive," she said. "But do you know why? He's going to lock me away until he kills my husband, and then he's going to marry me to shore up his right to rule St. Cloud. So even if your sad little plan succeeds, even if you get this province and every other little thing you wanted—have any of you stopped to think what will happen next? Because I know your faces, now. I know your name, *Lawrence.* I'm going to be your Governor's pretty little trophy. Someone he needs to stand next to him to smile for the cameras. You think your lives are worth more than my cooperation? You fools. When I tell him that what I want—the *only thing* I want—is your heads on a platter, do you really think he won't serve you up with pleasure? I promise you, I will have no mercy in my heart. I will take the knife and cut each of your throats myself."

Silence.

"But then again, you might be thinking, *That will never come to pass.* And you're right. We Duchamps will come out of this triumphant. Do you know *how* we will defeat you? Or did you all somehow miss our little presentation at the Palace of Fine Arts? You saw the power we wield. You think we won't hunt you down like dogs after we retake our rightful throne? What do you think that lightning rifle will feel like when we aim it into your chest? Into your sons' chests?"

The whisper again. "Lawrence . . ." Another soldier coughed. Another shuffled his feet.

She nearly had them.

"Tell me," Claire said, "do you know how it feels to be electrocuted? They say the first thing you smell is the hair on your arms, burning."

A muffled curse, and then at her wrists, a knife. Her bonds fell away. One of the soldiers was hollering for the driver to halt the wagon, banging on the wall between them and the cab.

They slowed, stopped. The wagon went silent.

It was only then, with injured dignity, that Claire brought herself to her knees. She regarded them evenly. "No matter how this ends, with me as the Governor's wife or the General's, *I will still win*. So help me now to save your necks later."

The boy soldier looked like he wanted to shit himself. "What do you want from us?" he asked.

"Tell me everything the General has told you. Tell me everywhere the General has been. Then tell me where you were taking me, and spare no detail."

The redcoats glanced at each other, terrified.

Finally the boy soldier leaned forward.

After the fight at the Palace of Fine Arts, the General had gone missing. For the first week or so, orders were still handed down from the top, but none of them were significant. The soldiers were told to fortify their positions. Then they were told to wait for more orders. But nothing more came.

"Round about that time," the boy soldier was saying, "the lads from Livingston-Monroe figured it was time for them to pick up an' go. Wasn't any push anymore. No—momentum, like. Leader's missin'. No one's gettin' paid. No one knows what's next. Y'all had those lightnin' guns, y'all had bluecoats here lookin' to raise hell, y'all got your Governor out west keepin' an eye on the border . . . naw, the Livmonians didn't like that none. And no one rightly knew if the General was alive or dead after that fight with his son. Miller just . . . laid 'im out, and for all we knew, the crowd'd trampled 'im."

"Lots of talk about where the General was," another soldier said. "If you all had him prisoner. If he had some little scratch on him or something, some wound, that he was being a baby about being all holed up in the mansion. No one knew for sure."

Claire kept her face impassive, but with effort. *We were more successful than we thought. If only we'd put more spies in place before we fled. If only Tesla—no, if only anyone had thought to confide in the Governor's wife.*

"Then what happened?" she asked.

The boy looked to the grizzled soldier beside him. "General came back," he said shortly. "Hell if anyone knew where he'd been, outside his aides, maybe. Limping. Bruised. Mad as hell. Good men got punished for doing nothing but being in his line of sight. Then he hears that the King has made a trip to that madman Tesla's tower, to go see *you* and the Governor, and if we thought the General was angry before . . . he talks to himself when he's mad. Paces around, spins out plans. Should've heard him. 'If I were King, I'd behead them both!'

"Then he told us to come here," the boy said. "Last-minute orders, just this afternoon. Said we was to take you to Adams Island."

The sanatorium.

She swallowed. "Why Adams Island? Why not . . . some dungeon, somewhere?"

The boy soldier cracked a grim smile. "Adams Island *is* a dungeon. Milady."

"It ain't the first time we brought someone there," another man said under his breath.

"Hate that place," another said.

"It's where the General . . . hides things." The grizzled one crossed his arms. "People. Sometimes girls, like you. Sometimes not."

"I am your Governor's wife," she said coolly, "and you will address me with respect."

"Milady."

"Thank you," she said. "Who did the General hide there?"

The soldiers looked at each other. "Can't rightly say," the grizzled one said.

"Can't or won't?" Claire asked.

"Can't," the young one said, "honest. We weren't told. Just that it was a dangerous man, someone who'd bring the whole place down."

"What did he look like?"

"Bag over his head," the grizzled one said. "And he didn't talk. Fought like a hellcat, though."

A dangerous man. "You're telling me the entire truth," Claire said. "Swear to it."

"Swear," the boy soldier said.

"Then I need two last things, and I will send you on your way."

"Girl—milady," the boy soldier said, "they'll *know* if you don't end up at Adams Island. They'll . . . they'll take it out on *us*." His voice broke on the last word.

He was a traitor. They all were. They had pledged to protect St. Cloud, and they had betrayed that oath. Instead, they'd thrown their lots in with the first strongman who'd come along.

All men ever wanted was babying after their own bad decisions. *How on earth is this my problem, you sad little insect?*

But what she said was, "Serve me well, and you won't be punished. But first I need you to fetch me a pen and paper, and a pair of fast horses that won't be missed." When no one moved, she clapped her hands. *"Now,"* she barked, and they scattered like the vermin they were.

She addressed the letter to Beatrix.

When they'd been girls, they'd written each other in code. It hadn't been play; it was out of necessity. After Beatrix had lost the use of her eye to that neighbor boy's stick, Claire's father had decided that she was a rotten influence on his daughter. He'd sworn that Claire wouldn't have been in that apartment—and in danger—had it not been for Beatrix, and perhaps he'd been right.

Still, it hadn't kept Claire from seeing her best friend. Under a rock in their tenements' shared courtyard, they'd left each other notes, detailing places and times they could meet. But Claire knew that her father watched her with the sharpest eyes. Had he seen her, from the window, picking up a scrap of folded paper, he would have snatched it from her hands and then beaten her if he'd seen it was from Beatrix. But had he done so, this is what he would have read:

BRIEF HISTORY OF THE POTATO

Any person can tell you that the potato is a vegetable. Keep in mind that they grow underground! Every potato tastes good when baked over an open fire. Really tasty potatoes can be left in with the coals. You'll know it is ready to eat when the skin is crisp! Three potatoes are enough to feed a family of three.

"I'm trading lessons with Beatrix's brother. He's studying plants right now." That was what she would have said, and snatched it back.

And then Claire would have taken the first letter of the first word in each sentence of Beatrix's letter and read BAKERY—and in the final sentence, she was given the time. THREE. The "meet me at" was implied. At three in the afternoon on the day the note was left (and if she couldn't check the rock every day, she did certainly try), the girls would share a French croissant in the bakery's alley, bought with pennies from Claire's complicit mother.

It was a delicious exercise for a child, exciting in its simplicity, its success—and it was a needless one as well. Because her father never saw her notes. Within weeks, he'd forgotten about Beatrix entirely. Her accident was just another in a parade of constant misfortune in their daily lives. By the time Claire's mother died, her father's whole world was his work, the one thing that couldn't betray him.

Until, of course, the Fair.

Beatrix and Claire's friendship had had more twists and turns than a triple-decker novel, and lately Claire had felt as though they'd reached its conclusion. Yes, she had flown her glider across the Monticello baseball diamond—but Beatrix would do anything for attention. Especially if her audience was wowed by her ingenuity.

What Claire needed now was someone who could understand self-sacrifice. But as much as she wanted to write Remy, or Tesla, and inform them of her plans, she knew that if she must send a message by enemy hands, it must go to Beatrix, and for this reason.

Bea,

All my admiration for your packing tips. Don't think I won't return the favor the next time you get to go on an exciting trip!

Any chance you can remind Georgiana to replace the lock on my desk drawer? My key turns and turns but nothing happens. See to it too that the servants' wages are paid through the next month—the date's tomorrow and I'm afraid the housekeeper will forget.

I miss you terribly and expect to be finished here in Monticello in perhaps a fortnight, perhaps three weeks. Say you'll come see me then, no arguments. Leave it to Tesla to overload you with so much work—really, if I was there, I wouldn't allow it, but I know you love immersing yourself in your projects, and I know too that the improved lightning rifle will be worth the wait. All I'll say is that when I see you next, I expect that you'll have an arsenal on hand! No need to start with a prototype—make as many rifles as you can once you have something you're happy with. Don't worry about cost, and don't shoot the messengers . . . maybe just have them go shovel manure for a while? Two weeks should do it.

All my love,
Claire

When she finished, she tucked the note inside the bodice of her absurdly luxurious dress. "Listen," she said, and the soldiers before her snapped to attention. "In an hour, you will take this note from me, and you will deliver it to Wardenclyffe Tower. You will all four go, riding double; you will ride through the night if you must. You will deliver this note directly into the lady Beatrix's hand, and no other." *That sounds sufficiently fancy; perhaps they'll take it seriously.* "Governor Duchamp will take you into his service. You will begin by mucking out our stables. If you betray him, you will be executed. If you try to leave his service, you will be found and executed. If you do anything other than follow his direct orders, you will be executed. Do you understand?"

When none of them spoke, just stared at the ground, she said, "I need to hear the words."

"We understand," they chorused.

The boy soldier clasped his hands. "But miss, you said two things. That was . . . more'n two things, warn't it?"

"That was *one* thing," she said.

"Then what's the second?"

"Ensuring that the General doesn't understand your betrayal until too late." Unbidden, her hand went up to touch her shorn-off hair. "Not that you deserve it. I need you to take me to Adams Island."

ELEVEN

Claire wasn't a military strategist. She wasn't a tactician. She wasn't even, as she'd just discovered, a decent flirt. The King had called all those bluffs, and more, and then he'd thrown a gauntlet before her: *I want a worthy adversary,* he'd said. All the world was a game to him, and he wanted a satisfying win.

What was it that the grizzled old soldier had said? That the General was hiding something on Adams Island?

A man. A dangerous man.

It was what he'd been pushing for in council meetings, the right of men to commit their relatives and take charge of their belongings; she understood why, now. He must have done it himself. Sent away someone who knew something he shouldn't. If the General were to become Governor of St. Cloud, he couldn't have any loose ends. And still it had to be someone he was unwilling to kill.

It could only be Captain Miller, recently missing in action.

And if he'd been put there, she'd find more of the General's prisoners, too.

Adams Island didn't allow visitors, didn't allow journalists. People were sent to Adams Island, and those people rarely came back.

After the spectacular failure of her gambit with the King, she knew that the Duchamps needed a new strategy. A military strategy. Knowledge she didn't have, knowledge she knew that Remy didn't possess.

What she needed was the one person the General was afraid of: his son, Captain Miller. And the only way to get him out of Adams Island was to do the very thing the General wanted her to.

She needed to go in herself.

When they brought Claire before the doctor in the sanatorium, she saw at once how things were there. How little she would have to act, to convince him that she was insane.

If she was allowed to speak at all.

The doctor peered at the soldiers over the spectacles at the end of his nose. "What did she do to you?"

A laugh cracked out of Claire, as hard as a whip.

"You see? She's mad. She's liable to come after us again, if you unbind her." The smallest soldier crossed his arms. "Bit us, scratched us. You can see my face. Landed a punch on Jimmy—on Private Oliver's neck. Look at that. She's a terror."

"And you did nothing to provoke her."

"No," the soldier said. "No, sir. We walked by this wretch on the street—we were down in the Levee, looking to have us a good time, know what I mean—and I suppose she took offense at our high spirits. Threw herself at us like a banshee. Whole way here, she's talking about how she's the Governor's wife or something. Delusional. The girl needs help."

It was a good story.

It had better be. I made it up myself.

The doctor made a note. "You've done a good thing today," he said. "This poor creature is certainly in need of help."

After a series of hearty handshakes and the doffing of caps, the soldiers left. Claire could hardly keep herself upright in her chair. For all she knew, they could be going off to report to the General.

Still, they had followed her plan so far, and what they'd told the doctor was true. She had gone for the softest, fleshiest parts of their bodies with her nails. Even after they tied her wrists, she'd flung herself against the wooden walls of the wagon, hollering for help. All of that before they had finally untied her, listened to what she had to say.

They had put on a good show, on the little leaky boat that brought her across the river to Adams Island. She had shouted and kicked and tried to fling herself overboard, but the two largest redcoats held her stoically in place, and when they pulled ashore, they dragged her out, panting, and hauled her before the sanatorium gates on Adams Island.

"We have a madwoman here," one of her captors yelled up to the guard, and slowly, so slowly, the gates before her opened. It was only when they shut behind her that she had gone quiet and shivery and watchful, like a dog left out in the rain.

In the doctor's office they had stripped her of the hat and the dress and the skirts below, and they had done so clinically. They hadn't groped her. It was still a violation, and now, forcing herself upright in nothing but her combination undergarment, she resisted the urge to cover herself with her arms.

She couldn't anyway, with her wrists tied behind her.

They aren't going to believe a word I say, she thought. *My story is so unbelievable. What if I just tell them the truth?*

"Sir," she said to the doctor. "I'm not insane. I have been very wronged by some . . . some terrible men, and I wish to be returned to my husband and my friends."

"Put out your tongue," he said.

"I'm sorry?"

"Put out your tongue. Now turn so I may see your hands. Move your fingers. Thank you, you may sit straight again." He made a note in his book. "All very abnormal. You poor girl."

Claire said, "Abnormal?"

"Who did you say your husband was?" The doctor was studying her, and he was not unsympathetic.

She squeezed her eyes shut, then forced them open. *The truth,* she thought, *the truth is wild enough.* "Governor Remy Duchamp. I am his wife. Formerly I was Claire Emerson, the daughter of Jeremiah Emerson, the inventor."

Sadly he shook his head. "My poor dear. You've had a time of it, haven't you?"

"Yes," she said. "Yes. I have."

As she'd spoken, the doctor had stood and walked to his medicine cabinet. He took out a blue flask and poured out a measure of its contents into a cup.

"Sir?" she whispered.

"You are overexcited," he said kindly, bringing the glass over to her. "When we are feeling as you are—as though our very souls are on fire!—it is easy to get confused. With all this unrest in our province, I must say I am shocked to not see more ladies needing to recover from a nervous ailment like yours. Much less some poor creature like you, so clearly ill-used by a man." He pressed the glass into her hands. "Here. Drink."

"What is it?"

"Drink, it will calm your nerves," he said, and when she said, "No, tell me what it is," he sighed and pushed his glasses up his nose. "Nurse!" he called.

A tall woman strode in as though she carried a yoke and buckets across her shoulders. "Dr. Kensington?"

"Would you please assist me in holding this woman down so that I may administer a dose of chloral hydrate?"

"That's a fancy way of putting it," the nurse said. "You don't need fancy," and before Claire could react, she reached out and twisted the skin of Claire's arm, hard, where the soldiers had grabbed her to haul her about.

Claire gasped, her eyes welling up, while the nurse took her by the nape—"A pity she doesn't have hair to hold on to"—and, with the other hand, pinched Claire's nose. Grimacing, the doctor poured the chloral hydrate down her throat.

"A nasty business, that," he said as she choked and sputtered. "Much easier to say yes. To let us take care of you. You want to be taken care of, yes?"

The solution was burning the back of her throat, the inside of her nose. She coughed and coughed and could not speak.

I want a worthy adversary, the King had said.

My province, the General had said.

Those bastards, Claire thought, and forced herself to swallow.

"The girl is insensible with fear," Dr. Kensington told the nurse. "Really, it's for the best she was brought here. I think Hall Six would suit her, don't you, Miss Grune? I didn't like what I heard those soldiers say about her behavior." The nurse opened her mouth, but the doctor went on speaking. "Yes, you're right, it's best to begin with Hall Six. Poor girl.

She can always be transferred to a gentler ward if she proves herself to be docile."

From a distance, Adams Island had always looked to her lushly green, with sprawling lawns that could be seen from the Monticello beaches in the summer. In the past, when Claire had heard the island spoken of, it had always been in the same breath as the Home for the Friendless, the orphanage where her father had adopted Margarete. That is, it wasn't spoken of often. When you took in the shape and makeup of a city like Monticello, your eyes caught on the extravagant restaurants and gardens and dance halls, on the skyscrapers and livery stables and the glittering stores by the lake, while the orphanages and asylums receded back into the landscape, shameful and invisible.

Unless you needed to lock away a very inconvenient girl.

Why would anyone want to consider those people in one's leisure time—the poor and unwashed, the unhoused and un-wanted? Though, of course, no one would admit publicly to such disdain. No good Christian, anyway, and Monticello was lousy with good Christians. Certainly Monticellans all agreed that these places must exist. The neediest of their populace must be cared for. Yes, they must exist, its citizens said—though of course it wouldn't do to give those institutions *too* much money. Why, to provide such luxuries as nutritious food and clean water and a comfortable bed might induce women to *feign* madness, to give up their children to the poorhouse so that they might all live off the government's teat.

When Claire's father had brought Margarete home from the orphanage, she'd been sickly and pale, with knobby wrists and knees. And yet she could carry in brimming pots of water from the pump. She could scrub the floor for hours, as tireless as a wind-up toy. At supper, twelve-year-old Claire had been surprised by how little the girl ate. Surely, even with her father's miserly food budget, they laid a better table than the Home for the Friendless.

One night when she was feeling brave, she asked Margarete why she had taken for herself only two slices of brown bread and no butter.

"Rich food makes me ill," Margarete had said, "after so many years without." Even today, the girl could not eat beefsteak, could not eat bacon.

It was a smaller complaint, so far as complaints go—it didn't speak to cruelty, as such; it didn't speak to outright deprivation—but it was enough to limn the rest of Margarete's life in the orphanage. At least in the way that Claire imagined it. She hadn't asked further questions. She told herself that it would pain Margarete to relive her former life, rather than admit the discomfort she would have felt to know the other girl's suffering. It was bad enough to watch her father treat her like a servant, when both Claire and Margarete had both been promised in the other a sister.

She wanted her sister now, badly. She wanted Beatrix. She wanted even her bluff and violent father to come roaring in, his Bible held above his head like an angry sun as he demanded these jailers release his daughter.

I made this decision myself, she thought, as Miss Grune dragged her through the Adams Island courtyard. *I cannot let this place—or my own performance—terrify me.*

She needed to master herself, to fully take in her surroundings. To observe, and then make a plan.

Here they were, the expansive lawns she had seen from the shores of Monticello, all that green. It was fenced off with a sign: DO NOT TREAD ON THE GRASS. Instead she saw women in rough dresses walking slowly about the dirt paths, some so old and wrinkled they looked like wizened pears. She saw a line of women tethered together with leather straps, ambling along like a long, strange centipede, and at first glance it was amusing until her mind made sense of what she watched. It was horrifying. *Why are those women bound?*

Who is in charge of this place?

Further still marched a set of inmates who appeared to be men. They were built one and all like those not accustomed to hard labor—soft limbs, chins tilted down in diffidence. They were digging, though for what Claire could not tell. They were all digging, all but one, who stood as still and straight as a flagpole, who shaded his eyes with a hand, who was looking directly at her.

Is that . . .

No, it can't be—

But she could not stop to make sense of it, not while Miss Grune heaved her along, and though at first she struggled against the larger woman's grip, she could feel her body growing heavy, lethargic. Chloral hydrate was a sedative, what the doctors called a hypnotic; it was given to you when you could not sleep. Beatrix's mother had taken it after the distress of her husband's death, and Beatrix had told Claire, in the imperious way a child speaks of death, that the doses had to be measured very precisely, because even a small amount too much could send you to a sleep from which you would not wake.

Beatrix was not even allowed to open the cupboard above the basin where the bottle lived.

And despite her effort to hold on to herself, Claire was no longer at the asylum. She was in the Lovells' tenement among the heavy smells of cabbage and pork fat, Beatrix's brother singing as he blacked his boots. Where was he? How old was he now? He had written her once about a potato. She felt scattered and slow. The chloral made her ankles turn beneath her, her feet skitter.

By the time they reached the heavy wooden door of Hall Six, Claire could hardly stand.

Focus, she told herself, *focus,* but her eyes were blurring. Inside, she had a confused impression of a church—so many pews in a line—before she was jerked into a side room, dark and smelling of mildew. There was a heavy copper bathtub. "Again?" a woman in white asked from the sink, where she was wringing out a dirty wet cloth. "We've just finished with the others."

"We don't know what they bring in with them, Agatha," Miss Grune said. "Get the brush."

The bathtub was full, and the water was not clean. The water was so full of oil and grease and dirt that it was thick, it was viscous like a soup. Claire was thrust into the cloudy, freezing bath, and something inside her roared back to consciousness, an animal awareness of herself. *This isn't right, this isn't right,* and she was saying the words out loud, kicking and screaming against her captors, and the woman called Agatha pinned her arms while Miss Grune roughly scrubbed her denuded head and body. She found every bruise, every scratch, and she scrubbed harder. By the end of it Claire was shivering so hard that her teeth mashed together. The only part of her that was warm was her cheeks from where her tears poured down.

They had never untied her hands.

It took the last of the fight left in her. It took the last of her thoughts, too, the last of the part that knew herself to be Claire. The chloral erased it all like a cloth across a slate, and without toweling her dry they dressed her in a slip that clung to her wet and frigid body, they laughed at her when she asked for a shawl. They marched her through the sea of pews and into a long hall with many doors and the one called Agatha said, "Put her in by herself tonight, she'll do a harm to one of the others," and as Claire, exhausted, shivering, stood for them to unlock the door to her cell, she could hear for the first time the other women.

Some of them were singing. Some of them were crying. One of them pleaded for mercy, pleaded again.

Miss Grune pushed Claire so that she staggered into her room, and before she could regain her footing, the door was bolted shut behind her.

I must hold on to myself, she thought, before the chloral clawed her down into sleep.

TWELVE

Even with the heady dose of sedative, she was plagued with terrible dreams.

Someone had soldered a crown to her head, and there was no removing it. She was made of metal, too, and when it came time to pry the crown from her body, the men couldn't tell the difference between her and the coronet. They came at her with a crowbar. *Apologies,* said the one in the doctor's coat, *but it's a family heirloom, and it must be returned to its rightful owner.*

She dreamed too that she was one of a team of horses being driven ever forward into the deserts of New Teshas. She had never been to New Teshas, never been anywhere, really, and now she was seeing the ground inch by inch, she was one of six mares towing a wagon of soldiers through the brushlands. The trees were low and stubby, the air punishingly hot, and as she ran and ran and gasped for air, she swallowed the dust that rose from all around her and badly wanted water. When she slowed, the men readied their whips. It was how this was done. Perhaps at the end of this endless journey there would be a soft bed of hay and a stream from which to drink.

When she awoke, she was in an ice-cold slip on a straw pallet in a cell on Adams Island, and at first Claire thought this too was a dream.

It was cold. It was ever so cold in her scrap of a dress that was still wet through and through. Even in the height of summer, it hadn't dried. St. Cloud's summers were famous for their humidity—Beatrix had once spoken of being in the "small hot mouth" of July, an image Claire had never forgotten—and that humidity crept into even the forgotten halls of Adams Island. She didn't know what time it was, as her room hadn't even a small window. All it had was this mattress overstuffed with hay, so unevenly packed that in her drugged sleep she had pretzeled herself into an impossible position trying to keep from rolling off.

This place is enough to wear at anyone's mind.

But the sounds were beginning in Hall Six, the booted footsteps of nurses and the clatter of keys, and she knew that they could come soon to let her out of her cell. And despite the pain in her back and her foggy head and the miserable shivering fits that overtook her, she knew that she wanted to face them standing.

When the nurse opened her door, Claire greeted her coolly. "Good morning," she said. "Could I bother you for a shawl? I'm very cold."

The nurse wasn't Miss Grune, or Agatha with the scrubbing brush. She was smaller and heavyset, with surprising green eyes. "I'm sorry," she said, taken aback. "We have no shawls for the patients. This is your first day, isn't it, Jane? If you come to the dining hall for breakfast, you will find it much warmer than this room."

Claire had been expecting many things, but she hadn't expected kindness. And yet the doctor had been kind too, in a fashion, until he was ordering her drugged and dragged away. "Thank you. But I would like some dry clothes. My name, by the way, is Claire. Claire Duchamp."

I will dangle that before her and see how she reacts. If they're in the habit of hiding away the General's prisoners, they might betray something, hearing his enemy's name.

"I see," the nurse said, as to a child. "But it says that your name is Jane Peabody on your records, and we do try to remind our patients of who they are, especially the ones who are in the grip of delusion. I'm afraid until you answer to your given name, Jane, it will be difficult for you to be granted release."

The nurse said it with such conviction, it set Claire back on her heels. "I see there's been some confusion. I am Claire Duchamp," she said, but the words came out as a whisper.

Oh, she was so cold, and hollowed out with sleeplessness. Once she was warm, she would be herself again.

The nurse regarded her with the sympathy one might have for a filly foaming and rolling its eyes. "Come," the nurse said, placing a hand on Claire's back, "we will begin with the names tomorrow. For now let's find you something else to wear."

As Claire was led through the warrenlike rooms of Hall Six, she found to her relief that the rest of the ward was indeed warmer than her cell. The heat buffeted her from all sides; it rose from the ground, wound in from the flung-open windows. And as her body warmed, so did her mind, until she was startled by her withdrawal into weakness. *My name is Claire Duchamp*, she thought firmly. *I have taken myself to this place by my own choice. I am looking to best the men who are trying to seize control of this province. To find and save Captain Miller.*

I need my wits about me now more than ever.

Claire hadn't thought often about insanity or its manifestations, though when she'd heard it discussed, it had always been within the fairer sex. In her childhood, she had heard stories of women who lived with nervous complaints that kept them from rising from their beds, but she hadn't seen any such afflicted in person. Occasionally other children would whisper about someone's mother, how she did not cook or clean, how she fought fiercely with their father, how some left their families altogether to seek something else—fortune, or adventure, or happiness—elsewhere. These women, too, were said to be mad.

In Lordview, one of her neighbors had a famous cousin come to stay, a young beautiful woman named Miss Alexandra, who had séances in their parlor where she could relay messages from your loved ones from beyond the grave. The whispers said she was dangerous, touched in the head, and yet those whisperers crowded her table on Sunday evenings. She had a lamp with a purple-fringed lampshade that rippled when there was a spirit in the room.

In truth, the only madman Claire knew of was her own father, and his madness too was something she doubted, for it masqueraded as grief for her mother. And besides, weren't brilliant men supposed to be eccentric? Weren't they meant to pace the night through, filling the air with pipe smoke, weren't they meant to abuse the lesser beings in their orbit? It was a consequence of genius; genius, splashing out like carbolic acid on those who came too close. The worst of Jeremiah Emerson's madness had been visited on her alone, but the whisperers noticed that too. Surely his daughter had brought it on herself. Indeed, that whisper of the chaos in her household—the debt collectors throwing bricks through the windows, the powerful men coming to call past midnight, the bruises ringing his daughter's wrists—had been enough to keep the rest of the neighborhood away.

Suffice it to say that the Emersons had never been invited to a séance. When Claire had passed Miss Alexandra on the street, they exchanged small, pained smiles.

It was much like the expression she wore as she walked again through the room she had mistaken yesterday for the main hall of a chapel. She had thought she'd seen it filled with pews, but these were just wooden benches, rows and rows of them. They had been constructed without backs, and they were high off the ground, and yesterday she had come during what must have been the evening walk, for they had been unoccupied then.

Today they were full of women.

There were perhaps twenty in that massive stone room, sitting in dresses of wool in the humid morning. Some were clearly in distress; one young woman picked continually at her clothing, and another laughed and laughed in a high childlike manner, while the woman beside her sobbed in German into a corner of her skirt. They all sat with their backs to the window, so they could not look out on the lawns and the glittering lake beyond; none of them held books, or magazines, or even a basket of sewing. Most of them, in fact, were merely staring at the wall. When Claire walked through with Miss Tennyson—she had been greeted as such by another nurse in the hall—none turned their heads to look. Only the bravest darted their eyes to the side to see who had joined them.

"Why do they sit like that?" she asked Miss Tennyson.

"It's to keep them from growing overexcited. We must maintain an atmosphere of calm."

"None of their feet touch the floor. There are no backs to those benches for them to lean against. It must be exhausting to keep themselves upright."

"Why, we can't have them falling asleep," the nurse said, "so they cannot be made too comfortable. No, this is a time for quiet contemplation. You will find it quite soothing, my dear."

"And where are the men housed?"

"The men?" The nurse looked surprised and dismayed. "Why ever would you want to see the men? I must say, if you are a loose woman—"

"To be wary of them," Claire said quickly. "I have been ill-treated by men."

She relaxed. "The men are kept in another part of the sanatorium entirely. You may only see them during your walks, and then from a distance."

They progressed to the Hall Six laundry, where Miss Tennyson dressed her in the same gowns as the other women wore, one of boiled wool that scratched against her skin, and within minutes of donning it all she could think of was taking it off. It was July, after all; it was the small hot mouth of summer, and how had she ever considered herself cold? She longed for the horrid wet slip even as Miss Tennyson bore it over to a pile of dirty laundry. The boots she was given were too large for her feet. "There," Miss Tennyson said with satisfaction, "you look a proper treat, Jane. Let's bring you to sit with the other Hall Six girls."

Claire struggled to keep her voice even. The nurse was kind, perhaps persuadable. Perhaps if she appeared to be sane (*I am sane,* she reminded herself), she could convince Miss Tennyson to confide in her. "What is the difference between Hall Six and the other areas?"

"Hall Six is . . . a place for close observation," Miss Tennyson said. "Eventually you may make your way to Hall Five, and so on, until you arrive at Hall One. And then onward to your family or friends, if they wish to look after you. Ah yes, let's introduce you to some of the other nurses. Do you know Miss Grune? Miss Studebaker?"

The two women were seated in comfortable chairs at the front of the room. Miss Grune, who just the day before had hauled Claire bodily into confinement, sat with her feet up on an ottoman embroidered with daisies. Miss Studebaker was cleaning her nails with a little knife.

Neither acknowledged Miss Tennyson. "Well," the younger nurse said uncomfortably, then bustled off before she finished the thought.

"Really they need to stop hiring girls from New Columbia." Miss Studebaker examined her hand, then chewed on a hangnail. "Thinks she's better than us."

"Uppity," Miss Grune said.

"Uppity," Miss Studebaker agreed.

Sweat ran down the back of Claire's neck, down her spine. It pooled at her lower back. Somehow this only made the dress itch more. "Where should I go?" she asked, regretting the words even as she spoke. Who were these women that she should be asking them for orders?

"Go?" Miss Studebaker inquired, popping her finger out of her mouth.

"Go to your *seat*," Miss Grune said, and Miss Studebaker laughed.

Gritting her teeth, Claire made to perch at the end of the nearest pew. Miss Studebaker laughed again, a rude sound.

"You need to earn the front pew," Miss Grune said, "you idiot child. Go take your place in the back."

It was like the words were a trip wire, and Claire plunged over into rage. *I put myself here,* she reminded herself, attempting to even her breathing. *I chose this debasement. I am here to gather information. To free a man. I should not draw attention to myself.*

And then she opened her mouth and said, "No."

It lifted her up, her anger, up and out of her body, and she wasn't in control anymore.

"No what?" Miss Studebaker asked.

"No," Claire said, enunciating. "You harpy." The hot pleasure in those words.

Miss Grune stood, her shoulders a farmworker's shoulders, her hands a farmworker's hands. "Take your *seat*, Jane."

Claire made a show of looking around her—the dirty flagstones, the light so weak and thin. "I see no throne here." Aloud, it sounded petty. It sounded delusional. "Where is my throne?" she said again, because it also sounded better than anything she'd said in years.

"Your throne is right here," Miss Grune said, looming over Claire, and she dragged her to the back pew.

Later, days would pass on that pew. Later, she would listen for hours on end to Miss Studebaker and Miss Grune gassing on and on from their overstuffed chairs, clambering to their feet only to seek out a lavatory or to take up their long wooden canes to whack at the legs of an inmate who had fallen asleep. The nurses knew everything. The obvious—which patients had screamed the night through ("Little Liliane Beaufort, it's always the frogs that yell when you throw them into the pot"), which picked at their skin and their clothes, which thought they were the Queen of England ("Almost as batty as that Jane Peabody—I'll give her a crown, all right!"), who needed a beating and why.

But they held forth too on other subjects. They fancied themselves the rare sort of experts, the ladies with the most discerning eye. To Claire, digging her nails into the wood of the back pew in an effort to stay awake and thereby avoid a clubbing, their words washed over her and broke into phrases she could never quite put together. For five minutes or ten, she would doze with eyes open, and jolt awake to hear the nurses discussing a man who might have been her father. "Became a preacher," Miss Grune would be saying, picking her teeth. "Now he rounds up the sad little harlots from the street and finds them husbands. Not *gentlemen*, mind you, but husbands all the same, and these are ones who'll beat some propriety into their little heads."

"A preacher? They said that in the papers?"

"They say plenty in the papers, Miss Studebaker." (They never called each other by their Christian names.) "*If* you were to read them. I read my papers every morning, that's how you know I'm a learned woman. They say the General is about to return St. Cloud to American rule. Give us a good strong man to look up to. Begone with this pussyfoot Frenchman, playing in his daddy's clothes."

"Ha! You know I don't trust the papers. They're wrong six ways by Sunday. One of 'em even said that that Nikola Tesla had invented some kind of lightning gun!"

"That man's a witch."

Miss Grune spit a stream of chewing tobacco onto the floor. "Heard too that he ran off with that little governess."

"Governess? Like a teacher?"

"Consort. Streetwalker, more like."

"Heard that she was the King's new mistress."

"Not half as pretty as that. No, I say that that's malarkey."

"Oh, boo-hoo, Miss Studebaker. You just have a little place in your heart for King Washington. Wishing *you* were riding along in the Royal Limited, warming his bed every night. Too bad for you that you look like an old shoe."

And then they broke into gales of laughter.

Every day after the first, she spent hours in that room, frigid and moist and overheated by turns, while Miss Grune and Miss Studebaker dissected, with incredible stupidity, the secret inner workings of the world. They never seemed to leave. They never seemed to eat. Night never came, or it never departed. Every morning Claire was given a dose of chloral—her outburst on the first day had earned her that dubious distinction—and in the hours that followed she fought it with her fists tied behind her back.

But on that first day, Miss Grune and Miss Studebaker didn't philosophize at the front of the room. Instead Miss Grune stood behind Claire with her cane, and whenever Claire slumped or twitched or curled her shoulders or yawned or lifted a single trembling finger, Miss Grune took a mighty swing and clubbed her on the back of the head.

THIRTEEN

"You need to eat something."

Jane's fingers listed in something lukewarm, lumpy. What was it? She wasn't sure. Swaddled in winter clothes in a punishing heat that pulled the last bits of moisture from her skin. Her brain was wrapped in a woolen blanket. It itched; the skin of her throat did too. She lifted her hand to touch it—yes, of course, her starched collar. Something warm dribbled from her fingers into her lap.

"You *must* eat."

Why could she see the same dress, the same collar, before her? Was she looking in a mirror? She began to laugh. She looked so *silly* with blond hair. And that delicate face, all freckled and clean, it looked nothing like what she remembered herself to be.

Another face before hers, both kind and stern. All

angles. Lambent eyes. Long elegant lashes, far too long for a man. *Unnecessary*, her mother would have said. *He should donate those to a girl in need*. He had kissed her in a palace. A palace of art? She had the sense that perhaps he had died.

Had she died as well?

"Don't just sit there. No, I don't care, she's been here days and they're going to let her starve herself if this continues. You hold the bowl, I'll feed her. Quick, before they see us."

Gentle hands (sweaty, but gentle) on Jane's chin, encouraging it to open. A spoon clacked against her teeth. Mush, foul; it had been horribly burned.

"Swallow. *Swallow.*"

Jane shook her head violently, but the hands—implacable now—kept her mouth shut so she couldn't spit the mush back out. This was a strange sort of palace, to treat its people so.

"You must eat. You will die if you do not eat."

Fingers plugging her nose—"I'll let go once you swallow." And she did, so she would be allowed to breathe.

There was a heat in her belly. Nausea rippled through her, then relief, then nausea again. The spoon returned to her lips. This time she accepted the gruel and swallowed before she could taste it; it kept her from gagging. For a vanishing second she focused on the girl beside her, penny bright and intent, shinier somehow than what surrounded her.

"Good," the girl said, holding aloft the spoon. "Again."

Jane (Jane?) opened her mouth.

Later, she decided she'd conjured up the girl with the spoon herself. That she had invented her own savior when she had been so close to being swept out to sea.

She had been a strong swimmer all her life. It had come on her by surprise.

Again she began to take notice of her surroundings. She was still, at turns, blindingly hot and cold; she was still half starved before mealtimes, and nauseated after. Sensation ruled her days, as it did so many of the other inmates'. (Claire refused to think of them as patients. Patients were provided with treatment.) When one's body was under siege, it was difficult to calm the mind, to try for critical thought. But after the day with the girl and the spoon and the gruel, Claire was determined not to lose herself again.

I want a worthy adversary, the King had said.

She didn't know how long she'd been in Hall Six, but by her best estimate, days had already passed. Days that the General could have used to fortify his position. For all she knew, the Livmonian troops had overrun the border. He'd ordered Miller shot, taken Wardenclyffe Tower by force, put Remy Duchamp to the sword.

Breathe, she thought. *I am where I should be. I will eat the rancid food. I will survive the heat and the silence. I will rescue Miller and seek his counsel, and we will put Remy back in his mansion.*

I will fight the feeling that I have flung myself into very deep water, very far away from shore.

Unlike many of the other girls who slept twelve or fourteen to a room, tended—guarded, really—by a lone nurse who read the Bible aloud to stay awake, Claire was roomed alone, in a ward with the women considered the most dangerous. At mealtimes nurses flanked their tables; when they sat in their pews, the inmates were clubbed for the merest whisper.

Another reason the girl with a spoon was likely an invention.

"Too much stimulation will make you ill," the nurses said.

"Only quiet contemplation will make you well," the nurses said.

"Conversation will only reinforce your delusions," the nurses said.

It wasn't until her seventh day that she discovered a time she could gather information without being beaten.

The walks on the Adams Island grounds. Those "constitutionals," in the white boating hats the nurses insisted they wear, as they clutched each other's hands and tromped through the heat and the rain and the rare glorious weather when the wind trailed the ridiculous ribbons hanging from the brims.

There was an art to it, Claire learned. Each day as they fell into the two long lines the nurses demanded, she angled to stand near the very back, the part that curved the closest toward the men's side of the island. Every day, she kept her eyes sharp for Captain Miller as she promenaded beside a different woman. Every day, as she waited for him to appear, she spoke softly to her companion, coaxing her to tell her story.

Perhaps they had been put here by the General too. And even if they hadn't been, she could listen. It was the least she could do in such a terrible place.

There were so many terrible stories.

Daphne had traveled with her sister to come to see the Fair; they had saved for months before embarking on their first train ride up from West Florida. Daphne could hardly sleep for days before the trip, but it wasn't excitement that drove her. Her sister, Phoebe, had a secret beau she refused to speak much about, though the two of them had traded letters for a year at least. His name was Isaiah; he was in the West Floridian army; Phoebe had met him at the greengrocer's—that much Daphne knew. She imagined they'd marry when his service ended. But in the midnights before their journey Phoebe rose silently from her bed, and into her traveling trunk she stuffed every rolled-up gown and cape and set of stockings that she owned, far more than she needed for their weeklong trip.

Phoebe had a temper. Daphne didn't dare ask questions for fear that she'd be left behind. She so badly wanted to see the Fair. Besides, their train journey was dusty and long, but uneventful, and all Phoebe spoke of was seeing the great Tesla's light show. Daphne basked in the sun, glorying in this time away from her long days as a locksmith's apprentice. Perhaps she'd misunderstood. Perhaps Phoebe wasn't planning something in secret.

But other shoes dropped—that's what they did. It fell out that, on the first morning at the boardinghouse they'd taken rooms in St. Cloud, Daphne came down to breakfast in a panic. Phoebe had vanished in the night; of course she had, without a note, and having taken their coin pouch with her, along with Daphne's good pair of shoes.

Daphne had gone to the landlord to ask for assistance.

I regret that the most, Daphne said to Claire out of the side of her mouth, as they skirted the lush lawn they weren't allowed to walk on. *Given the choice now, I would have burned his boardinghouse down to the ground.*

Daphne was diminutive, hardly five feet tall, with brown skin and braids, with large dark eyes that made her look years younger than sixteen. The landlord wouldn't believe she was of age. He asked Daphne again and again, "Where is your mother?" The other lodgers crowded around her. One was still holding a morning bun, little flecks of cream on her chapped lips. Daphne remembered that especially. "Where is," they asked, "your mother?"

The night before, Daphne and Phoebe had arrived close to midnight, hadn't properly introduced themselves to the landlord. Daphne had no money secreted away to pay their bill.

"My mistake," Daphne said now, soft and steely. Claire could hardly make out the words over the wind that whirled across lawns.

When the landlord called the police to transport Daphne to the Home for the Friendless, she insisted she wasn't an orphan, she was a woman grown. She had struggled mightily, all ninety-two pounds of her, and so they did not take her to the Home for the Friendless, they took her here instead.

The nurses would not send a telegram to her parents. They would not send a letter, would not allow her visitors. "I know I've had visitors," Daphne said, not crying. Daphne did not cry for fear that the nurses would see, and send her into isolation as a "rest cure" for her distress.

"I don't ask what will become of me," Daphne said, "for nothing will, unless I myself will it. No one is coming for me. I will get myself off this island, and punish those who put me here, and I will never be made a fool of again," and as she spoke, Claire believed her.

No, Daphne wasn't the General's prisoner.

The other girls let themselves weep. Why wouldn't they? They knew they would never leave this place; another week of isolation wouldn't matter. Liliane Beaufort, who the nurses had so mocked for screaming the night through, spoke little English, but Claire had enough French that she could understand bits of the girl's story. Liliane had been a dancer, in a traveling show. Claire said "dance hall" and the girl nodded;

Claire said "opera" and the girl nodded. She nodded to every suggestion Claire made. Perhaps she had danced in all of them. Perhaps it was all the same.

One night in her dressing room after a show, she had been taking off her Marie Antoinette–sized wig ("Grande," Liliane said, "très grande," extending her arms into the sky), and a man had come in. Men generally weren't allowed in. ("Seulement?" Claire had asked, meaning "Were you alone?" Her French really wasn't that good. The girl pursed her lips, levered her hand back and forth. It was the right word and it wasn't. She reframed it for Claire in her elegant voice—"Étais-tu seul?" This girl who had screamed the night through.) She had, indeed, looked up to find that for the man she was alone.

The man.

"General?" Claire had asked, her heart in her mouth.

Liliane frowned. "En generale?"

"Non," Claire said. "Militaire?"

The other girl thought, then shook her head no. She slumped her shoulders. With her hands, she clutched an imaginary gut and waddled. "Ce n'était pas un militaire."

The General was lean, powerful. He did not slouch. Still, Claire pressed the girl further; you didn't know where a story might lead.

It was muddled in the telling, but perhaps the experience had been muddled too. Money had changed hands. The usher had taken a bribe, perhaps. The man had seen Liliane doing her pirouettes on the stage and selected her as though from a menu. She had fought back; she wouldn't go quietly. But he had been an important man, behaving as so many important men did. Important—the word was the same in English. He brought her home by force.

"Important how?" Claire had asked.

"Big house. Grosse. Servants en plus."

She spent many nights in his bed, unwilling; he talked on and on and on, fed her bad food. She never saw the sun. Finally she had had enough and went after him with a fireplace poker.

If she did not want to be forcibly made his mistress, she must be insane. The inevitable wagon had been called.

It filled Claire's throat with acid. "Where is this man," she asked, "and when can I take off his head?"

Liliane made a fist, said, "Je suis là. Nous sommes ici."

I am there. We are here.

As was Tilly Goldman, who gave her full name in a work-aday manner, actually extended a hand to shake. Her story was a simple one, if any of their stories were simple. She'd gone to a doctor on the recommendation of her friends, as she was feeling nervous and afraid after the death of her husband. They had no children, and their large estate was difficult to manage alone. Her husband's younger brother had seen her distress. He'd recommended a short stay on Adams Island.

She'd arrived two years ago.

She'd never been allowed to leave.

Her husband's brother, she assumed, controlled all her estate now.

On and on it went, this parade of women in misery, marching up and down the island. Claire bore witness as best she could. She had no useful advice—not like Daphne, who told her that if you raised your voice to the doctors, they'd forever brand you a hysteric, or Tilly, who said that if you pleaded your case too quietly, they'd claim you suffered from a lack of feminine feeling. When asked for her own story, Claire said only that she had trusted the wrong people, which was more or less the truth.

As they marched up and down the length of the island, gulls wheeled overhead. Water lapped at the sugar-sand shore. They did not, did not, did not tread on the grass.

And in the distance, those same male inmates with shovels, digging, no matter what time of day. Always one with his head flung up, staring. But sometimes he was tall and lean, like a librarian, and sometimes he had the proud shoulders of a soldier, and the closer Claire came to him, back at the end of her line, the less sure she was that this was the man she was seeking.

She had to get closer, to find out for sure. But she hadn't yet found a way to sneak over to the men's side of the asylum. Every night she was locked in, and every morning she was drugged.

But she waited. She watched for her chance. For now, she focused on listening to the women who wanted to speak. To be sure, there *were* women on Adams Island who were ill and needed help, and oftentimes all Claire could do for the inmate she walked with was to hold her hand and listen. Some didn't want to be touched, and so she didn't. Some were in the grip of very real delusions, were a long way away from here. Not a single one of their stories led back to the General.

Perhaps Miller was already dead, and she had been seeing his ghost on this island.

She was making no progress. She was running out of time.

Claire wondered, as she ate the gruel and the bread and the rancid butter, as she began to ask questions of the doctors during her examinations, as the days slipped one into the other, how many of the girls in Hall Six had lost their grip from their treatment in this facility. She had never thought that insanity made one worth less as a human being, but she had thought before—incorrectly, she knew now—that there was a firm line that separated the sound of mind from those who suffered. That once you went over into that dark ocean, there was no swimming back.

"But as you can see," she told Dr. Harmsworth, "I'm perfectly well." She kicked her feet a little from her perch on the examining table, trying for sprightliness.

The doctor ignored her.

A man, she thought, looking at his Adam's apple. A flash:

her father, asking her to bless her. Remy's sudden recovery from his illness. *I'd been surrounded by only women and for so long, I'd forgotten—*

"Hold out your arms," the doctor said, and took up a ruler. He aligned it with one wrist, then the other. "Good."

He was so close to touching her skin. What did he want, this man? Could she influence him? Could she make him want what was best for *her*?

She began to lean in to his touch, then jerked herself back. Jerked back her train of thought.

This too is a kind of madness. I must rely on my brain, not on men's delusions.

"My apologies," she told the doctor. "The ruler is cold."

He ignored her. "Now stick out your tongue for me."

Claire obeyed. Pushing his spectacles up on his nose, he peered into her mouth. Dr. Harmsworth was a doctor she hadn't met before; he was younger, blithely handsome. He had blue eyes and a lovely smile and he paid no mind whatsoever to the words of his patients. Or at least, he paid no attention to her.

There had to be a way to get information out of him. Gossip, even. Perhaps if she were prettier—less skeletal. Perhaps if she still had her hair. Her hand stole up to touch the brushy growth along her scalp.

Not too passionate. Not too dispassionate. Smile like a normal girl would.

How does a normal girl smile?

"What is the ruler for?" she asked him.

"Patient continues with nervous fondling of her head," he told the nurse over his shoulder. Miss Studebaker made a note in her file.

"I'm only self-conscious about my hair," she said. "It wasn't my choice to shave it."

"Patient is lying," he told Miss Studebaker.

Again the nurse made a note. "You have a keen eye, Doctor."

"I work best under *your* keen eyes."

The nurse giggled like a child. She was forty if she was a day.

"Tell me," he continued, "what would your diagnosis of this patient be?"

"Oh, I could hardly—"

"Your intellect is really wasted on this place, Miss Studebaker. Do give your opinion."

At this buffoonery, Claire's eyes began to unfocus. She tasked herself with staying present. This was, after all, a room she hadn't seen before. In here, the walls weren't made of cinder block, but plaster; the ceilings stamped tin, a fleur-de-lis pattern embossed into the tiles. Around them the bookcases were crowded with texts on hysteria, nervous excitement, the weakness of the female form. Ceramic models of the human skull dotted the shelves, painted and labeled with markers she couldn't quite read. The doctor had rolled his chair out to examine her, and behind him the desk was thick with files: *Irina Ivanovich, Tilly Goldman, Hermione Ann Pappas.* Her fingers itched to flip through them, to see once and for all what kind of racket Adams Island was running.

To find out if Miller's file was in there, somewhere.

And even as she wished it, Dr. Harmsworth stood and asked Miss Studebaker to show him her notes. He crowded her close into the corner.

With the two of them distracted, Claire leaned forward to rifle through the files—and then her hand stilled. The doctor had a subscription to the *St. Cloud Star.*

In Hall Six the news was far too excitable a subject for its inmates; all Claire learned of the outside world was through the misinformed gossip of the nurses. But here, spread-eagled across an anatomy textbook and a dusty-looking stethoscope was the front page, dated August 5, 1893—*August,* she thought dizzily, *how on earth is it already August? How old is this newspaper?*

SEARCH CONTINUES FOR THE MISSING MRS. DUCHAMP
Part six of our eyewitness account of Lady Duchamp's abduction

The byline was John Mackenzie, Lizzie Cochrane's pen name. But the ink of the front page was smudged by the doctor's sweaty hands. From her distance, she couldn't read it. She longed to pull it closer to her, but she'd surely be noticed by the pair flirting in the corner.

Her eyes roved. Any scrap of news, anything she could learn—there, on the back page:

DAUGHTERS OF THE AMERICAN CROWN HOST CHARITY EVENT

There was a photograph of women in white dresses, but unlike the inmates', these were gauzy and light. She recognized some of their faces from the D.A.C. meeting Beatrix had brought her to, before. The most memorable one, of course, was Rosa Morgenstern, her hands delicately resting on the shoulders of the women about her. She smiled with shark teeth.

This esteemed group of patriotic ladies will, this Saturday next, host a charity auction to support their new initiative for the betterment of women's lives.

"I wouldn't say women's rights, I'm more for women's lives!" Miss Rosa Morgenstern told this reporter with a laugh. "We're just trying to make our sisters' lives a little brighter with our work."

The Daughters of the American Crown want an expansion of the Married Ladies' Property Act, which currently allows a woman's assets to be given into the trust of her husband if she dies or is declared mentally infirm. They would like the law to allow the sisters, daughters, and female friends of such a woman to offer that assistance as well.

"If a woman is institutionalized," Miss Morgenstern said, her hair becomingly pinned about her head, "and she has no male relatives, surely her finances must still be tended by a loving relation! We're not talking about inheritance. That's only meant for men. But wouldn't it ease a poor sick woman's mind, to know her things were being looked after by her friends?"

At the luncheon, shrimp cocktail was served. . . .

Miss Studebaker shrieked with laughter. "Oh, thank you for noticing, that new nurse is just a pain. Such a bleeding heart!"

"And disfigured, as well," the doctor said. "I won't allow her on my service. Really, it's distressing for the patients to look at her. . . ."

Claire had another minute with the paper at least, while they continued their vile gossip. But she could only read snatches—Livingston-Monroe, and men's rights, and Governor Duchamp—while she processed what she'd just read about the D.A.C.

They had done what they did best: aligned themselves with the nation's worst impulses, and for their own personal gain. Rather than fight against an unjust law, they had bent it to their own advantage. The D.A.C. had deep enough coffers to buy off any doctor they so chose. With those physicians in their pockets, they could have any inconvenient person declared insane.

And once that person was locked away on Adams Island, the D.A.C. could take everything they owned. What better way to dispose of one's political enemies?

It hadn't escaped Claire's notice that, at the moment, the most powerful woman in St. Cloud was *her*. And that the sharks of the D.A.C. would be smelling her blood in the water, now that the papers were reporting her kidnapped. It made the Duchamps look like easy prey.

Bless Lizzie Cochrane, and damn her too.

The most powerful woman in St. Cloud, and she was sure that if she asked these nurses for so much as a drink of water, she would be denied.

You chose to be here, she reminded herself. *You are a worthy adversary.*

The doctor had tired of his flirtation sooner than she'd thought. When he turned back to her, Claire's color was still raised from the news of the D.A.C. To explain it she feigned indignation. "I'm sorry," she said, pointing at her file in Miss Studebaker's hands, "what on earth does it say about me in there?"

Her ploy worked. For the first time, Dr. Harmsworth met her eyes.

Then he winced.

"It says that you are a nineteen-year-old woman named Jane Peabody. It says that you were married, and that you ran away from your devoted husband," he said, and motioned for Miss Studebaker to bring her notes. "It says you were found raving in the street with a straight razor. That you injured the two worthy soldiers who bundled you up and brought you here for help, and that since you have arrived, you have been suffering from delusions of grandeur and inflated ideas of your power and worth."

It was a fun house mirror of herself, fit for one of the Fair's midway rides.

No, there was no need to put on a show to convince these doctors that she was mentally ill. She could tell them the baldest truth, and do it without fear.

Why not?

"My name is Claire Duchamp," she said, "formerly Claire Emerson. My picture has been in the newspaper, in the *St. Cloud Star*—I see you have a subscription? If you don't believe I am who I say I am, you simply need to look. I was photographed on the steps of the Governor's Mansion—of course, that picture was taken before I was starved nearly to death and battered by the nurse you call Miss Grune." She could hear herself speeding up, breathing faster. *Calm,* she thought, *calm.*

The doctor stole a glance at the nurse, but said nothing.

These fools.

"Answer me. Am I not speaking clearly?" Claire said.

"Hasn't anyone said anything about the way I was kidnapped from the King's Box at a rather public baseball game? Hasn't my likeness been on the front of every newspaper?"

He cleared his throat. "I'm really not at license to say—"

"How many inmates have ever left this place? How much does the General pay you to hide away his dirty secrets?" She crossed her arms. "Is it enough to let you sleep at night?"

"Enough," Miss Studebaker said, and took Claire's ear in her pincerlike grip. "Doctor, I apologize for the behavior of this disturbed young woman. We'll be going now."

"Of course," he said, pulling out a handkerchief to wipe his brow. "I mean, yes. Yes. Please show in the next patient. I don't think we'll need to see Miss Duch—Miss Peabody for at least another month."

In a month I will be back in the mansion, and this hell house will be forever closed. Galvanized by the thought, Claire fought hard as the nurse jerked her to her feet. At the door she dug her heels in heavily, clawed her fingernails into the soft wood of the doorjamb. "Have you stopped to think, for one single moment," she hissed as Miss Studebaker grunted with the effort to pull her away, "what I will have done to you when I am restored to power?"

It was already August.

If Beatrix had in fact received her encoded letter, if she chose, this time, to help free Claire from her captivity, Claire would be an inmate on Adams Island only a day or two longer.

I only have that much time to find Captain Miller.

Dr. Harmsworth's lip twitched. "Remove her," he was saying.

"You don't look very powerful to me," Miss Studebaker told her then, and still it took three nurses to drag Claire away.

It was the norm after any small infraction to be tossed into her cell like a bale of hay. But Claire had crossed an invisible line this time. Perhaps she had simply misbehaved in front of the wrong man.

She thought, for some strange reason, about Remy.

Down the dark, damp corridor, feet scrabbling in her too-big boots around corners she'd never been allowed to see; down a flight of stairs and then another. Down and down into the bowels of Adams Island.

Here the floor was packed earth and there were no electric lights. Claire had stopped struggling. Instead she went limp so the nurses had to haul her down the hall like cargo.

A door. They put her through it, threw her to the ground. There they dosed her with chloral for the first time in days, holding her nose until she was forced to swallow, but this time Claire had the presence of mind to vomit the moment they left. Her arms braced against the hard-packed floor, she breathed in staggering breaths, determination filling her lungs.

Then she looked up.

Where on earth am I?

FOURTEEN

Hall Six, the nurse had told her, was where the very worst cases were kept. Who then did they keep in Hall Six's basement under lock and key?

No lamps, no windows. Claire steadied her breathing. Some of the chloral had made it to her blood, of course, but she could fight off the drowsiness by pacing her new cell. By crafting a plan.

Her eyes began to adjust to the dark.

There was a bucket in the corner. There were manacles bolted to the wall—too rusted, thank God, to be used. Little winged insects flittered through the air, and she heard the low thrumming pulse of others rubbing their legs together.

In the middle of the room a shallow hole had been clawed into the earth, and as Claire squinted into the darkness, she saw that hole held a woman's body.

With a shout, Claire scrambled to her feet.

"Easy," a voice breathed into the darkness. "Easy, girl, easy. That's what I always say."

Claire waited for her heartbeat to slow. "Who . . . what's your name? Did they put you in that hole? Can I—" She stopped. A pale stick of an arm was emerging from the hole, then the other. A knotted mass of copper hair.

"I'm Aislinn Kelly," the woman said, from a mouth like a gash in the darkness. "That hole is my bed."

It had taken her months to dig it.

"I kept my nails long," she was saying, as Claire walked a tight circle to shake off the chloral. "Like tiny shovels! Plow, plow, plow. All of it was flat in here, before, and all I did was sleep. I wanted contours. I wanted an elegant little bed. It took me months to dig myself a little nest." Aislinn scratched at her face. "Then I chewed my nails off. No need anymore. Got in the way. They grow back. Did you know they grew back?"

"How do you keep time in here?"

"Sleep, wake up. That's one day." The woman cocked her head to the side, grinned. "I can count the days now by talking to you. One talk, that's one day now."

Terror cut through Claire's sedative haze. Terror for Aislinn, and terror for her. "We'll talk about getting you out of here."

"Silly child," Aislinn said, and grinned again. This time

Claire saw she was missing most of her teeth. "I'm here forever."

"Why? What could you have possibly done for them to throw you away like this?"

"I'm Aislinn Kelly," she said again. Rhythmically, almost. Like she spent her hours chanting it in the dark to not forget. "Aislinn Kelly. I loved the wrong man."

That name. Claire knew that name. She tried to search her mind and came up with bruises and grime instead. A headache behind her temples, the collar of her dress twisted around her neck. "Aislinn . . . Kelly?"

"Aislinn Kelly," the woman whispered. "I used to love the King."

She'd been all over the society pages, with her daring dresses and updos and her lion tamer's smile. Aislinn Kelly, on the King's arm at a baseball game, pointing at a home run cresting through the sky, her parasol over her shoulder. Aislinn giggling behind a hand in Orleans's finest chophouse, the King whispering something in her ear. Aislinn, all freckles and big sweet eyes, caught spinning dizzy circles on a bicycle (a bicycle!) in the King's private rose garden. Washington with his arms full of flowers on the sidelines, his face lit from within. A man who couldn't believe his good luck.

Across the First American Kingdom, girls styled their

hair like hers and bought their own lace-trimmed parasols. They stayed daringly long in the sun to try for that same insouciant spray of freckles. Claire, age nine, had followed Aislinn's adventures along with the rest of the country. Her mother hadn't yet died, and together they would steal away the newspaper's society section each week and read about her exploits. AISLINN AND THE KING, OFF AGAIN TO FRANCE! Sunday mornings on the sofa with her mother and the gossip column, like a serving of strawberry shortcake after the meat and potatoes of that week's schoolwork.

It's a harmless diversion, her mother told her father when he protested the frivolity of their interest. *How else am I going to see Paris? Besides, Claire and I are waiting for the King to propose to her. It's a good way for a girl to learn the value of marriage,* she'd said, the argument that had sold him.

But the King had never proposed.

For a few years, Aislinn Kelly was everywhere. Then she wasn't. Claire vaguely recalled hearing she'd taken ill, but by then Claire's mother had died. Her Sunday mornings with the society pages were a thing of the past. If Claire thought about Aislinn at all, she'd assumed what everyone had, that the King had tired of his mistress and settled her somewhere with a kiss on the cheek and a cute little cottage in New Columbia. Maybe someday Aislinn would write a book about her life for bored old ladies to be scandalized by.

Claire had never once imagined her on Adams Island, digging a hole in the ground to sleep in.

A hole she was proud of.

"I convinced them too to bring me new water once a week," Aislinn was saying, her arms wrapped around herself. "And now that you're here I think maybe we'll have more food? More than bread. Bread and water. Do you like bread?"

"I do," Claire said gently. She settled on the floor by Aislinn's bed. "What else can you tell me about your days?"

"Nothing."

"Nothing?"

"My days are full of nothing," Aislinn said. "I have to fill them with the memories of before. There was everything, then. I try to bring in the everything."

"Before? When you were with the King?"

"The King?"

"Did the King put you here?"

Frowning, Aislinn looked at the ground. "They told me not to say that."

"Who did? The nurses?"

"I was told and told and told not to say that. I am not Aislinn Kelly, they said." She stole a glance up at Claire. "I am, though. At least I think so."

"I think so too. I saw your picture in the paper when I was a girl."

"You did?" At that Aislinn smiled, a bit shyly. Even in these depths of hell, she had a touch of the ebullience that Claire remembered from the photographs. "What was I doing in the picture? Was I pretty?"

"Very pretty. Let's see. I remember seeing you eating a lobster at a fancy restaurant. You were by the ocean."

She didn't speak for a long minute. "In New Columbia," she said finally. "Up by the border with Canada. *Brr*, it was cold. They gave me odd little tools to eat it. Lobster. It's peasant food, you know."

Claire said, "I remember too seeing a picture of you at a zoo. You had on a straw hat with ribbons. You were posing with a . . . giraffe? Or an elephant?"

"A giraffe." Aislinn coughed. "A tall one. My head hurts."

"We don't have to talk if your head hurts. We can talk later on." *God knows we're likely to have plenty of time. How on earth do I get us out of here?*

"I want to. I want to, I never talk. I mean I do talk, but I talk to myself." She scratched at her tangle of hair.

"What else do you remember?"

"I played croquet. There were photographs of that. The King would come when there were photographers, other times he was away. If I wanted I could go to the ball club to see him and I would sit and drink lemonade. Lemonade! I used to drink lemonade. They would throw the ball and catch the ball and I never cared much, but I knew I'd lose my head if I said so. So I didn't say so. He met me in a baseball park, you know, I was a ticket taker. The first time. So he thought I liked it. Baseball. Him. But it was a job. Just a job. I was a ticket taker in New Teshas. He used to say that to me very fast like a rhyme. 'A ticket taker in New Teshas, a ticket taker in New Teshas—'" Her speech was winding up faster and faster, like a pitcher's arm, until she exploded into a coughing fit.

Claire went to get the bucket from the corner. The water was brackish, dirty. With the air of long practice, Aislinn drew it into her cupped hands and drank.

"You left New Teshas?" Claire asked.

"I went with him when he left. He wanted me to. You know I went with him everywhere? To the moon! We went to the moon. I lived in a crater, it was be-au-ti-ful." She drew out the word with relish. "Much nicer than *this* crater. I had fairy dust in my hair. . . ."

She went on like that for quite a while. At times she'd spin out a plausible-sounding memory, and at others she was clearly in the grip of some fancy. Mostly, though, her stories dwelled in the in-between. She'd taken a riverboat one summer—with a team of dancing monkeys. She'd eaten a French omelet for breakfast every single morning—while the King ate nothing. "Nothing ever, he supped on air—the very finest air!"

Still, Claire listened. She listened to every word until Aislinn's words ran out, even when her own eyes grew heavy from the chloral. It was the smallest kindness she could offer.

Eventually Aislinn talked herself to sleep, her head drooping lower and lower until it rested on a pillow of her arms, there in her hollowed-out bed of dirt.

She had come here seeking the General's secrets and had found the King's instead. A worthy adversary, that's what he had wanted.

Well, he would get his wish.

A little voice inside her was asking, *Why settle for the seat of St. Cloud when you could topple a King from his throne?*

Claire stood and took herself to the door of their cell, where a little light bled in from the slot for food. There were so many possibilities, now. The King's treatment of such a beloved woman would cause an outcry. Once Aislinn had been freed, Lizzie would gladly put her and her story on the front page of the *St. Cloud Star*.

A plan. She was suffused with a strange sense of calm. *Though I can't do anything until I escape,* she thought. *And they might have planned to leave me here only a day or two, to scare me. I should ask Aislinn if she's had cellmates before.* But Claire didn't know if she could take Aislinn's answers for truth. *It's not her fault. She believes everything she's saying. Every last word.*

A little voice whispered in her ear: *And if rescue does not come for you, and if you cannot then rescue yourself, you could easily become her.*

Her calm fled, and cruelly, the last of the chloral had

burned away. It was many, many hours until she could fall into sleep.

"Wake up wake up! Wake up wake up! What is your name? I've named you Edith." The patting of Claire's head, as though she was a dog.

Claire blinked herself awake. Surely it wasn't already morning.

"Such short hair. Is that in fashion now?" Aislinn made an effort to wash her face with the dirty water. It looked, too, like she'd tried to wash her dress. Now it was both falling apart and damp.

"It's not," Claire said. "It was a punishment."

"That was your punishment?" she asked guilelessly. "Mine seems worse."

"Why are you being punished?"

Aislinn laughed. "Do you want some bread?"

The hours ran on like that. Claire didn't want to call them days. She had no sense of time down in Aislinn's room; even more than the absence of sunlight, the absence of order was torturous. Like being lowered into an abyss on a rope, inch by slow inch.

Claire kept trying to steer the endless conversation back to Aislinn's years with the King. It didn't seem to hurt her, Aislinn. She was eager to recount her memories. But one memory tangled with another, and that memory tangled with fantasy, and soon Claire didn't know where or when Aislinn was. Finally the woman grew hoarse, then went silent. The two of them lay on their backs, breathing in the cool. After some time—ten minutes? ten hours?—the butt ends of a loaf of bread were pushed through the slot in the door. They fell—*one, two*—into the dirt.

Claire yelped.

"Scares me too," Aislinn said. "Like gunshots."

Claire stood and collected the bread. "Did you hunt game with the King?" she asked, passing Aislinn hers.

"No," she said. "He's afraid of rifles. Doesn't want anyone to know. He's afraid of lots and lots. No, I went shooting with my daddy when I was a girl. Though I'm not supposed to tell. Women aren't supposed to."

A prickle, then, on the back of Claire's neck. "The King is afraid of rifles?"

Lightning rifles, the King had said. *Like something out of a nightmare.*

"Ohhh," Aislinn said, gnawing on the hard bread. "Rifles! Not just rifles. He's afraid of bees, but maybe because their sting makes him swell up something fierce. Like he could die. But sometimes I think he wants to die? He's always out in his garden. He grows columbine and indigo and wild bleeding heart. He has roses too. Bees everywhere. The gardeners are supposed to tend it, but he does the roses himself." She stopped chewing. "I'm not supposed to tell that."

Claire kept her smile steady. *The King is allergic to bees. He could die.* "I won't tell anyone," she assured her.

Aislinn relaxed. "Good. It was an accident that I found out. Saw him running. He keeps hives on the grounds because of the honey and because he's a fool."

"He's a fool?"

"An utter fool," she said. "Oh, he's smart, but he's not smart. A fly would get into his chambers and he'd hear the buzz and think it a bee and run. Poof! Out into the hallway, hollering for his butler. Strange man." She mashed the stale bread between her hands to soften it, then tore off another hunk. "All the time with people he's so calm. Hand on my back, shows me where to go, makes sure I know what to say. Then we go back to his bedroom and he double-checks the window locks. Not the door! The window. Roses always by his bed. He cuts fresh ones every morning. Even in the winter in his hothouse."

"He must love roses."

"He doesn't love anything."

"Anything, or anyone?"

"No one," she said with her mouth full. "He loves no one. He has no family. Not me! I had my daddy. I loved him. It was him and me, always. Did I tell you about the time he taught me how to ride a horse . . ."

Aislinn began to wander back through her childhood in New Teshas. As Claire listened, half frustrated, half intrigued, she kept returning to Aislinn's insistence that there were things Claire wasn't supposed to know. It wasn't common knowledge that the King was allergic to bees, or that he was superstitious—in fact, Claire was sure the King worked very hard to keep those weaknesses private.

But his mistress, living day in and day out with him for years, would know all those things, and more.

". . . and my daddy died the year after I went to Philadelphia on the train." Aislinn had long finished eating. She eyed Claire's untouched bread, and Claire gave it to her. The gruel they served upstairs was gourmet fare compared to this.

"Did you ride the train often?"

"The King always rode the train. Always always. He didn't want to be in Philadelphia. He said that house was haunted." She paused. "I'm not supposed to know that. Avert."

Claire watched, bemused, as Aislinn pressed two fingers to her lips.

"What does that mean?" she asked. She'd seen the King make that gesture at the baseball game.

"Ward off bad luck. The house is haunted. The King is haunted. He does it to send the bad spirits away."

"Haunted?"

"He has no family," Aislinn said again.

"He has a cousin living in Russia—"

"Far away. Far, far away. As far as she can get." Unexpectedly, Aislinn giggled. "She took a hot-air balloon all the way there! I love hot-air balloons."

"He has an uncle—"

"That old man? He doesn't know what day it is," Aislinn said. She seemed unaware of the irony.

"No family." Claire was so close to it, now. "No family," she repeated. It was true that the King had no close relations, but Claire hadn't ever questioned it. Her own mother and father were both only children; her father was the only one of five siblings to survive childhood illnesses and accidents. Claire's experience of family was that few made it out alive.

If the King died without producing an heir, there would be chaos, Claire realized. She had been so myopically focused on St. Cloud that she hadn't given the matter due thought. But he seemed blithely unconcerned. Perhaps he had an illegitimate child by one of his mistresses?

Besides, the King was not yet thirty. Perhaps he felt that he still had time?

"No family," Aislinn was saying. "No family *now*. No one close to him. Did I tell you I learned to ride horses from my daddy? I was only thrown once."

"The King has no family now." Claire leaned in. "And then?"

"He used to have a brother. A bigger brother. Ernest. Ernie. Smaller now than Gus. Augustus. King Augustus." She giggled again. "Silly name."

Claire tried to follow. "He died when they were young, yes?"

"I learned to ride—"

"The King," she redirected, gently.

Aislinn frowned. "I am *trying* to *tell you* about the *King*."

It was the first time she had seen Aislinn frustrated. Claire apologized.

"I learned to ride," Aislinn began again, "when I was young."

And as she spoke, Claire began to understand.

It was a sad story, well known. Ernest and Augustus Washington, the young princes only a year apart in age. Ernest had been the elder. Stories of them running amok in the palace in short pants, putting frog spawn in their tutors' beds, driving their nurses mad. Everyone loved to hear of their exploits, and the newspapers knew it, gave them endless column inches. The boys had been the darlings of the nation.

Until during a day's ride on the palace grounds, Ernest was thrown from his silver palfrey into a fallen log. He broke his neck. He was fifteen years old.

He died in the night, and the next morning, Augustus became the heir to the First American Kingdom. The nation mourned Ernest for weeks; Augustus ordered that there be no body on display at the funeral, for fear that frantic, grieving mourners might fight through the crowd to touch it.

"You were thrown from a horse," Claire repeated. Her pulse throbbed in her temples. "Like Ernest was."

"I told Gus. The King. I told Gus the King. He was so sad sometimes and I wanted him to talk about Ernest. I thought he missed his brother. I thought it would help. Talking helps! But he held me like this"—she clasped her own throat—"and said, 'Who told you, who told you?' And I said everyone knew! And he said, 'No one knows.' And I wondered about it forever until I realized that—"

"There hadn't been a riding accident," Claire whispered.

"I said it to him. After I finished wondering, I said, 'What really happened?' I said boo, I guess. Next day I came here."

"What *did* happen, Aislinn? What happened to Ernest?"

"Ernie says this, Ernie says that. The King quoted Ernie all the time. 'Hiley, don't let them forget you're the King!' Hiley this and that."

Claire shook her head. "I don't understand—"

"Augustus Hiram Washington. Gus doesn't want to be Gus. Everyone else does, but not Gus! Thought it was undignified and so Ernie called him Hiley, always. After Ernest died he was Gus again. Changed his face."

"How did he die, Aislinn? I need to know."

She shrugged. "He stabbed him. The King spends every one of Ernest's birthdays in the rose garden, by the Carolina roses. The fairies buried him there."

With a groan, the door to their cell eased open. Claire had to put her hand up to protect her eyes against the dim light.

"The door," Aislinn muttered, "the door the door the door. The door never opens at this time. The door!"

"Jane Peabody," a stentorian voice said. "We are taking

you back up to Hall Six. If you struggle, you will be returned to this cell. If you continue to tell lies about who you are, you will be returned to this cell."

"But Aislinn . . ." Claire reached out for the other woman. "Aislinn can't stay down here by herself. It isn't humane!"

Miss Studebaker strode into the cell. In the hall, a team of nurses waited. "Stand, Jane."

"No—"

"*Stand*, Jane, and if you make me ask again, I will leave you here and throw away the key."

The decision was a wrenching one. *I can't help Aislinn— I can't help anyone if I'm left down here.*

Shakily Claire stood. "I'm sorry," she said.

Aislinn looked back up at her, unblinking. Then she stuffed the rest of Claire's bread into her mouth, and laughed.

FIFTEEN

She had only been down there a day. Had you told Claire she'd lived in Aislinn's cell for a year, she would have believed you.

The gruel the next morning was the best she'd ever tasted. The room with the benches, with the nurses' unending gossip—it was a cathedral. They bathed her in the tub of filthy water, and it felt like a baptism. The nurses watched her carefully, and in their eyes Claire was once again a docile patient.

But Daphne and Tilly and Liliane kept close to her as she moved through her day. In snatches, she told them what she'd seen. What she'd learned.

The King killed his brother. It was a secret for which Aislinn had been locked away forever. *The King killed his brother, and he mourns for him in the rose garden.*

I know how to save St. Cloud.

Claire wasn't a confident swimmer, had only been in a

boat as a passenger. It didn't matter. She didn't have time to wait to see if Beatrix would save her. By hook or by crook, she would get herself off this island. Then she would present herself to the offices of the *St. Cloud Star*, sit down with Lizzie Cochrane to prove she was still alive. Together they would free Captain Miller; they would free Aislinn Kelly, and put her in the hands of a real doctor, perhaps the lady doctor that Cochrane had praised. It seemed likely that, with *real* care, Aislinn would likely come back to herself.

And an exposé on the King—

If the *Star* was brave enough to publish Aislinn's story, it could change everything.

It was decided. During her next constitutional walk she would make a break for the pier. The only woman who looked athletic enough to catch her was Miss Grune, and Claire planned to be fast.

The worst they could do was lock her up again with Aislinn Kelly. At least the two of them could keep each other company.

The next morning, she forced down a full bowl of gruel before she took her place beside Tilly in the line. In front of them were two elderly inmates, a pair who kissed, daringly, when the nurses weren't looking; today one tucked her hand in the other's elbow. In the row behind Claire, Daphne was comforting a poor young newcomer who muttered continually to herself. "I can't," she was saying, "I can't, I can't," and she twisted strands of her hair and pulled them from her head. Daphne comforted her in a quiet voice, and still the girl continued pleading.

All of this was the normal way of things on Adams Island. Ten o'clock struck, and the nurses unbolted the door. In hushed words behind their hats, Claire told Tilly what she had planned.

"There are guards at the pier, and they will shoot you before they let you in that water," Tilly said in her straightforward way, and clasped her hand.

Claire squeezed her fingers. "They'll need good aim."

"You won't succeed."

"But if I do, I'll come back with an army of my own."

Either way, at least she would be taking action. Claire was at peace with her decision, despite Tilly's darkening eyes and the mewling of the young woman behind her. As they all marched out onto the grounds, Claire counted the minutes. Soon their long line of women would wheel toward the pier, she and Tilly near the end, and then she would have the shortest distance to sprint to the water.

It wouldn't be long now.

But perhaps she had spoken too loudly to Tilly. Perhaps she should have noticed as they walked how the chanting of the woman behind her sped up and sped up, as staccato and desperate as a horse's hooves as it ran with a whip to its back.

"I can't," she said, "I can't, I can't—" And then she was stumbling forward toward the water, scrabbling against the granite path in her ill-fitting boots. Her white woolen dress was sweat stained and brushed gray with dust, she was falling again and pushing forward.

The two guards at the pier watched with interest and not much worry. One lifted his rifle, looked down the barrel.

"No," Daphne was whispering. "No, no," a drumbeat much like the other girl's chanting, and before she could move, before Claire could move, Miss Grune had tackled the girl to the ground.

The guard lowered his gun. "Pity," Claire heard him say. *He* wanted *to shoot her,* she realized, as Miss Grune hauled the girl to her feet as she kicked and flailed and screamed.

Miss Studebaker was muscling through the line. "Watch the line!" she told the guards, and grasped the runaway girl by the arm. "Someone send for a straitjacket!"

The girl, struggling against her captors, jerked her elbow into Miss Grune's nose. The nurse doubled over, blood spewing down her dress, and Claire wasn't sorry to see it.

Now, if ever, would be the time for Claire to run, but the two guards that stood between her and freedom had their rifles at the ready. More uniformed men were coming over from the men's side to help guard the line; at a distance, a few curious male inmates trailed them.

Close enough that, for the first time since she'd arrived, Claire could begin to see their faces.

Thank God, she thought.

Captain Miller. He was alive.

She hadn't been seeing his ghost after all.

He shook something loose from his sleeve. It fell to the ground. Claire waited a moment, then dodged forward to pick it up, swiftly, before she was seen.

Laundry, the note read. *Tonight*.

One of the men's guards must have caught the end of her interaction—he swooped in to seize the note from Claire, then elbowed her hard in the side.

"Tonight!" Miller yelled.

A buzz went up among the women; some began to cry. One of the men's guards ran back to herd them to their side of the island. Miss Studebaker ordered the women to about-face and return indoors.

This had never happened before, not in lashing rain or wind. Claire's stomach felt like it was crawling up her spine.

The doors to Hall Six were flung wide open, and the voice of the runaway girl spiraled out. "Tonight!" she chanted now as they dragged her away. "Tonight! Tonight! Tonight!"

That evening was the first that neither Miss Studebaker nor Miss Grune was on duty. After that afternoon's proceedings on the lawn, they had both been given the night off. Instead Miss Tennyson sat alone in an overstuffed chair, reading to them from Proverbs. In the pew next to Claire, Tilly nodded along, the very model of piety. Daphne, beside her, had perfected the art of sleeping with her eyes open.

Tonight, Claire was thinking. *Tonight*. She allowed herself her latest vice—resting a hand behind her back, as if to balance herself, and then tapping her index finger against the wood. She hadn't dared fidget for weeks; it wasn't worth the clubbing from the nurses if you were caught. To do it now was a comfort on the level of stepping into a clean, steaming bath.

Tonight.

Miller. Miller was alive. And moreover, the girl with the spoon who had fed her—she'd known, in the back of her mind, that there was only one person that could possibly be.

Beatrix.

Had she sent that letter to Beatrix as a dare? *Prove to me you are still my best friend. Despite what you have done. Despite how you have failed me.*

Prove to me you are still the one who knows me best.

If so, Bea had proven herself more than worthy.

Claire had to find a way to get down to the laundry.

The nurses in the sanatorium all seemed to subscribe to a kind of errant Christianity, one that called for judgments and moral pronouncements rather than good works. Miss Tennyson, alone among them, showed empathy for the inmates in her care, but like all the other nurses, she demanded from them cleanliness, modesty, and silence. The only way to prove that you were well enough to leave Hall Six was by erasing yourself entirely.

And still.

It left her an opening.

With any other nurse, it might not work—it might not even work on Miss Tennyson.

Claire took the hand behind her back and sent her fingers slowly questing one way, then the other. The soft wood grain flaked under her fingernails. But she was looking for an edge, a splinter—better yet, a nail—

There.

As Miss Tennyson droned on, Claire slowly, slowly began to scratch away the wood.

The unexpected friction made Daphne jolt awake. The pew shifted beneath them. Miss Tennyson's eyes darted up. "Please, ladies," she said, "I need you quiet and attentive to the word of God."

Daphne's head nodded back down onto her chest. Her eyes were open, but she was napping again.

Miss Tennyson cleared her throat. "A cheerful heart is good medicine," she read, "but a crushed spirit dries up the bones. . . ."

Claire dug more vigorously. There were splinters, now, stabbing her under her nailbeds, but she gritted her teeth and kept on. There. *There.*

She'd freed it.

Claire spread her skirt modestly around her and, with quick fingers, twisted the hem around the tack.

Then she took a deep, dusty breath in through her nose, and sneezed as hard as she could, flinging herself forward with the force of it.

There was a tremendous sound of ripping fabric.

"Oh!" Miss Tennyson said, dismayed. She pushed herself to her feet. "Jane! What have you done?"

Claire widened her eyes. "My modesty!" she cried out, trying to gather her torn dress around her. "I can't be seen like this!"

The other inmates had swiveled to look at her. Tilly's eyebrows were in her hair. "What on earth are you doing?" she mouthed.

For her part, Daphne was still sound asleep.

"Certainly you can't," Miss Tennyson was saying. She looked uneasily at the Bible in her hands, at the dozen inmates before her. "Though it has been a strange day, and so you may have to wait until another nurse comes . . . I cannot leave your sisters here alone. . . ."

Claire broke into loud, anguished weeping. "My modesty," she cried again. "My only remaining virtue!"

It wasn't her finest performance, nothing near as good as when she had persuaded her father not to hit her. But it was good enough, it seemed, for the little theater of Hall Six.

While Miss Tennyson hesitated, Liliane Beaufort, in the front row, began to sob. Then the German grandmother who had so little English, and the woman beside her. The wailing spread as though they were infants in a nursery.

It wasn't hard to understand why. Even though her tears were a sham, Claire was still surprised by how good it felt to cry.

Miss Tennyson flushed red. Wringing her hands, she said,

"I don't . . . however do I . . . *go*, Jane, go to the laundry and find yourself a new dress from the laundress, and I will tend to your sisters here—"

Claire didn't need to be told twice. As she fled the pew room, she heard Miss Tennyson fluster to a new chapter in her Bible. "The Lord is my shepherd. I shall not want. . . ."

She hadn't ever walked the halls of the asylum alone. It struck her, as she sped down the hall to the stairway, that this might be as good a time as any to make a thorough break for it. Out the front doors, into some shadowed crevice, wait for nightfall, and then go.

But there was still the problem of Captain Miller.

The laundry was in the bowels of the Adams Island sanatorium. The inmates' clothing was collected once a week, on Saturdays, so that they would have a clean dress for the Sabbath. The bathing room was where they made the exchange. A laundress collected the white dresses in a heap of dirty snow, while her assistant pulled a clean one from the waiting dumbwaiter. That was how they transported the clothing: a hole in the wall big enough to roast a fattened calf, with a pulley that lifted and lowered the compartment.

Claire wondered sometimes if the laundresses themselves were inmates, from Hall One or Hall Two, perhaps. They had that pinched, scuttling expression, that refusal to look anyone clear in the face. The nurses, save Miss Tennyson, regarded them as a half step above vermin.

And so when Claire came pelting down the stairs and through the door marked LAUNDRY—just around the corner, she knew, where Aislinn Kelly lay wasting away in her hole—one of the laundresses threw her head up from the iron she was using, and then threw her hands up as well.

There were others in the room, Claire could feel it, but she kept her gaze fixed ferociously on the laundress before her. *Don't let her register that I'm not a nurse.* "There is mayhem," she panted, "up in Hall Six, and no nurses to spare. I've been sent to fetch help. We need everyone you can spare!"

The laundress hesitated.

"Look how they ripped my dress! They're behaving like *animals* up there," Claire said. "Go!" She held the door open and ushered the bewildered woman out. Across the room, an older man was steadfastly ignoring her, head bent over a pile of mending.

And behind him, another man, a young one, with his back to her, stirring a giant vat of wet clothing with a stick.

"Didn't you hear me?" Claire said to the man, advancing. *If I must, I'll—I'll subdue him, gag him, and tie him up in the hall, I know I can—*

"James is deaf," the man said, not turning around. "And unless you keep jumping around like some mad acrobat, he'll let us have our conversation in peace."

"Miller," she said faintly.

"In the flesh."

She laughed a little, disbelieving, and after a moment, he did too. "Dear God," she said. "Didn't we meet in the Governor's Mansion?"

"Back when you were a fancy lady?" he said.

"And you my loyal guard."

"Camelot, this ain't," he said. But he didn't turn around; he kept on stirring the vat. "Listen, we can't draw attention. Keep your tone even and find yourself something useful to do. I'm bluing these ridiculous outfits of yours."

"You say it like it was my idea." Claire took up the laundress's station at the ironing board. "How did you get leave to work down here?"

"Weeks of good behavior. They don't let the male prisoners idle."

"Prisoners," Claire echoed. It was as good a word as any.

"Pretty much. Our side's full of the General's enemies. He's been stuffing them all in here, men he needs to give a good scare. Clerks, customs officials . . . hell, even a reporter or two—too much grumbling from any of them, and the General lets 'em know who's in charge. They're freed after a week or two of cooling their heels."

Claire barked out a laugh. She'd left the iron too long on the dress in front of her; it had burned a dark triangle into the fabric. "The women come in, and never leave."

"Neither will we," Miller said, stirring, "unless we get ourselves free."

"That laundress will be back any moment," Claire told him. She was listening hard, but the hall outside was silent. "We need a boat."

"We have a boat."

Claire's heart leaped. "How—"

"Just trust me. We have a way off the island. That's not the hard part. The hard part is finding—"

"A way out of the sanatorium."

"Right. There's nothing on the men's side that isn't guarded by armed men. No doors, no windows. But from what I can tell, the women's quarters aren't that way."

"You're right, they aren't," Claire said absently. There was something tugging at the back of her mind, something she'd heard while half sleeping. Something just out of her reach.

"What have you seen? What do you know?"

A memory.

Miss Studebaker tormenting Miss Grune as the Hall Six women dozed open-eyed in their pews. Something about ghosts. About spirits that would never rest.

Something about catacombs below the sanatorium.

Down in the depths of Hall Six was the entrance to a world of death.

Hidden there, behind a locked set of gates, lay a set of catacombs that had been constructed alongside the Adams Island asylum a hundred years before.

There were other sanatoriums in the First American Kingdom, but this had been the first. Adams Island provided an elegant answer to the question of where good upstanding citizens would want to house the insane: a location both beautiful and remote, so they could fondly imagine the lives of the people they sent there while never once having to clap eyes on it themselves.

But supplying such a place was an issue. Outside of what the asylum's small garden could provide, all food came in by boat. Rarely did a passenger arrive as Claire did, alone; usually they rode in with the grain shipments. The nurses lived on the island, as did the island's administrator, and the doctors came in once a week, stayed the night, and left on the boat with the morning supplies. And those crafts were laden down with other goods as well, as Adams Island was only one of many stops they made on their route along Lake Michigan.

Once things arrived at Adams Island, they rarely left. On the rare occasion the asylum had an export, it wasn't food or trade goods or crafts. It wasn't an inmate being discharged— never that.

Most always, it was a patient's body in a coffin. Something too unwieldy and unimportant for the supply crews to bring along with them. No, the architects of Adams Island had thought through the logic of this carefully. They built catacombs into their plans for the asylum's construction so that the bodies of the dead could be brought to the lowest level and abandoned, much as they had been in life, where no one would ever see them.

There was a boneyard there. That was the story that had so tormented Miss Grune. That the women they tortured in life would become vengeful in death and come a-hunting their tormentors.

Tonight Claire was going on a hunt of her own.

She cast around quickly for something to write with, and found a pencil on the sewing table. "I'm making you a map," she said, "of what I saw when I was sent down here in isolation. There's really only one place where the entrance to the catacombs could be. . . ."

James glanced up again from his mending. Claire smiled at him, then bent so the man couldn't see what she was doing. She sketched a rough map of the women's side, marking the catacombs with a star. "I'm folding it up and leaving it under the sewing table," she told Miller.

Footsteps on the stairs.

"Quickly," Miller warned.

"You'll need masonry tools to get through the catacomb wall, like the kind you've been using in the courtyard," she said. "Can you do that?"

"I can do that," he said.

"When do I meet you?"

"I need time to cut through—midnight. I can do it by midnight."

"And where do I meet you? The catacombs?"

"You'll know," Miller said. "They'll find a way to tell you."

The laundress slammed back into the room. "*Miss* Peabody," she said, panting. "Miss Tennyson would like you, please, to take some clothing, and *go to your cell*."

Claire's head was spinning. She accepted a dress with shaking hands.

They'll find a way to tell you.

Beatrix *was* here.

And maybe, just maybe, Remy was too.

Miss Tennyson was waiting for Claire outside her cell.

"You must know," Miss Tennyson said, running through her ring of keys, "how highly irregular your earlier behavior was. Destroying the lovely white outfit so kindly given to you. Terrifying that poor little laundress—"

Claire lowered her eyes, hugging the clean dress to her chest. "I apologize. I was frightened by all the noise. I thought to send for help."

"Perhaps this is a good time to tell you that a priest will be coming tonight to hear your confessions." She unlocked the door and pushed it open. "You would do well to confess to any . . . mischief, then."

"A priest?" Claire asked. "Since when?"

Miss Tennyson looked pleased. "The director of the sanatorium thought it best for you all to unburden yourselves after today's . . . excitement. All ladies will meet in the Hall Six dormitory. The father will see you behind a screen. Then those of you housed individually will be returned to your own rooms. I do hope that your changed bedtime—from eight o'clock to eight fifteen—will not be too disturbing to your systems, and that you will find the expiation of sin to be a balm for your poor souls. Now *change*, Jane."

If you only knew the sins I plan to commit, Claire thought, and smiled her very best angelic smile.

That night, inside the largest of the women's shared dormitories, Miss Tennyson ushered the inmates one by one: Tilly and Liliane and Daphne, the German grandmother who repeated counting rhymes to herself, the lovers who could only touch on their twice-daily walks before the guards, and others Claire hadn't met. Miss Tennyson arranged them all in a single-file line between the rows of beds and ordered them not to speak. Then she shut the door and placed herself before it.

Claire heard the unmistakable sound of someone bolting the door from the outside, as though they planned to set the room on fire.

They'll find a way to tell you, Miller had said. Claire's stomach was curdling with nerves.

The priest waited for them behind a wicker screen that would shield him and his confessors from view. From where she stood, only his outline was visible, and Claire could see that his head was bowed where he sat. The room was long enough that they wouldn't be able to hear the women's confessions, not if both parties were whispering. A nurse had been stationed at the front of the line to call the next sinner forward.

"The priest would like to see the Catholics among us first," Miss Tennyson was saying, "and then he'll speak to the others about conversion."

"Conversion?" Claire asked from her place at the back of the line.

"We can arrange for a baptism, if you'd like. Please do hear him out." Miss Tennyson gave Claire a conspiratorial smile. "I've been trying to arrange for Father Matthew's visit for weeks, but even with the director's approval, some of the other nurses made it . . . difficult. Thankfully, the incident this afternoon during our walk showed those nurses the error of their thinking. Indeed, our Lord's grace is very much needed on Adams Island."

"Indeed," Claire echoed, and left it at that.

One by one the inmates shuffled forward in their white dresses, but Daphne hung back to keep pace with Claire. "Always in a line," she said. "Are you going to confess?"

"To what?"

Daphne waved a hand. "To anything. Can you imagine— a man who actually wants to hear what we have to say?

It's been months. I'm going to dredge up every last impure thought I've ever had."

They stepped forward, slowly, as inmate after inmate processed to the makeshift confessional, spoke to the man behind the screen, and departed, clasping a new rose-bead rosary in her hands. Some prayed to themselves as they walked, counting out their Hail Marys with their fingers. Some shoved the rosary under their pillow and tried to go to sleep.

In the corner, one of the girls who had fits seized and seized, with a wooden spoon between her teeth to keep her from biting her tongue. When the fit stopped, she spat it out and lay, shaking, on her side.

Claire tried not to imagine the runaway girl from that afternoon, where she was sleeping tonight. What Grune and Studebaker had done to her in retaliation for their injuries. What Aislinn was feeling now, down in the bowels of the building.

Even if I escape tonight, they will all remain here, for now. Daphne and Tilly and even Liliane—my friends.

Claire's heart ached.

I must find a way to free them.

At the front of the line, a nurse directed their movements, her blond hair pinned up under her cap. There was something familiar about her. Her posture like an army commander's, straight and true. The twin moles on the back of her neck. Her clever, capable little hands beckoning the inmates forward.

And when she turned her head, the edges of a piratical smile.

It's another delusion, Claire told herself. *Like glimpsing an oasis in the desert.* A wish she couldn't even express to herself, she'd wanted it so.

The unruly nurse, the "deformed" one Studebaker and Grune had so complained of. The girl with the spoon.

"You go before me," Daphne was saying, stepping to the side. "I'm still thinking up something scandalous to say."

Claire hardly heard her.

The girl who'd fought dragons. The girl who could fly. The girl who'd left her in the Governor's Mansion to fend for herself, who regarded Claire now with her ineffable mix of conspiracy and ebullient joy.

Beatrix.

"Hello," she said, biting back a smile. "Are you already a Catholic, then?"

"Yes," Claire lied, and tried not to grin like a fool.

"I thought so," she said. "So are you ready to see the priest . . . tonight?"

SIXTEEN

Behind a flimsy screen, in a cane-backed chair, in a set of black robes that hung down to the floor, the priest had his hands clasped on the Bible on his lap. He stiffened when he saw her, made to stand. The princely bearing, that oddly beautiful mouth—

Remy.

Her Remy.

"We have to stop meeting like this," Claire said.

"You're alive." He reached out to touch her cheek, her ragged hair. "You're *alive*," he repeated, his voice catching on the words. "My God. I didn't let myself hope. I—"

She leaned in to his warm fingers. So few had touched her gently since she'd come to Adams Island. "You came."

"You sound surprised." Remy withdrew his hand, his long black sleeve trailing behind.

"I only expected Beatrix," she told him truthfully. This

man who had said he couldn't love her. This man she was sacrificing so much to save. (*Only because it's convenient for you*, the little voice told her, *if he's still alive*.)

"I would be surprised, too. I haven't . . ." He searched her face. "I've been a passenger for so long in my own life."

"Yes," Claire said. She didn't have the energy to equivocate. "I let you take the risks."

"You were," she said with a half shrug, "shot in the chest."

"I let you take the risks," he repeated. "All of them."

"All of them? You did bring in the lightning rifles."

Remy's lips twitched. "A small point in my favor."

There was color in his face, in his lips. He watched her with none of the languor of the sickroom or the throne room; his blue eyes were startlingly avid, and they were fixed on her. Again he reached out, but this time Claire was reaching too, and their hands met between them.

To her surprise, she was trembling. "How long do we have?"

"I'm not sure," Remy said. "How much do you have to confess?"

Claire knew she had become something else since she'd seen him last. She had a strange sense of herself as an ear. An ear that was trained to listen to herself and to women who were like her, rather than waiting to be filled with a man's instructions. She had a sense, too, of herself as a buoy in rough water, small but determined, riding the tides. She had been shown unknown depths of cruelty on Adams Island, had also seen and given kindness.

And Remy was looking at her. He cataloged her bruises, her exhaustion, the gauntness of her face; he unclasped their hands and touched, gently, her midsection. She had wasted away where he had grown strong, but she knew as well as anyone that the body could tell one story while the mind told another.

What was this she was feeling? Was she so overwhelmed with joy at seeing a friend and ally that she could again mistake it for love? Had she even missed him while she'd been in the asylum? She'd missed her best friend more.

As much as I feel as though I know you, I do not, he'd said, and she knew herself now under the same delusion.

There was one thing in particular she was coming to realize. If the two of them took back St. Cloud, she would once again be subject to a man's demands. And Claire didn't *know* what Remy would do with such power.

In Claire's experience, power made its wielders into tyrants. And Claire could never bring herself to love a tyrant again.

I will have to find a way to keep him in check.

"We are getting you out," he was saying, and she warmed through with the words she'd waited so long to hear, even as she reminded herself to keep her head.

"You and Beatrix, and . . ." Claire sighed. "Miller. Captain Miller. For a moment I thought I'd imagined him."

"You were in a bad way, Beatrix told me."

"They had me convinced, for a time, that I wasn't myself. That my name was Jane Peabody. I was nobody, to no one."

His eyes glittered. "Miller knows we have a boat. But we need to find you a way out of here—"

"We found it," she said. "Through the catacombs. Miller should be there now, carving a hole in the wall."

Remy sighed. "That was the last piece of it. We managed to smuggle him in a note to tell him we'd be coming, that we had a boat at the ready, but you—Claire, the security on these wards is stricter than what we keep for the mansion. No wonder the General's been storing his dissidents here. Listen," he said, lifting the book from his lap, "we only have a few minutes. We leave tonight. At midnight."

She took the Bible from him.

"Open it," he said.

Heresy upon heresy. Remy done up like a priest, taking her confession; the architectural plans to the buildings at Adams Island sewn in between Numbers and Deuteronomy. Claire recognized Beatrix's small, perfect stitches.

For once, for *once*, her friends were stepping up to the plate. They weren't leaving her to bat for the team by herself.

Even if it wasn't necessary.

"Midnight," she said. Red ink circled a small dock at the northern end of the island.

"We'll be on the other side," he said. "There's a boat big

enough for the four of us, and a doctor back in Monticello waiting to look you over. To take stock of what . . ." He shook his head. "What they have done to you."

"I don't need pity," she said. "I'm far better off than most of the girls here."

"Don't say that. I'll never forgive the General for this."

"I put myself here, Remy. I chose this. I came to ferret out his secrets. And God, what I've found . . ." Why had his statement of support made her feel so suddenly furious? "It's more than just the General. This place existed before him. There are so many men just like that out there, and *women* now, too, and they can do whatever they want with us, we're useless to them—"

"We don't have time," he said gently. "Not now. We'll discuss this further when you are free."

Another flash of fury, and this time she buried it. It was a skill she had honed from years of practice.

"Midnight, then," she said instead of arguing. "So what *is* the plan?"

Remy told her.

Her eyebrows went up, and then up somewhat higher.

When he finished, Claire snapped her Bible shut. "I'll meet you there," she said.

That night in her cell, as she traced again the path she'd take to freedom, her only thought was that they'd buried Aislinn

Kelly alive. *Her cell is just across the entrance from where they keep all their dead.*

It was ten till midnight. Claire was in the black shift and boots that Beatrix had left her, smuggled under her pillow. Now Claire tore out the map and stuffed it inside the collar of her dress, then sat a moment and forced herself to breathe. Her thoughts were turning in a tight circle. *I can't leave Aislinn here. I can't leave Daphne or Tilly or Liliane or any of them. I can't. I can't do it.*

But Remy had said the boat was big enough to hold four. Four. Neither he nor Beatrix had considered the hundreds of other inmates in their plan, and why would they? They'd been entirely focused on Claire.

The Governor's wife.

It wasn't fair. But she knew too that a craft any bigger would attract the attention of the guards, and then none of them would escape at all.

The situation was impossible. *I'll come back for the other women,* she told the knot in her stomach, and stood.

I will.

Beatrix had already taken care of the lock on her cell, but she'd told Claire to wait. *I can't promise that Miss Tennyson will be asleep until midnight,* she'd whispered, walking Claire back to her room from her "confession," *and she patrols the halls until then.* Beatrix had learned the intricacies of the nurses' schedules in the last few weeks. *They've kept me on*

Hall One except when Six is shorthanded, like tonight. *Claire,
I am so sorry, it took us a week to even smuggle me in, and
then another to learn the fastest way to get you out. Remy is
too recognizable, so we couldn't pass him off as a doctor and
have him, well, un-commit you, and then I learned the hard
way that the doctors who do work here can't be bribed, not
for money or for—how do I put this?—my feminine wiles.*

Claire had struggled not to laugh. *I've seen those doctors,*
she whispered back. *You must be a good actress.*

*Lots of batting my lashes. One kept calling me disfigured,
as though he could convince me that I'm not the prime article.*
Her eyepatch glinted in the light. *I'm gorgeous, and he's a fool.*

At the end of the hall, Miss Tennyson ghosted by, and
Beatrix made a show of shoving Claire into her cell. *I love
you,* Bea whispered after her. *See you soon.*

The path they'd detailed took Claire through the winding
corridors of Hall Six, past the pew rooms and the laundry, the
bathing room and the kitchen, past the two communal bedrooms
where most of Hall Six slept. The boots Beatrix had left her fit
her feet—a small, significant marvel—but they tapped against
the stone floors no matter how quietly she walked.

(*Move quickly, not quietly,* Beatrix had said. *No one will
hear you.*

What about Miss Tennyson?

*A nip from her own bottle of chloral, and a lovely cham-
omile tea to hide it in. She comes back to her room at half*

past eleven to study her catechism. If all goes to plan, she'll be fully sedated by midnight.)

And still, as Claire slunk through the halls, she cringed each time she set a foot down. As she passed one of the dormitories, she lingered at the door, fingering the deadbolt. These larger bedrooms didn't have locks that required keys. You only turned a knob, and just like that, you hid a woman away.

Just like that, and you freed them.

Like that.

Claire turned the lock; she didn't let herself think about it any further as she hurried on to the staircase.

Down and down she went, clinging to the shadows against the wall. Down into the asylum's depths, down where the earth was packed with dirt, where Adams Island buried their dead.

God willing, Miller will have made a hole through the brick big enough for the two of you to escape by midnight. We'll have the boat on the other side at ten past twelve. The guards begin their next patrol at quarter past.

That leaves us five minutes. Five minutes, Claire, to get you both from the building to the boat. There is no margin for error.

I'll meet you there, she'd promised.

But now, in the basement, her hands shook too hard to check her map. Where was it, the entrance to the catacombs? She tried one door, another—brooms and mops, a boiler, an empty cell that stank of death, another. By all accounts, it should be here.

I'll be left, I'll die in this place—

Time speeding up, her breath beginning to labor. Surely it was now ten past twelve. Surely the boat was even now turning into the greater dark of the lake.

Was it her imagination, the voices that echoed above her, the sounds of heavy impact, doors slamming, fear? She didn't think so. *A river of women, building and building until it overcomes the dam—*

The next door she came to had a deadbolt and a food slot.

Aislinn Kelly. *There's a boat big enough for the four of us*, Remy's voice reminded her. And still, Claire's hands reached out and again turned the lock. Then, for good measure, she opened the door as well.

Inside, Aislinn was facedown in the hole she'd dug. She jerked up at the sudden light. "Edith," she croaked, her eyes all pupil. "Edith?"

There isn't time. "Come with me," Claire said, "or don't, but choose *now*," and then around the next corner she halted.

Cast-iron gates more than doors, an intricate spiral of flowers and vines through which she could see—*yes*—the long curved lines of the catacombs beyond.

But there wasn't a handle on the gate, not on this side; this was an exit, not an entrance, and Claire fumbled the map from the neck of her dress and stared at it like the architecture could rearrange itself before her eyes. There wasn't another way in from the women's side. There was this. Only this.

Nearly in tears, she stuffed her hand into the scrollwork of the grate and flattened out her fingers, straining to grasp the doorknob beyond. She couldn't do it. *You would need a child's hand to reach through.* She cast around her for a stick or a rod or a railroad tie, anything she could use to jimmy the door open, but there was nothing in the hall but mouse droppings and dirt.

"Edith?"

Aislinn had crept out of her cell. In the electric light, the full extent of what had been done to her was staggering. She was taller than Claire and yet perhaps half her weight, the result of years of deprivation. She had been deprived of light as well, and she rubbed her watering eyes. "I can help," she said, and shooed Claire from the door. Her wasted-away hands fit easily through the ironwork. "Do you want me to turn the handle?"

"Yes," Claire breathed. "Yes."

Aislinn frowned, leaned in. With a horrible groan, the door swung open toward them.

Claire stepped through, then hesitated.

"Where are we going?" asked Aislinn, in her guileless way.

"Yes, Claire," said the voice behind them. "Where *are* we going?"

SEVENTEEN

Daphne's white dress was streaked with blood. Leaning on her elbow was the girl—sweating now, wan—who'd been seizing unnoticed in the corner of the dormitory. The girl still clutched the wooden spoon in her right hand.

"Please," the girl said. "My fits are getting worse."

"Jana needs a doctor, a proper one." Daphne drew the girl nearer, footstep by fumbling footstep. "It's chaos up there. No nurses. The guards—they've just discovered the women loose in the halls. From the noise outside, I think the men have been freed as well. And—"

"Tell me," Claire said, as there wasn't time.

Daphne hesitated. "There isn't any chance that . . . you might be who I think you are?"

A boat that can only hold four, Claire thought, but what she said was, "If you want to leave here, come quickly," and when she slipped into the vaults, the three other inmates were at her heels.

The castoffs of Adams Island. Them, and what surrounded them: the line of rusted gurneys, the racks of moth-eaten dresses, the shelves of tonics and unguents and potions left open to degrade in the dank air. A metal basin turned upside down, a hole punched through it, and a behemoth laundry press that listed to its side, all its gears snaggletoothed and broken. The smell grew stronger as they walked, a smell of black earth and decay, and behind her, she could hear Jana gagging. Then a quick series of sounds—*rip, rip*—as Daphne tore the collar off her dress and Jana's. They pressed those makeshift handkerchiefs to their mouths to keep out the stench.

For now they were coming to the catacombs, down in the horrid heart of the vaults, and though Claire had seen lately so many unimaginable things, what lay before them was dredged up from some new nightmare.

Bones.

A bleached-out sea of bones that lay everywhere before them.

Some were piled into alcoves that had been built into the brick walls, and though those skeletons were stacked three or four together, they still seemed the more fortunate. Worse were the cairns that lined the dusty path they walked, bones piled upon each other without any semblance of care or respect. And worse—those bodies still recognizable as bodies, earth-dark and degraded, dumped here and there along the path.

This is what they think of us. This is the sum total of what we are worth.

It took only minutes to pass through the space, but those minutes accordioned out and out as the four women walked in a single-file line through the valley of the dead.

All the while, before them, a sound beat through the silence, the tooth-grinding clang of metal against brick. Claire's pulse rose to meet it. *A ghost,* her mind cried, *a ghost*—until she forced herself to breathe. *Captain Miller. Miller, who is working to free us.*

Her vision swam. It was nearly too much. Daphne was swearing under her breath while Jana said a quiet prayer.

A worthy adversary. I am a worthy adversary.

Then Aislinn began to laugh. And at that barren sound, Claire broke into a run.

"Over here!" a man's voice bellowed.

It *was* Miller. The two of them had never quite seen eye to eye. He was unpredictable, and had you asked Claire only weeks before, she would have said that she'd had enough of unpredictable men for a lifetime. She hadn't understood him—his rangy energy, the intensity of his convictions, his disdain for what he'd seen as her privilege—until she'd learned he was the General's illegitimate son, and even then, he wasn't someone she'd ever counted as a friend.

But she hadn't even been able to see his face in the laundry.

Tonight she cleared the distance between them in a trice before launching herself into his arms.

"There, there," he said, surprised, as he patted her back. His hands were so rough and work bitten that she could feel their calluses through her dress. "You're not hurt?"

"Yes, but the women with me—" Claire stepped away. "I'll explain once we're free. You've—dear God, you've done it."

Behind him, the asylum's wall was in pieces. He had attacked the mortar with the trowel and metal pick now at his feet, using the trowel's handle to hammer out a section of brick large enough for him to crawl through. "Then I kept going," he'd tell her later, "for lack of anything else to do." The opening was now large enough for a marauding elephant. All around them, the humid night air crept in.

Miller was frowning past her at Daphne and Jana and Aislinn, all waiting in an uncertain line. "Claire," he said, the first time he'd ever used her Christian name, "are these women coming with us?"

She had been bargaining with herself for hours now. To leave these women with a promise to return that she didn't know she could keep, or to risk none of them escaping at all. Inside her, the machinery of rage was lumbering back to life, the roar in her ears not unlike one of Tesla's generators. *I cannot make another compromise,* she thought, and then: *so I won't.*

She didn't know what he saw in her eyes, but Miller retreated from her—one step, another. "They could come," he said. "It's a risk, but—"

Before he could finish speaking, she motioned the other inmates through the hole in the wall and outside into freedom.

Scrub brush and broken brick underfoot, or perhaps they were rocks washed up from the shore. Around them, cicadas buzzed in an infinite choir, one punctuated by the shrieks and cries of the patients in the asylum above them. She heard, too, guards' voices shouting orders, and when she looked up, she saw the hot light of a fire on the men's side of the building.

Jana was crying into her makeshift handkerchief. "It's too terrible," she sobbed, but Claire was past grief. In the weeds before them in the shallows of the lake, a little rowboat was bobbing up and down.

Remy stood at the bow, waving his arms, but he stilled as the women approached. From this distance, she couldn't read his face. She was thankful for that.

Miller helped the girls aboard—Jana first, who huddled in next to a bewildered-looking Beatrix, and then Daphne, who clutched at the sides of the boat for balance.

"Be *careful*," Miller warned her as their craft pitched back and forth. He held out a hand for Aislinn, but she hovered behind Claire on the shore.

"It's not going to hold us all," Remy murmured, as the women around him made themselves as small as possible. "Claire."

"We need to try," she said, as Miller waded up to his knees in the water to try to steady the boat.

They all turned at the light that went up behind them. A bonfire had begun to rage on the asylum's flat roof. Flares whistled up into the sky.

"Ten, eleven, twelve," she heard Aislinn say, and realized that she was counting silhouettes. *Guards or inmates?* Claire didn't know.

"We came for you," Remy was saying. "You, and the captain of my guard. That's *all*. What is happening up there? Did you start some kind of insurrection?"

Daphne crossed her arms. "She only unlocked our door," she said. "We did the rest."

"Give me one reason you couldn't have come back for them! Why this needed to happen tonight!" His whisper may well have been a shout.

"Not to interrupt," Beatrix said from the boat, "but by my estimation, we're all about to die."

Jana mewled, her face buried in Beatrix's shoulder, and Daphne threw an arm out for balance. "She needs a doctor," she said, as the little boat shuddered back and forth. "She's ill. And—"

It was clear she didn't know what to say about Aislinn.

"And Aislinn has been locked away on Adams Island for years," Claire said to Remy, quietly. "Aislinn is the key to everything. She has a secret that can topple the King. Trust me, we can all fit on the boat."

Remy's eyes were fiery. "I love you too much to let you do this, to sacrifice us all, for strangers. We're not leaving with them on board." He got out of the boat to face her.

"Strangers? These are your people," she told him. "You are their governor. Aislinn, get on the boat!"

"No, Claire. I came for *you*." He reached out to take her hands, but she snatched them away.

"If you can't do it because you're a good man, do it because you're a selfish one! We can secure our position! Come on, Aislinn, *get on the boat*—"

"Since when do you give orders?" Remy demanded.

"Every woman has been put here because a man has *tired* of her," she hissed. "Because her being alive was inconvenient. Because the tiny amount of power she had over her own life was judged to be too much. Because she was in the wrong place, or because she was rich and someone couldn't stand it, or, yes, sometimes because she needed help—but that isn't a place that can help anyone!"

What went unspoken between them: *I may be under your protection now, but that is worth nothing if you can one day, on a whim, decide to take it away.*

"We need to be in charge of our own destinies," Claire said. "I don't care if I die. Frankly, I don't care if we all do."

(Beatrix made a small sound of protest.) "It's worth the risk. Let's get in the boat and go. Come on, Aislinn."

Miller, who had been silent, said, "She's gone."

"*What?*"

Jana began again to cry, and Remy swore under his breath. But she couldn't care about them now.

Aislinn wasn't waiting behind her, bare feet in the scrub grass on the shore. She wasn't wandering with her arms open, looking up at the quarter moon. At first it seemed she had disappeared into another world. It was cloudy and hot, moist, the kind of night where the shadows melted together. But Aislinn, like the rest of them, was wearing white, and despite the weather, she should have been like a beacon on the water.

"Oh my God," Daphne said, her arm flung out to point.

For Aislinn had turned back to the asylum. She walked like a selkie, a mythic creature emerged from the lake. Translucent skin, seaweed hair. As Claire watched, dumbstruck, Aislinn ran toward the guards. "I'm here!" she yelled, darting through the bonfire's thrown light. "I'm here!"

Claire could see the men lined up at the edge of the roof. "Who's there?" one of them called back. "Who is that? Is that Joseph down there?"

"It's a woman," another spat. "Not a guard," and the rest of them shouldered their rifles.

"It's Aislinn Kelly." She stood, defiant and calm, below them. "Aislinn Kelly. I am the reason for all of this."

One of the guards shot his rifle into the air, and another yelled, "Hold!" But it was too late—spooked by the noise, the rest of the men began to fire.

As the gunshots cracked out like corn kernels over a stove, Miller hauled Claire bodily into the boat, a hand clamped over her mouth to keep her silent. Remy pushed the craft out into the water, and when he jumped in, he brought some of the lake in with him.

She sobbed into her wet dress, useless, as Remy and Beatrix rearranged their passengers, everyone climbing over one another until the boat was more or less balanced. Enough of her was aware to notice that they floated just fine. When Remy had made his calculations, he must have done so for men's bodies. He hadn't taken into account that the women, save Beatrix, were all so malnourished that they added far less weight than they otherwise would have.

There would have been room for Aislinn. Aislinn, and one or two more.

Miller took up the oars. "Who was that?" he asked, in that voice she'd always thought disinterested. She wondered, now, if he'd seen so many horrors that no atrocity could surprise him anymore.

"She was the King's mistress for years," Claire said. "Then she spent years more on Adams Island, she's always been a captive—"

"Aislinn *Kelly*." Beatrix's eyes were round as she put it

together. "That's who that was? My God, imagine what she knew."

"She was a person!" Daphne protested.

"She was. And she was also a weapon." Miller grunted with the effort of the oars. "You should have boarded her first."

"You should have left her in the asylum, where she was safe," Remy said.

"Safe?" Claire wanted to slap him. "They threw her away. Into a cell, where she lived in complete darkness for years. She slept in the *dirt*, and all because the King picked her up in some little New Teshas town and whisked her away—"

"She agreed to go with him," Miller said.

Beatrix snorted. "We all know what would have happened to her had she said no."

"She was a prisoner from the moment he laid eyes on her," Jana whispered, and to that, the men said nothing.

EIGHTEEN

It wasn't yet dawn when they tied up the boat in the little fetid harbor in the meatpacking district that Beatrix swore would be abandoned this time of day.

No one was there to see them disembark. Jana and Daphne sat on the dock while the rest of them dealt with the boat.

"My workshop used to be here," Beatrix said, tossing Miller a tie rope. He caught it. "Spent a lot of long nights working out plans on this dock, admiring the sunrise. Well, that, and trying not to vomit at the meat smell."

"Workshop?" Miller asked.

"Oh, just the place where I built my gliders. You might remember my gliders? I think one saved your bacon back at the Palace of Fine Arts?"

"My bacon? More like Duchamp bacon." Miller grinned. "Look at you. You're like a lady Tesla."

"He's more like a gentleman Lovell," Beatrix said. She

gave the rope an experimental tug, then straightened slowly. Miller snuck a look at her bottom, and flushed.

Claire smothered a laugh. *It could be the end of the world, and Beatrix would still be Beatrix.* So many weights hung from her shoulders—Aislinn, the kingdom, her frustration with Remy. She would snatch a moment of joy when she could.

It felt good to trust Beatrix again.

At the edge of the dock, Remy stood in his priest's cassock, arms folded as he watched the horizon. "I cannot tell if that's a boat out there. If someone has successfully followed us."

"Let's not wait and see," Claire said. "We need to get Jana to a doctor. Follow me, we need to get rid of these dresses. We look like inmates."

Monticello, in the still and early light. Nights in her cell on Adams Island, Claire walked these streets by memory. She had missed even the meatpacking district—foul and crowded, the cramped doorways of its factories, the starveling little cats scavenging for scraps.

For Beatrix's workshop was within this warren of streets, a safe haven if she'd ever known one.

Between the two of them, Claire and Beatrix had enough clothing stashed away to outfit all the girls in short order. Bea chopped off four inches from the hem of a dress so it would fit tiny Daphne, while Jana rooted around for bonnets to cover their shaved heads. Claire donned an old pair of Beatrix's brother's trousers and a worn-in, comfortable shirt. After the constant discomfort of the asylum's heavy dresses, she wanted to cry with relief.

As the women changed, Miller paged through Beatrix's old sketchbooks, that same little grin on his face as before. He had rowed the heavy oars for hours, bringing their boat to Monticello; he should have been asleep on his feet, but he somehow had the same rangy energy he always did.

Remy, on the other hand, looked half dead when Claire found him on the pallet Beatrix kept behind a ragged curtain. He'd done his share of rowing too, but unlike Miller, the Governor was healing from both a gunshot wound and the infection that had followed.

Plus he'd likely never done hard labor in his life.

"How are you feeling?" Claire asked. She was almost surprised by the rush of acid up her throat. She couldn't quite forgive him; it seemed she'd traded one grudge for another.

Aislinn on the shore, in the open air. Aislinn brave enough to save all their lives. The King thought he'd never met his match? How wrong he'd been. Aislinn Kelly had been a force to be reckoned with. They could so easily have brought her back to Monticello, had Remy not resisted.

"What did she know?" Remy asked her, as though he'd read her mind.

"Enough," Claire said. "I'll tell you, but first, we need to get Jana into a doctor's care. Can we get a message to Lizzie Cochrane, the reporter from the *St. Cloud Star*? I need a favor, a referral to a Dr. Eliza Blackwell. Is that possible?"

"The reporter will do you this favor?"

"Haven't you been reading the papers while I've been away? Lizzie's been leading a crusade to find your missing wife."

Remy snorted. "We should send her a gift. Perhaps some chocolate oranges."

She ignored him. "I can offer Lizzie an exclusive interview in exchange for the referral. I just need to know if we can get out a message to her."

"You know, we are not entirely friendless," Remy said, surprised. "My household staff, my business partners—they are all still in Monticello."

"Oh, good," Claire said. "Excellent. Wonderful to learn that just now. Weeks after I might have used them to gather information, or spy, or—"

His lips quirked. "You never asked me."

"*You* were too busy malingering to see me."

"Dear God," Miller said, looking up. "Children, will you please stop?"

Remy's eyebrows flew up.

"Sir." Miller quickly corrected course. "Do you want me to round up a few page boys, your valet, perhaps—if the General hasn't scared them all into hiding? And I can deliver Mrs. Duchamp's message myself. We can have the lady doctor meet us here."

Beatrix appeared next to him. "Are you going to bust some heads open, then?"

"It's what I do best," Miller said.

"Excellent. I'll bring my boxing gloves." With that, she strode out of the workshop like a prizefighter. Miller's eyes followed her.

"See something you like, Captain?" Remy asked him with a smile.

"Something I'm scared of, more like," he said, and hurried after Beatrix.

When the cavalry finally arrived at the stockyards, they didn't look anything like cavalry. For one, they were carrying little lace parasols, and they had a full complement of men to ease their way. A cheerful-faced photographer trailed them, a boy to help carry his equipment. A bored-looking off-duty soldier—a husband? a brother?—was there, presumably to protect their virtue.

As they toured the grotesqueries of the meatpacking district, they made loud pronouncements about the injustices they saw: the working conditions, the poor suffering animals, the smell that surely would waft northward to the more genteel districts of the city, districts where they themselves lived. Their photographer captured them, grim-faced, in front of the Livestock Exchange.

They drew no attention. The world in 1893 was so upsetting

and upside down; there was too much that needed fixing. It made sense to choose a single cause and commit yourself to it, and so reformers were a dime a dozen in Monticello. As they walked through the warrenlike streets, all the stockyard workers saw was another gaggle of do-gooder feather-headed women.

It was by design. That was all the General's spies would see, too.

And when the reformers stopped at the offices of one Barnaby Lovell, inventor, the white-haired woman in the plaid dress exclaimed, "Oh! I think this is the man who has invented a more elegant way of slaughtering cattle! Let's pay him a visit!"

At that, the soldier rolled his eyes, took the arm of the blond lady with the eyepatch, and strode off as the others filed into Barnaby Lovell's place of business.

Which was, of course, *Beatrix* Lovell's.

"Lord have mercy," Lizzie Cochrane said, dropping her parasol unceremoniously on the floor, "but you are a terrible actress. How did you ever convince the medical school that you were a man?"

"Confidence. Bullish confidence, and some straw stuffed into my trousers." Dr. Eliza Blackwell plucked the hat from her head. "Elmer, will you unpack my bag on the table there, that's a lad." The boy scurried to follow her directions.

"The girl Jana is back here," Daphne said, rushing to meet Dr. Blackwell. "She just had another seizure, she's sleeping now, on that pallet behind the curtain. She still has the spoon in her mouth, I don't rightly know if that's safe—"

Beatrix and Miller had only come to deliver their guests; now they were off to track down the remaining members of the Governor's household. The Governor himself was in the corner, having taken the giant stack of *St. Cloud Star*s that Miller had procured, smuggled here in one of Elmer's bags. "I've never read it before," Remy had told Claire, who'd goggled at him.

"The paper?"

"I had advisers who kept me abreast of important happenings—"

"How on earth did you govern this region?" she'd asked.

He had smiled at her wanly. "I do ask myself that question sometimes."

The women paid the young Governor no mind; to them, he was an afterthought. Instead, Lizzie's gaze lit on Claire. "You're alive," she said. "My God, I couldn't believe it until I saw you for myself."

"Took a holiday at Adams Island," Claire said. "Haven't you heard? It's lovely this time of year."

Lizzie was already rooting around for her notepad. "Tell me everything. Bill? Some photographs?"

But Claire held up a finger. "Wait. I know you don't owe me anything. I know you traded me an interview for Dr. Blackwell's assistance, and I will give you that interview. But I can't let you run a story about me yet."

The reporter shut her eyes briefly. "You're not in charge of me," Lizzie said. "I mean that on a fundamental level. The independent press can't answer to the Governor, Mrs. Duchamp."

"Listen to me. At Adams Island, I uncovered something. Something incendiary."

"If you uncovered it," Lizzie said, "then I can too."

"Not when the woman in question is now . . . dead." Claire surprised herself by blinking back tears. Aislinn, so proud of her hole in the dirt. "And not if you want a firsthand account of how Adams Island became a war zone last night. Or would you rather wait for the sanatorium director's version?"

The women stared each other down.

"What is it that you want, Mrs. Duchamp?" Lizzie asked abruptly.

"Call me Claire, please," she said, not looking at her husband. "What I want is for you to withhold the story I'm about to tell you—to let the General think that my piece is still off the chessboard—until the end of next week."

"Next week? Next week is the King's birthday celebration in Philadelphia! I have a full slate of activities to cover—not to mention the wheeling and dealing that's going to happen on the sidelines. My editor would have kittens if I broke another story instead, especially one that's based solely on one girl's word."

"On the word of your Governor's *wife*," Claire said.

"What are you, then?" Lizzie asked, sinking down into a chair. "You have to decide. Are you Mrs. Duchamp, lady of St. Cloud, silent in the gold dress beside the Governor's throne—or are you Claire, the inventor's girl, a little unloved scamp from Lordview? Because you can't be both."

"How do you know those things about me?"

"Everyone knows them!" Lizzie glared at Remy, busily reading a six-month-old newspaper. "How are you both so naive, so disconnected from your day-to-day reality? Who on earth allowed the two of *you* to govern?"

"Lizzie—"

"No. Listen to me. Do you know what's happened since you've disappeared? The General's taken control of the narrative. He keeps holding these . . . rallies in front of the mansion. He's been whipping the Monticellans up into a frenzy, talking about how you and Remy fled out west to live high on the hog on taxpayer dollars. Telling them that he stayed—the General, that *he* stayed, and that he's taking care of St. Cloud. Looking out for the little man."

"That's a bald-faced lie," Claire said.

"Well, they believe it. No matter what we dig up and print about him, the people believe he's a hero."

Claire looked to Remy for a reaction, but he only quirked an eyebrow and turned a page of his newspaper.

At that, Lizzie rolled her eyes. "That's why he's succeeding. You sit there with your little continental affectations, acting like any real politicking is *beneath* you, when that is quite literally your only job, Governor."

"Neither of us chose this! Don't you understand that? He was born into it, and I—I didn't want to die." Claire dragged her hands across her face. "Do you know what I am?" she said finally. "I'm just another madwoman from Adams Island. Say the wrong thing in front of the wrong man—in front of the wrong member of the D.A.C.!—and you can be one too, *Mr. Mackenzie*. All I want is the chance to take the General down while he thinks I'm still locked away."

Lizzie groaned.

"It isn't only for me. I need to speak for the rest of the women that were locked away in Adams Island. So many of them were just . . . jailed there, and I want to drag their jailers into the light. I want to do something for these people, Lizzie. Please."

"I'm sorry to interrupt," Dr. Blackwell said. Her face was wreathed in kindly wrinkles, but her eyes were as bright as knives. "I've finished examining the patient, Jana."

"Will she recover?" Claire asked.

The doctor spread her hands. "I'm afraid I'm not an authority on seizure disorders myself, though I do have colleagues who have had success administering low doses of sedatives to those who suffer from this affliction. Jana agreed that she would like to consult with them. For now she's resting. I doubt she's gotten a good night's sleep since she was sent to Adams Island, and I know for certain that none of you did last night. And lack of sleep is dangerous with a seizure disorder. Once she wakes, I'll take her with me, and anything she chooses to do—or not do—will be of her own free will. She could be restored to her home if she would like."

Claire frowned. "I don't know her story, or if she'd want to go home."

"Her husband said her fits were a sign of madness," Daphne said, joining them. Her voice was raspy with exhaustion. "They married young, I think. Jana came from money."

"Who is he?" Remy lowered his newspaper.

"Treasury clerk," Daphne spat at him. "You've likely met. I imagine you all play cards."

Remy startled. *No one's ever spoken to him like that before,* Claire realized, watching him struggle to form a response.

Lizzie held up her hands. "Peace. We're *all* exhausted. Once Jana wakes, Dr. Blackwell and I will take her to a specialist. He knows to be discreet. And the rest of you—"

"—will get some sleep here," Claire said. "We'll wait for whatever news Beatrix and Captain Miller bring us. And then in the morning we'll make our next move."

"Which is?" Daphne was still seething.

"We can decide together," Claire said. Already, she had an idea.

The King's birthday party. A week's worth of activities. A week's worth of wheeling and dealing, of trading information for influence.

I wonder what he would give us for what we know.

A worthy adversary, indeed.

NINETEEN

Daphne shook her awake in the middle of the night.

"Get dressed and follow me," she hissed. "And don't say a word to the others."

On the pallet beside Claire, as Remy slept, his chest rose and fell. She rose as quietly as she could.

Beatrix must have returned sometime after they had all gone to bed; she dreamed at her desk, her head pillowed on her arms. And like a true soldier, Miller slept with his back against the door. The rest—Lizzie and Dr. Blackwell and Bill and the boy and Jana—had all left in the late afternoon. Lizzie Cochrane had promised to book them a berth on the train to Philadelphia the next day.

They were going to meet the King on his own playing field.

So why was Daphne rousing her in the middle of the night?

"Come *on*," Daphne was urging.

Claire pointed with her chin at Miller, sleeping in his

clothes, blocking their only exit. Daphne shook her head, then pointed to the open window and the alley outside.

Why must it always be a window, Claire wondered, clambering outside after her. "What do you need, Daphne?" she asked, once they were both outside.

"I couldn't sleep. I kept thinking that . . . I don't know you." Though the night was warm, Daphne hugged her arms to her tiny frame. "Not really. I don't know who you are out here in the world. What you're actually like. I still can't . . . I still can't quite believe that you're married to the Governor of St. Cloud."

"If it helps, I can't quite believe it either."

"In the asylum, we were friends. Out here I don't know." Daphne took a breath, looked up. The sky was thick with clouds, the moon a bright smudge above them. "But you made it a priority to get Jana a doctor's help. A *lady* doctor, even. I didn't know there was such a thing."

Claire shrugged, one-shouldered. "I think there are many things our sex could accomplish if we were the ones who made the rules."

"But that is precisely what I don't understand."

"What is?"

"Why are you trying to restore Remy Duchamp to power?" Daphne asked, and there was an ache in her voice. "General Montgomery is a terrible brute, I'll grant you that, but Remy Duchamp is worse. Remy Duchamp *does not care* about his people. Was I correct in hearing that he hadn't read a newspaper in the last year?"

"Possibly ever," she admitted.

"Can he even read?"

Claire struggled against the urge to defend him before giving in. "He's brilliant, Daphne. Let's not shortchange him. He writes scientific articles, he can converse with Nikola Tesla about superconductors. The lightning rifles that saved us all at the Palace of Fine Arts were *their* idea. But when it comes to political maneuverings . . . you're right. Remy is a babe in the woods. I think he'd be at his happiest in a schoolroom somewhere, doing mathematical equations into infinity."

"You say that like it's a lovable part of his character. But it's not, Claire."

"Daphne—"

"No, it's selfish. Can't you see? That kind of absorption is well and good for a man who is alone in this world, but the Governor of a province must care for his citizens. I don't see why these are our only choices to rule us—brute force or selfish naivete."

"They're not our choices," Claire said, "because we don't have a choice. We can do what we can to influence the outcome, and to save our necks, but in the end, it isn't up to us. It's Duchamp or Montgomery, and if we don't settle it ourselves, I know the King will. All we can do is make our case."

"Well, it should be up to us. I've had enough of being treated like a child just because I'm a woman."

"Do you think I enjoy it? But how do we prove our adulthood to them, Daphne? Do we ask them very politely in our daintiest voices? Do we trick them into marrying us and then hope they'll take care of us and not send us back to the wolves on Adams Island? Do we try to outstrategize a general, us and our merry gang of women and boy librarians? No—we take this to Philadelphia. We take this straight to the King. We find a way to confront him, we force his hand. We put Remy back in power and we take it from there."

"And in the meantime, the General stages these—these rallies in front of the mansion, telling the people he's their savior. Didn't you hear that reporter? Every night he's out there, drumming up support. He's consolidating his power!"

"His power doesn't matter," Claire said. "Only the King's power matters."

"Washington is a tourist, not a king. He rides around in that little train, with his little trained men, amusing *himself*, and himself only. He's just like Governor Duchamp. The King won't lift a finger to help his kingdom. No. Local power matters. Provincial power. What's going to keep your citizens from tearing you apart, limb from limb, when you come back from the west with some royal pronouncement saying that the Duchamps are in charge? You have no popular support!"

She has a point. "Then we need proof. Indisputable proof

that the General has been taking advantage of the common man for years. That he's not their hero. My God, the protection money he takes from business alone—that's how he built himself that giant house out in Lordview."

"And who knows about this?"

"Business owners do," Claire said. "He talked about it openly on the council. If there aren't financial records we can access, I know there are records of the meetings."

"Where?"

"In the mansion," she said, slowly. "But . . . Daphne. We don't want to go there. It's going to be surrounded by his supporters. We took all this trouble to make it here, unseen— what's the point of any of this, if we're caught and hanged before dawn?"

"We'll be armed." Daphne looked incandescent with purpose. "We'll fight our way out."

"With what weapons? The only weapons we have are men's secrets!"

Someone cleared their throat behind them.

"Um, I have weapons," Beatrix whispered, her golden head stuck out the window. "Brought a wagonload of lightning rifles, on Mrs. Duchamp's orders. Do you all need a few?"

Claire glared at her, but Daphne was clearly considering her offer, as though it wasn't made in jest. "Think I could strap a pair to my back?"

"You're funny," Claire said. "What a funny joke."

"Claire, this isn't a bad idea. We can be in and out of the mansion before anyone knows we're there. Back in Orleans, I was a locksmith's apprentice."

"You don't need to get inside something to destroy it," Beatrix said. "Claire's father worked in munitions. The two of us know a lot about explosions."

"Destroy it? Dear God, Bea, we're talking about getting in there and grabbing a *logbook*. Not blowing it up."

"You might want a diversion," Beatrix said. "An explosion's a good one."

Daphne shrugged. "Makes sense to me," she said.

"Thank God! Finally someone who wants to *do* something!" Bea crowed. "Let me pack a bag."

Panic. It crept up her arms and into her chest, and Claire forced herself to breathe.

Think logically. You can talk them out of this.

She had a plan for blackmailing the King, yes—but the more she considered it, she had the creeping sensation that it was a plan handed to her by the General himself. The General certainly kept his prisoners on Adams Island; his soldiers hadn't been lying about that. Miller himself had told her of the political prisoners who came and went in the men's ward.

No, what didn't make sense was why the General hadn't killed her out of hand. Had he actually wanted to marry her, the way the King had suggested, the General would've kept her close to him and on display, a target to lure Duchamp and his forces into an ill-fated rescue mission. Everyone knew the Duchamps couldn't best the General when it came to force. The General could have killed Remy, married Claire, and secured St. Cloud in a single move.

But he hadn't.

Instead he'd sent her to Adams Island. And maybe it was mere convenience for him, maybe it really was the most secure place for him to store such a threat as her, but . . .

Did the General know about Aislinn Kelly? Does he want me to confront the King with what I learned?

And what is the General planning for when I do? Does he want the Kingdom for himself?

My God, I might be playing directly into his hands.

"Remind me. How is this a better plan than just going to Philadelphia tomorrow?" Claire asked Daphne.

"Your *plan* was to walk up to the King and inform him that you know his darkest secret. What did you think would happen next, other than him putting your head on a pike?" The girl looked at Claire like she'd grown horns. "I am not putting another man in power. We are taking them *off* their thrones."

"So you want to declare war not on the General, but on the governorship." Claire clenched her fists, with terror and with excitement. "Not on the King, but on the monarchy itself. We're going to take down the General and then . . . and then what, Daphne?"

"Rule," Daphne said, simply.

Beatrix dropped her bag out the window, then clambered out after it. "Gunpowder, flares, a saw, two hammers, a brick and some twine, oh, and some apples from the market! Miller and I picked them up earlier. They're lovely. Claire, do you want one?"

Claire swore loudly enough that an alley cat began to scream.

She'd thought they would need to make an elaborate plan to get to the mansion unseen, what with the General's soldiers swarming the city—underground tunnels, disguises on the El train, a stolen horse or two—but then Beatrix had pulled out a handful of coins and hailed them a hackney cab two blocks west of the stockyard.

"The Governor's Mansion, please," she told the driver, hefting her bag. "We have a late delivery for the kitchens."

The three of them crowded into the cab together. "Simplicity itself," Beatrix said.

"You don't know he's not an informant for the General," Daphne said, shifting her weight around. As the smallest, she'd been stuck with the middle seat.

Beatrix responded, very reasonably, "I don't know that *you're* not an informant for the General. You're the one who told me to pack a bag full of gunpowder to blow up a palace, remember?"

"A distraction," Daphne said. "That's only if we need a distraction."

"Do either of you have a plan?" Claire wanted to laugh; she wanted to weep. She thought her head was going to explode. "Are you just going to sneak behind the General while he's ranting on that stage and pick the lock on the mansion's front door? I think we might draw just a *little* attention, don't you?"

"I could offer the cabbie an extra few pennies to wait for us," Beatrix said. Daphne snickered.

"Dear lord," Claire said, "you're going to have us all killed."

"The General's been sleeping soundly in that mansion every night. He's had no opposition for weeks now, Miller told me. Walks out there on that stage like he's immortal. Someone could just shoot him, and no one does." Beatrix juggled the bag on her lap. There was gunpowder in there, one of the most dangerous, finicky substances in the known world; Beatrix handled the bag like it was full of teddy bears. "We were cooling our heels out west at Wardenclyffe, and you know it. We tried it your way, Claire. You ended up in an asylum."

"I chose to go to that asylum!"

"We'll be fast, and silent," Daphne said. "We'll get in and get out. Through the kitchens. Bea was right, that's the easiest way."

"We should have left a note for Miller, at least, to tell him to alert whatever soldiers we have left in Monticello for potential conflict. If we get caught, this is a powder keg. God, *do* we have any soldiers in Monticello that the General hasn't caught? Are they still all out at Wardenclyffe?" Claire put her head in her hands. "I've been away for weeks, and I don't have troop tallies, I don't know what new intelligence we have. I haven't spoken to Remy about any of this! We shouldn't be doing this tonight, we should have taken the time to plan—"

"The longer it takes for you to wrest power back from the General," Beatrix said, "the longer the Duchamps are dithering away in the west, the less likely your people are to accept you as their rightful leader once you return."

"If that's what we want," Daphne said darkly. "To put a man like Duchamp back in power."

The hansom cab clattered to a stop, and Beatrix reached up to give him another handful of coins. "Enough to stop your ears to anything you might have heard tonight?"

"Damn horses are so loud. Naw, I heard nothin', saw nothin'," he said, and grinned, a line of dark uneven teeth. "Evenin', girls."

"That sound," Daphne said. "I don't know if the cabbie could have heard us at all. Where is that *roaring* coming from?"

"There," Claire said, pointing. She felt ill.

A line of redcoats idled outside the mansion in the electric light. Someone had set up a stage behind them, a rough thing of boards and brick. A podium stood lonely in its middle, lit by a pair of electric lights that they must've taken from Tesla's laboratory. There was no sign of the General. Not yet.

By the way the crowd was acting, you'd have thought that God Almighty was about to address them in the middle of Monticello-by-the-Lake.

Washerwomen and prostitutes, priests and day laborers, the occasional man in vest and cravat, fat off the toiling of his workers—they were all jammed in together, shoulder to shoulder, and some of them had thought to bring torches. Claire had a confused sense of them as a many-headed hydra, mouths agape, eyes wide and frightened, waves of sound coming off them like the roar of some massive wounded creature. She remembered reading her mother's copy of *Frankenstein* by candlelight, the mob coming up the hill to kill what they saw as a monster—

But here, the monster and the men were the same.

Her sense of self-preservation took over. "Get out of the light," Claire hissed to them, falling back across the street and into an alley. As Daphne and Beatrix drew up beside her, she craned her head to keep an eye on the growing crowd.

They kept coming, swarms of them, traipsing down Prairie Street in high spirits, clutching blankets and sandwiches and their children's hands, and if it weren't for the torches that some of them carried, Claire would have thought they were headed off to see some entertainment in the park. In the distance, she heard the telltale bells of an El train pulling up to a platform, and knew that more were on their way. More, from hansom cabs that lined up at the corner of Prairie and State, more peeling off from a crowd of merrymakers meandering over from the Fair.

The General, then, was just another attraction.

Motion, up on the stage. An honor guard, guns drawn, flanked the podium, and the crowd grew louder. They knew from experience what came next.

"MONTGOMERY!" the people were chanting. "MONT-GOMERY!"

General Montgomery strode up to the stage. He grasped the podium as though it was a steer he was wrestling. When Claire had last seen him in the King's Box, he'd been battered and old, but here the gaslight smoothed out his imperfections. Tonight he looked craggy. Formidable.

"My people," he said. "My people of St. Cloud."

They roared, with one voice.

"I come to you with a heavy heart. I come to you with sad tidings. I come to you with a story, about an act of destruction. An act of war.

"Did you know that with every passing day, our alliance with Livingston-Monroe grows ever more fragile? They were our brothers-in-arms, once. They too understood the importance of military strength. They were willing to lay down their lives for a First American Kingdom they believed in. The Monroes ruled their province well; why, just weeks before Remy Duchamp fled the city—"

Yelling, booing. "Hang him!" a man howled. "Traitor!"

"You said that," the General said. "I didn't say that. But yes, yes, I do think he's a traitor. . . . Where was I? When Remy Duchamp fled the city, the Monroes were still our valued guests! And then, overnight, the beautiful Abigail Monroe—such a lovely ornament on her husband's arm, don't you think?—Lady Monroe *vanished*."

The crowd gasped.

Claire's hand stole up to her throat. She'd seen Abigail Monroe moments before she'd vanished . . . to some dungeon somewhere below the mansion, a place only Captain Miller knew.

"We've been keeping this information secret," the General was saying. "Didn't want to cause a panic. But I thought it was important that you knew. Because the people who did this to Abigail Monroe—they're here. Right now."

Claire swallowed. Beside her, Beatrix drew back further into the shadows.

The General had his audience in the palm of his hand. Women were hugging their children, men were patting down their pockets, looking around for criminals. "Tell us!" someone called out. "Tell us who they are!"

Under his mustache, the General was beginning to smile. "They've been in this city for years. They've eaten our food, slept in our houses, walked on these very streets. They've been right here under our noses this whole time."

"Tell us!" the voice yelled again.

"Immigrants," the General said. "Aliens. From *Europe*. Hard-drinking, soft-handed, un-American *immigrants*— and no wonder! Look at the man who this province called its leader! No, he let them in. He made it very *comfortable* for them to be here. That mad scientist Nikola Tesla that he keeps like a pet—that man could level this city with his experiments! You heard the stories of what happened at the Palace of Fine Arts! Lightning rifles. Unnatural weapons! Yet another immigrant that Duchamp has at his command.

"And poor Abigail Monroe was this man's *guest*. She even challenged Duchamp in front of his court! Challenged his Francophile sympathies! And Duchamp couldn't take it. He called in his gang of immigrant toughs, and he made her *disappear*."

"How can he do this?" Beatrix was whispering. "He's just . . . lying. I was there! I saw what happened to Abigail Monroe! Remy doesn't have *gangs*, does he?"

"No. Of course he doesn't," Claire said. "Why do you even have to ask that?"

Daphne said nothing, her arms wrapped around her waist.

"Our allies," the General was saying, "they're *upset* with us. Livingston-Monroe blames us for the death of their lady Abigail. They're mad enough to make war—and who could blame them? But I'll tell you what." He leaned forward, as if to whisper a secret to a little boy. "I think if we just give them *Monsieur* Duchamp, all of this will just . . . *poof*. Go away."

"And that little bitch of his, too!" someone yelled.

"Why not?" the General said. "Might as well. Without those frogs, we'll make St. Cloud a mighty place to live again."

The crowd was chanting something that Claire couldn't make out. She thought she was going to be sick, right there on the pavement. Somehow—somehow—the General was still talking, but Claire didn't hear a word.

She'd been so naive. So certain that, after years of indifferent leadership, all it would take to make it up to St. Cloud would be an apology and a logbook that proved the General's sins against them.

But if God himself came down to tell this crowd that General Montgomery was a crook, they'd tar and feather him and send him packing back to heaven. They wouldn't listen to reason now, not when they had someone who spoke to their rage instead.

If this crowd caught Claire and the others breaking into the mansion, they'd hang them on that stage.

Claire swayed a little. "Give them what they want," she said.

"What, your head on a platter?" Daphne asked.

"No," Claire said. "They want a war? Give them a war. Burn the place down."

In the torchlight, Beatrix's eyes were glittering. She lifted the bag in her arms. "I'll be back," she said, and slipped into the crowd.

Claire could make out, now, what they were chanting. "MAKE THEM PAY!" they said. *Make them pay.* She didn't know if they meant the Duchamps, or the Duchamps' imaginary immigrant toughs, or both. She didn't know if the crowd even knew who they wanted to pay for their crimes. The General had whipped them up into a jingoistic fury.

He was making his goodbyes, flanked by his red-coated guard as he strode off the stage and into a waiting coach. *A pity,* Claire thought, but at a strange remove from herself. It would have been too easy to expect him to walk into a waiting tinderbox.

At least there was still a chance that she could slit his throat herself.

"MAKE THEM PAY! MAKE THEM PAY!"

The city—her city, the place of her birth, whose streets she'd walked by day and night, the city that she was a steward of, now—it wanted her dead.

They only stopped chanting after the first explosion.

After the second, it was pandemonium.

She couldn't hope to find Beatrix, not in the stew of screaming children and men unholstering their weapons and women, red-faced, bawling in the road; not when the crowd's bloodlust had turned to frenzy. She and Daphne huddled together in the alley and waited.

She couldn't stop staring at the mansion.

Smoke was coming out of it in great black columns. Claire watched, transfixed, as the fire raced from the main hall through the open doors of the ballroom. Through the oversized windows, she watched it twist and coil, a bright spreading path. Curtains went up, and divans. A pianoforte folded into itself. A painting flared up, and then a second, and in the light of their immolation, she could see where the fire would leap to next. In that way she watched the painting of Remy's beloved father curl up into a blackened scroll, then fall into nothing.

Then the windows went too, one two three, like gunshots.

Remy had said that his household staff had gone into hiding, and it appeared to be true; from Claire's hiding place, she only saw a handful of uniformed people escape out into the night. They carried their belongings on their backs, in the drape of their aprons; they stumbled, they fell, they ran.

"If anyone's still asleep in there—"

"They chose to work for the General," Daphne said to Claire. "That man. That awful man. And anyway, the mansion would have been our first target when we retook the city."

Claire shook her head. "How do you find comfort in that? We are *responsible* for any of their deaths."

"This is war. It can be the right decision, and it still can feel terrible," Daphne said. "Both of those things can be true."

Only a few minutes had passed, but to Claire they felt like

hours. There were calls for the fire brigade, a line assembling to bring buckets of water from a pump, lost toddlers mewling in the road. Claire made herself watch. She watched it all.

Whatever projects and notes that Tesla had left in the mansion would surely have been destroyed; he claimed that he was cursed to be followed by fire wherever he went. This time it was her fault. She had deemed his work a worthwhile sacrifice. The kitchen and all the beautiful food in the cellars, Remy's library with its two hundred volumes, all the dresses he'd saved from his beloved sister who had died in Europe only a few years before. She watched a pair of cats escape out a high window onto the roof, and she thought about Aislinn Kelly, and she cried.

Why am I mourning this symbol, when it stands for so much I hate? But there were so many things she wanted to mourn, and here was a vessel for that mourning.

Daphne put an arm around Claire's shoulders. Her own face was dry.

Monticello was a city that was afraid of fire, and rightfully so, after so much of it had burned just a few decades prior. It mobilized quickly. The fire brigade arrived in short order, their bells tolling loud and long, and those Monticellans who had skipped the General's rally were certainly awake now. All around the square, their windows winked into light.

"There's going to be violence," Claire said. "Where's Bea? It's been too long—Daphne, we need to find her and *go*."

Daphne took her hand, and together the girls slipped down the street, heads down, hugging the storefronts to avoid attention. But Claire stopped short at the corner. Something was happening, though through the smoke she couldn't see what; she flung her arm up to keep Daphne behind her. A commotion within a commotion—a trio of horses pulled up, rearing, a laborer with his hands thrown up against their hooves.

"*Move*, damn you," one of the riders said, and the man staggered off down the road, back into the crowd.

Remy. He'd seen her first. He struggled to rein in his horse; it was rolling its eyes and stamping its feet and clearly wanted to run. Remy's face was like iron. "Did you think we couldn't hear you, giggling like a set of murderous schoolgirls right outside the window? Have you any idea the *damage* you've caused?"

"Sir," Miller said, on the horse beside him. He was struggling to keep the riderless mare they'd brought calm. "It isn't safe. We need to take the girls and run."

He was right. The roar behind them was growing louder and louder; it was hard to tell what was the fire and what was the crowd.

"No, I think we should look upon their handiwork. At this!" Remy flung his arm at the mansion. "At my *home*! At your home, Claire! At the very thing you've been fighting for!"

With effort, Claire clambered up on the saddle in front

of him. "Does this look like the time," she asked, "to talk about this?"

Another explosion.

"Duchamp!"

Someone had spotted him.

"That's Remy Duchamp!"

"The traitor!"

"We need to go," Daphne said urgently, climbing up onto the riderless horse. Miller was cursing.

"Wait!" It was Beatrix's voice. She was soot stained, red in the face, running full out at them with her bag flapping against her back.

But the crowd was converging on them, a crowd of men in their shirtsleeves, fire in their eyes, fires burning at the ends of their torches. "What should we do with them, boys?" the man in front shouted. "I think we should make them scream."

"Now, sir!" Miller was yelling. "Now is the time!" He cantered forward through the crowd, grabbing Beatrix's arm and swinging her up in front of the pommel. She was half on the saddle, half dangling over the side, but his horse kept going, its hooves a sharp tattoo against the cobbles of Prairie Street. Daphne's followed.

But Remy didn't move. As the men with the torches began to regroup, surge forward, Claire spat at them. She dug her heels into the horse's sides; it shied and whinnied and then took off after Miller, Remy clinging to her back.

"Those are your people," she shouted to her husband, willing him to understand. "Those are your people, like it or not. Don't you see? This is what the monarchy has done to us! Tell me, Remy—did you really ever want to govern St. Cloud?"

Remy's voice was shaking. "Mon dieu, I do not . . . I . . ." He couldn't seem to settle on an answer.

"Don't you want to be free of it all?"

"My family is gone," he said. "I am left alone. Now my home is gone as well, and by your hand. Is this what your freedom looks like?"

"You have lost more than any of us have ever had."

"Claire—"

"I don't know," Claire said, with effort, "if you would make a better ruler than the General. I don't know if I want a ruler at all."

At that he went silent.

Slowly, like a house collapsing, Remy put his arms around her body, and as they fled through the burning streets of Monticello-by-the-Lake, he wept into her dark and streaming hair.

TWENTY

In the morning, Remy was nowhere to be found.

They spent the night again in Beatrix's workshop in its little brick building in the stockyards. Claire noticed the brick specifically; she was relieved it wasn't wood, and couldn't burn. Still, they had all agreed it was the final time they could safely stay there; even this night was a risk. Beatrix Lovell was far less of a nobody than she used to be, and the building was registered in her brother's name.

The crowd last night had wanted their blood.

If the General wanted to, he could find them there, and so Miller insisted on keeping watch in case any avenging redcoats made their way to the stockyard. But he must have fallen asleep. That, or he was lying when he told them he hadn't seen Remy leave. He and Daphne had gone out early to assess the damage from the fire and to pick up provisions for their trip to Philadelphia later in the day.

Without Remy, apparently.

The young Governor had left a note on Beatrix's workbench: *I don't know anything about this world,* it read, in his beautiful penmanship. *How can I hope to govern it well?*

"What is it?" Beatrix asked, trying to read over Claire's shoulder.

"We have to get over to the *Star* offices. We have an appointment," Claire said, trying to tuck the note into her bodice, but Beatrix snatched it from her hand.

She scanned it, then dropped it on the table. "Oh. Well, I'm sorry, love," Beatrix said, in a tone that said *I saw this coming from a mile away.*

Claire forced herself to keep her tone light. "Don't you think it's a bit of a liability, having our sad young Governor wandering around, ripe for the kidnapping?"

"And what would we do with him if he was here? He says right here that he's not fit to rule, and for once I happen to agree with him."

"I do too, Bea, but I don't know what we're doing instead." Claire scrubbed at her face.

"Are you feeling okay?" Beatrix asked.

"I'm fine."

"You don't look fine." Beatrix folded her arms. "It's not every day you hear an angry mob calling for your execution."

"It was . . . invigorating," Claire lied. The whole horrible scene was there every time she shut her eyes. "I don't want to talk about it, Bea. It was . . . it was out of control. When we see Lizzie today, I want to make a detailed plan for Philadelphia."

"We're going to run off to blackmail the King of our great nation. Isn't that enough? Cheer up, love. Remy will turn up."

Claire had nothing to say to that. Instead she sank down to the floor. She needed to comb through the trunk to see if there was anything she should take along with her. Right now, the sum total of her possessions were a stained white inmate's gown and a heartless best friend.

Beatrix sighed, then knelt down beside her. "I'm sorry. I'm punchy this morning."

"You are. And your timing for that is awful, by the way. I feel like I took enough punches last night."

"I'm nervous. That's all. This is . . . this isn't just sitting around in some powder room, scheming with the D.A.C. bigwigs. This is frightening. I feel like I need to be frightening to meet it."

"You just burned down the Governor's Mansion. You're not frightening?"

Bea chewed her lip. "It almost feels like someone else did that," she said quietly.

Claire met her eyes. "So just be Beatrix. Be my best friend. That's what I need right now." She pulled a blanket out of the trunk and tucked it into her bag. "The rifles. Miller has them, yes?"

Beatrix nodded. "If you don't mind my asking—what is he to you now?"

"Miller?"

"Remy. A lover? A meal ticket? A way to keep your head out of the guillotine?"

She didn't know how to answer that question. "He's . . . he's my oldest friend, other than you. And we burned down his house last night. And he's in pain. That's all."

"Can I say something?"

Claire braced herself. "Can you keep yourself from saying it?"

"Fine then. I won't." Bea kissed the top of Claire's head. "We should go. We need time to get to the *Star*, and who knows what we'll see between here and there. I don't rightly know what Monticello will look like in the light of day."

It looked like disaster.

The Gold Coast was a smoldering wreck. The fire had spread down city blocks in every direction, radiating out from the mansion. Women wandered through the street, soot covered, carrying their belongings on their backs, their children clutching their dresses. People's houses had burned, and so had their businesses. Livery stables had burned down, and stationers, and milliner's shops, and fruit stands, and their wares were scattered in the streets. As Claire walked alongside Beatrix, she found herself kicking along a half-charred apple like it was a stone.

We did this, she thought. *We did this to Monticello.*

On the corner of Division Street a boy was hawking copies of the *Star*. GENERAL MONTGOMERY GOES TO WASHINGTON, read the headline. SEEKS MILITARY AID. She went to pay for one, and realized she had no money. She'd been wandering the city like a king would, expecting others to tend to her, flowers to be thrown under her feet.

Beatrix gave the boy a coin for a paper. She read aloud as they walked. "Headed to Philadelphia by special train . . . hooligans and anarchists, he was quoted as saying, him saying he wants to build things, not burn them down . . . clear difference between me and Remy Duchamp . . . sources say that Governor Duchamp is still in exile at Wardenclyffe Tower."

"Either the paper has bad sources, or the boys working the wires at Wardenclyffe are spreading misinformation," Claire said.

"That, or he's run back there, tail between his legs, and someone found out about it before us. There's another article, farther down. People are pleased as punch that the General is bringing 'a true American patriot' into 'this battle.'"

"The King?"

"The King."

"Terrific. Look, we're in Printers' Row—the *Star*'s up ahead. I think we're late, we should hurry."

The *St. Cloud Star* newsroom had the feeling of a clubby men's-only establishment, the kind that women only saw inside to clean. Papers were scattered across the parquet floor, and the walls were lined with bookcases that groaned under the weight of reference guides and records. Desks were everywhere, pushed head-to-head or tucked away in nonsensical little corners. Only half of them seemed to have chairs.

Everywhere, there were men. Men with walrus mustaches in their shirtsleeves and suspenders, men gathered around a squawking telephone, taking furious notes, men shouting over one another in their need to be heard. "What do you think of this?" one man boomed. "Anarchy in the streets! St. Cloud under siege!"

"General runs like a little goose girl!" another said, and they all howled.

"I need a lead boy," someone called, and in the doorway Claire and Beatrix were nearly run over by a child in a cap. He ran to pluck the note from the editor's outstretched hand, then took off again at speed.

"Give the boy room!" the editor snapped at them.

"I don't see Lizzie anywhere," Bea said to Claire.

"Excuse me," Claire said, waving at the editor. "Do you know where we can find John Mackenzie?"

He glanced at her, then did a double take. "Aren't you . . . ?"

Dammit, I'm supposed to be missing. "Who?" she asked guilelessly.

"Anyone ever tell you you look a lot like the Governor's wife?"

"It's why she gets double from her patrons at the dance

hall," Bea said, stepping up to put her arm through Claire's. "You should see the wig we put on her, she's a dead ringer. Poor thing sells her hair to pay her landlord and then this fire? She's in a hard way. We're supposed to see John Mackenzie, he wanted to write a story about it. Human interest."

Claire did her best to smile like a girl with a broken heart. It wasn't that hard.

The editor had already stopped listening. "Mackenzie's upstairs. Has a bunch of other hard-luck cases up there already, they're probably spilling into the hall by now. Room two oh two." He loaded a fresh page into his typewriter and lit a cigarette.

Claire stepped around his wastebasket, filled with crumpled paper, and headed up the stairs. It was quieter on the second floor; perhaps the man below hadn't been an editor, or an important one anyway. There certainly weren't "hard-luck" girls waiting out in the hall. Here there were nameplates next to the frosted-glass doors. The publisher, the managing editor—there it was, JOHN MACKENZIE, PROVINCIAL EDITOR.

"Lizzie didn't make it sound like she was this fancy," Claire said, and knocked on the door.

It opened immediately. "I got a nice fat promotion," Lizzie Cochrane said, "selling papers with your face on them. America loves a missing white girl. Come on in, both of you. I want to show you what I've found."

She opened the door wider.

"Liliane!" Claire cried, and pushed past Lizzie to hug her friend. "You got off the island? How? And . . . Tilly? Tilly! My God! And oh, I'm sorry, I don't know either of your names, hello, I'm Claire Duchamp, I was on Adams Island with the rest of you. If you were there too, that is. Oh, this is my friend Beatrix. . . ."

Once introductions were made and everyone was settled into their chairs, Lizzie sent down for some tea. "One of the benefits of my new position," she said. "The tea's awful, by the way, don't expect much. I drink it for the principle of the thing."

Liliane was curled up in her seat like a cat, eating a biscuit. Tilly looked better than she ever had, flush with sun, her cropped hair curling at its ends. The other two women were middle-aged, one lanky and eager, leaning forward, the other with kind blue eyes and a thick scar that cut across her cheek. They'd been introduced as Hattie Wilde and Diana Anastos.

"Lizzie, how did you get everyone off the island?" Claire asked.

"I didn't."

"That was down to us," Diana said quietly.

"Tell the story, Hattie," Tilly urged, as Lizzie took out her notepad and a pen.

Hattie leaned forward on her elbows. "By the time Miss Cochrane arrived, we'd more or less sorted it out ourselves.

Diana and I had been in Hall Two together"—she clasped the other woman's shoulder—"for God knows how long. At least two years. Maybe three? And we'd always talk about what we'd do if we had the chance. Figured it might happen the way it did: doors left unlocked, whether by accident or design, and the women thinking to free each other until there were enough of us to swarm the whole place proper. Men don't necessarily do that, mind. Stop to let the others out on their way to freedom. But us girls, we look after our own.

"Shouldn't say that the men were useless, because they weren't. By no means. After the girls from Hall Six fanned out, broke into the other wards, men's and women's, and opened the dam, so to speak, we gathered together a bunch of us old-timers in the women's mess. Went into the kitchens, ate some real food for the first time in God knows how long. The stuff the nurses had saved for themselves."

"Bread," Diana whispered.

"Bread." Hattie squeezed her eyes shut, remembering. "Gave us the strength to do what we had to. Some of us who were feeling stronger, who hadn't been sick or had the life beaten out of them, we went and lay in wait for the guards. Years in that place, you know where to linger to not be seen. I took out a pair of them with a chair leg. Got their guns. One big fella on the men's side, he had four of their rifles over his shoulder when I saw him next. Didn't ask. Didn't need to know.

"Locked all the surviving guards in solitary. There are a few rooms like that in the basement of both sides, men's and women's. Horrible places."

"I've seen them," Claire said.

Hattie whistled. "Have you? Not nice. Secure, though. Guards in one, nurses in another. Mercy me, no, those ladies did not like that."

Tilly grinned wolfishly. For one glorious, effervescent moment, Claire let herself imagine Miss Grune being dragged by her ear into Aislinn's cell.

"And then it only was a matter of seizing the morning delivery when it came in, taking the doctors and locking *them* up, making sure no messages got back to the city. But we had some desperately ill folks with us, and none of us wanted to spend a minute we didn't have to on Adams Island. We had to get to Monticello, but we had to do it in a way where no one saw us. And there were a *lot* of us. Not an easy ticket. That's when Miss Cochrane here came in."

"Some fishermen owed me a favor," Lizzie said. She put down her pen. "I reported on their working conditions last year. Shamed their employer. They ended up with better wages. After I spoke to you, Claire, forgive me—I couldn't wait to find out what was happening on Adams Island. I asked the fishermen to keep watch as they were out in the early morning, and one of the captains came to me when he saw the chaos at the sanatorium."

"I never expected you to stand idly by," Claire said. "I only wanted you to hold back my part of the story, for now."

Lizzie nodded. "Took our five trawlers six trips apiece to get everyone out of that hellhole, and we're still sorting everyone out. No idea how we would've pulled it off in secret, but there was some gigantic fire last night. Started at the Governor's Mansion? After some asinine rally the General was having?"

"How about that?" Beatrix said from beside Claire.

Lizzie shook her head. "I don't want to know any more. Well, some inmates were healthy enough and had places they wanted to be. I appealed to a friend of mine whose husband has more money than he knows what to do with; she's helped me out in a pinch before. With her help, we gave those inmates some coin—enough for a train ticket and a few nights' lodging—and sent them on their way. Bless them. And Dr. Blackwell took charge of the ones who needed help, sent them to hospitals under false names. Got them good doctors, sympathetic ones. As for the rest—"

"There are so many of us," Diana said.

"We took each other's stories," Tilly said in her matter-of-fact way. "Those of us who knew how to write. I must've taken twenty, myself."

Claire's eyes fell on the stack of paper on Lizzie Cochrane's desk. "Stories," she said.

"Detailed stories," Hattie said.

"With names," Tilly said. "We have so many names of

powerful men who damned these girls to hell because they knew too much."

"My God," Beatrix said.

"And we've hidden the inmates across the city," Lizzie said, "in boardinghouses and hotels, so that they can't be found and silenced before we do what we need to do."

That euphoric feeling again, that lightness, like she'd been lugging a bag of wrenches all over Monticello and had finally put it down.

"And what's that?" Claire asked, though she already knew the answer.

Liliane had finished eating her biscuit. "Il faut appeler un chat un chat."

"What did she say?" Tilly asked.

The French girl smiled. "We tell the world—comment dit-on? We tell them who these men really are," she said, and licked the crumbs off her fingers.

TWENTY-ONE

The first story would come out in the *Star*'s evening edition, but Lizzie Cochrane had an early copy. She'd written it, after all.

As she waited her turn to board the train, Claire kept checking her reticule to make sure the newspaper was still there.

"My God," Beatrix said beside her. "Do you think it's going to escape?"

"No, I just can't wait to read it," Claire said.

"Out loud, please. The moment we board the train," Daphne said.

Beside them, Miller snorted. "You realize that, in those get-ups, the glee in your voices is obscene."

"Thank you," Claire said gravely, trying not to fuss with her veil.

Their run-in with the newspaperman at the *Star* reminded Claire how careless she had been. She was a wanted woman; her disappearance had been front-page news. She couldn't be walking around town wearing her own face. It would be ironic indeed to put together a bulletproof plan to take down a king . . . only to be recognized by a train porter and handed over to her enemies. Beatrix was far too recognizable as well, even after she had replaced her cloth-of-gold eyepatch with a plain one. ("It's the swagger in your walk," Miller had told her, and Beatrix beamed. Claire had rolled her eyes.)

When Claire had pointed out their problem, Beatrix had immediately begun concocting a plan for spirit-gum mustaches and big fancy hats. Laughing, Claire had held up her hands. "There's a much easier way," she said. "How much money did you say you had again?"

"Emptied the coffers before I left," Bea had said, plucking a purse out of her bodice. "As per your instructions, sir. Have I mentioned yet how lovely it was to see our old cipher again, in your letter? And those amazing fabulisms you came up with! You lie beautifully. You lie like a rug."

"I learned from the best." Claire grinned. "Think you can pretend a little more?"

When they arrived that afternoon at Unity Station, the girls were dressed in full mourning garb. It was fiendishly hot, the black silk dress with its neck that came up to the chin, and the long crepe veil that sat stiffly an inch from your face. The dye used on its fabric stunk to high heaven, and Claire felt her lungs constrict each time she tried to breathe in. She couldn't quite believe that it was still expected that women so obviously carry the full brunt of mourning the dead. Men wore precisely the same suit of clothes after their wives died; women had to muffle themselves away for a full year.

But it certainly made for a terrific disguise.

I wonder what Remy would make of me now, she found herself wondering. *If he would be disgusted, or delighted. Or simply overwhelmed.*

Miller directed the porters to stow away their less-important luggage, the clothing and supplies that he and Daphne had scouted out that morning. Daphne and Lizzie both wore half mourning, grays and lilacs, while Tilly had dressed herself as a lady's maid. (Lizzie's photographer, Bill, had taken an earlier train; his equipment made him far too conspicuous.) If anyone asked, their party was traveling to Philadelphia for a funeral. Despite the unrest in Monticello, Unity Station was full of merrymakers arriving for the Fair and landed gentry headed off to New Columbia for the King's celebration.

Claire and her friends were a sober patch in all that brightness. They were politely ignored, which was, of course, what they'd wanted.

Once they'd all settled into their berth, drawn the curtains, and locked the door, Beatrix flung her veil across the room.

"Ew, please don't put that near me," Tilly said, flinging it back. "It smells like a latrine."

"Can we please act like adults for one minute?" Claire

grumbled, but when she pulled out the paper from her reticule, she was hiding a smile. "Lizzie, would you like to read it out?"

"I've spent enough time with it," the journalist said. "Daphne, why don't you?"

With gusto, Daphne shook out the paper like a man in his club in his favorite wingback chair.

Sources have exclusively informed the *St. Cloud Star* of a malignancy hiding among the province's upper echelons. . . .

"What with the General going missing, and his soldiers doing nothing to track down the arsonists who destroyed our glorious Gold Coast district, it feels like the right time to weed out the other undesirables in positions of power across Monticello-by-the-Lake," one of our sources said.

"What source was that?" Beatrix said.

"Me," Tilly said.

"You?"

"I'm the source for Liliane's story. Lizzie needed a quote and I was still in her office. So."

Daphne cleared her throat to continue.

Lizzie had decided to begin her series of exposés by reporting Liliane's story. It had been the one she could investigate and verify the fastest. Lizzie spoke fluent French, enough to be able to ask Liliane the questions needed to identify the man who had had her kidnapped from her dressing room. Though Liliane had been blindfolded when she'd been taken by carriage to the man's house, once inside, her eyes had been wide open. From Liliane's description of everything from the chintz on the settee to the paneling on the stair wall, Lizzie had been able to ask her society insider if she knew anyone who owned a home that was less than a ten-minute carriage ride from the Levee, and who had done the entire place over in the Japonism aesthetic.

"The place with the enormous Hunzinger sofa?" the insider had said. "Oh, I know exactly who that is."

His name was Albert Wallinger. It wasn't a name that Beatrix had been familiar with, but it was one Claire certainly knew. The man sat on the Governor's council. He was St. Cloud's secretary of the treasury, and though he seemed staid and sober during the workday, there had been dark rumors about his carousing in the Levee district for years. This exposé would only serve as confirmation of something that the public already knew.

But that wasn't the worst part of it for Wallinger. The worst was that unbeknownst to him, his wife, Kitty, was a prominent member of the D.A.C. She had been in Toronto visiting her sister while her husband was abducting Liliane.

"That fool. If we don't get him, Rosa will," Beatrix said.

Lizzie had lined up a full complement of witnesses, from the Wallingers' housekeeper down to the boy who delivered their fish. Unsurprisingly, Liliane's abduction hadn't been the first time Wallinger had treated a girl like a necklace that he could smash and grab from its glass case.

"Government officials are already calling for his resignation. We expect official statements by the morning." With a flourish, Daphne folded the newspaper.

"And who were those officials?" Claire asked Lizzie.

The reporter laughed. "Who else? The two men in the treasury department who would be the natural successors to his position, after he's dismissed."

"This is how the sausage gets made," Miller said. "It's unbelievable."

"It *is* unbelievable," Beatrix said. "Because by the time tomorrow morning comes, we'll see consequences for Wallinger's behavior. Can you imagine living in an America where that happens?"

Claire's gaze had turned inward. "There's more to it than that."

"More stories," Daphne said. "We all have so many. The *Star* could rake enough mud to redo the Levee. The series could run for weeks."

"Not all of your stories can be proven as easily as Liliane's," Lizzie warned her. "I'm good at my job, but I can't make miracles happen. So many of the Adams Island women were put away by a man they had a close relationship with. They had a brother or a husband 'begin to notice their insanity.'

Brought in doctors and lawyers, did the thing properly and by the letter of the law."

"And once a woman is labeled mad," Daphne said, "no man will believe her. Not ever again."

Lizzie cracked her knuckles. "From the stories I've reviewed—and I've reviewed them all—I have maybe two or three home runs like Liliane's. I can't speak to the rest, not yet. I certainly can't report them on the timeline you're hoping for."

"We have something more than verifiable stories," Claire said again.

"And what's that?" Miller asked.

"We have the *threat* of them."

Every face in the train car turned to her.

"Right now we have train tickets to Philadelphia without any clear idea of how we'll get close to the King when we arrive. Lizzie has access to him as a journalist, but the rest of us? He'll be well guarded during his birthday fete. We've been putting off making this plan because we've known we have nothing to work with. But now we do.

"Lizzie," Claire said, fighting down that familiar rush of glee. "I need the name of King Washington's most disgusting, wretched, low-down hanger-on. The worst of the worst. The one who's a single accusation away from a vertiginous fall from grace."

The reporter guffawed. "Wait. You only need the one?"

TWENTY-TWO

The journey from Monticello to Philadelphia by train was lengthy and slow going. Out the window of their berth, Claire watched day wind into night and into day again. As she sat with her legs tucked up to her chest, she marveled at her own exhaustion. She had been on the run since before the Fair opened its gates. Not a night had passed since when she hadn't been in danger.

Tonight, she felt that rarest of things: safe.

But she knew that feeling was a flimsy one, predicated on assumptions she couldn't quite afford to make. She was married to the Governor of their province, who was currently missing; the other claimant to his throne wanted her dead. She was on what was likely a suicide mission to make the leader of this country pay for his crimes. And even if Claire were to consider how safe she was in this precise moment, consider it long and hard, she wouldn't come up with a reason for relaxation. Oh, the women with her were wily and brave; they'd proved that a thousand times over, and if it came to an entirely physical threat, Captain Miller would certainly defend them. But he was also a wanted man, one who'd been walking around Monticello wearing his own face. Hiding in plain sight. Had someone followed him to the station, and boarded their train—

They could burst in at any moment.

Deep breath in, deep breath out. The door is locked. A stack of suitcases is piled before it. If everyone else feels safe enough to sleep, you should too. It's not as though you're going to feel safer once you get to Philadelphia.

It was the hour after dawn. Light climbed up the walls of their berth. Claire heaved herself off her bed, thinking she'd perhaps go in search of a glass of water.

"Can't sleep?" a low voice asked.

Miller had the bunk below hers. To her surprise, he was sitting awake.

"No. I wish I could."

Miller inclined his head. "Come talk awhile." At her hesitation to sit beside him on the bed, he said, "Believe me, if I wanted to make a pass at you, I would've by now. And anyway, one squeak out of your mouth and the rest of these girls'll be at me with knives. Especially your friend Beatrix. She's a real corker."

Claire chuckled and climbed in beside him. They sat with

their backs against the wall, jostling a little with every movement of the train. "I don't know why I still have this sense of propriety. It wasn't like I was born rich, where that kind of thing would matter. My father just had . . . ideas."

"It's hard to shake what you're taught when you're young," he said. "It gets into your bones."

"He had so many ideas of how things should be. About me, about the world. None of them were ever tethered to the here and now. I used to think that all great geniuses were like that, you couldn't follow their train of thought because it led up into the sky. That it was my job to applaud him. Not to understand."

"And now?"

"I think he was always insane," she said after a moment. "I think my mother managed him because she had no other choice. She considered it her job, I think, to tell him what he wanted to hear. It kept his rage in check. 'I'm teaching your daughter to work a laundry press,' when she was teaching me calculus instead. 'That landlord should be thrown in jail for talking to you that way,' when my father came home raging over the injustice of paying what was owed. She'd clean up behind him in secret. And then, when she died, there was no one to remake the world to suit him anymore."

Miller huffed. "Seems to me that . . . well. That your father was a right asshole. I hope you don't mind me saying so."

"I don't," Claire said, laughing a little, "but yours isn't a peach, either."

"We have that in common, don't we? And also the fact that my dear old pa thought the best place for both of us was Adams Island." Miller tipped his head back against the wall.

"What was it like for you there?"

"Different, I think, from what it was like for you girls. In my hall, at least, the nurses seemed afraid of us, and maybe they had reason to be. There were guards stationed there to keep us in line, inside and out. It was like being at a work camp, honestly—had us out there breaking rocks all day and then they'd pen us up in our cells. They'd give us our evening meal in there; our morning meal too. I was too exhausted to do much but sleep. And the only time I could talk to anyone else, it was in the yard, and even then we were under the eye of the men with the guns. They didn't have you working, did they?"

"Mostly they starved us and beat us with clubs."

"Yep," Miller said equitably. "Yours was worse."

She looked at him sideways. "Did you see your father before he sent you there? How were you caught sending us messages, anyway?"

Miller made a face. "I was a fool. Kept going back to the same wire station. I had some buddies from the Governor's guard who'd crossed over to my father's side—but you know how it is, with this kind of conflict. Hate the sin, love the sinner and all that. I'd go over to their digs and dice and drink all night—it was where I got most of my information, since they'd all forget after a few beers just who it was I worked for now. And then when the place started to empty out, I'd sneak upstairs to use the telegraph. Did it one too many times. Friend of mine followed me up there, and once he realized who I was sending messages to . . . it was a foregone conclusion. They tied me up and came in an hour later with the order. I didn't see the General at all."

"Brave of him, having his lackeys do his dirty work."

"Can you blame him? I had the chance to kill him, you know. That night in the Palace of Fine Arts. I had his throat in my hands. I could feel his pulse under my thumbs."

"Why didn't you?"

"Not for his sake," Miller said. "And I guess it wasn't for the sake of St. Cloud, either, because we'd all be better off without that maniac. No, I suppose I . . . I kept him alive for myself. I don't need to go courting my father's ghost. I have enough blood on my hands."

Claire looked down at hers.

"You know, he wants to be King," Miller said. "My father's men were saying that he's set his sights past St. Cloud. Those rallies at the mansion, all those people chanting his name— he's begun to believe he's been chosen to lead. Apparently he thinks he can get the support to have the King declare him next in line for the throne, since the King doesn't have any heirs."

"All these men think they're chosen for something grand," she said. "Imagine, to think yourself so endlessly important. My father was the same way."

"Do you know where he is now?" he asked her.

"No," she said. "If you had told me a few months ago that my father would be the least of my worries . . . I don't know how I could have imagined a world like that."

"That bad?"

She shrugged. "It's tempting, now that I'm free, to say that it was fine. I survived it, didn't I? He didn't beat me. Not often, anyway. I don't have scars. And I've seen plenty of things since him—like *your* father—that scare me a hell of a lot more. But . . ."

He didn't speak, just sat with her while she sorted out her thoughts.

"My father had me convinced for a long time that I had this power," Claire said finally. "That my touch could grant his wishes. He invented this whole . . . ritual around it, this laying on of hands. At the Fair, that's what he made me do when his cannon wouldn't fire. He had me 'bless' him. To Remy, it must have looked like I was whispering advice in his ear, or something like that. Anyway, it worked; the gun fired, and Remy took my arm, and holding on to me, he gave this amazing speech to open the Fair. First decent speech he'd ever given, judging by the crowd's reaction. And on the strength of that . . . that hunch about me, he kidnapped me."

"You're still angry about that," Miller observed.

"I don't know if I ever *won't* be angry about that."

"Do you believe it? That you can grant wishes?"

"No," she said. "I don't really know what I believe. Only that, ever since Adams Island, I don't see myself the same way I did before. I thought sometimes, living with my father, that I was the only thing standing between him and disaster. One wrong move on my part, and he'd fail, or scream at the wrong person, or blow up a whole city block. That we'd starve. When he identified this . . . ability of mine, to make his wishes real, it was like he was making me an equal partner in all that misery he created."

Miller stared into the dark. He said, "There are a lot of ways to break somebody's spirit. Especially when that person is a child."

"I know."

Unexpectedly, he grinned at her, a flash of white in the dark. "Take my hand."

"Sorry?"

"Take my hand."

He held his out to her, and after a moment, she clasped it.

"Now shut your eyes," he instructed.

"You better not try anything—"

"For the love of God, *Lady Duchamp*, just shut your eyes, okay? Concentrate. Can you feel the wish I'm making right now?"

"No," Claire said petulantly.

"Could you ever feel the wishes your father was making?"

"That's hardly the same thing!"

"Hush. Sense has no part in this." He made a low humming sound. "Okay. You can open them."

"What did we just accomplish?"

"I convinced myself that the thing I wanted most dearly in the world—"

"Oh no."

"—was for you to turn into a purple hippopotamus."

"Oh, for crying out loud!"

"I'm very serious."

Claire choked on a laugh. "It doesn't work like that, and anyway, that *is not* the thing you want most in the world."

"It isn't? Think how many problems it would solve! With you a hippopotamus, and Remy Duchamp run off into the hinterlands, I could finally in good conscience step away from this carnival ride you've kept me on. I could go back to being just another soldier, not thinking twice about his orders, not having to think at all about how bad you women have it—I could get back to enjoying myself! And you know what else?"

"What?" she said.

"You wouldn't just be a hippopotamus, you'd be a *purple* one. A very *bright* purple, that was what I wished for, just for clarification—"

"Yes, thank you."

"So I could sell you to a zoo and I'd be rich."

"You've really thought this through, haven't you?"

Miller snorted. "I don't do things by halves. Anyway, then

I'd have enough dough to take your little blond friend there and get her to marry me. All my problems solved. Tell me again that this wasn't what I wished for."

"Wait . . . Beatrix?" she asked. "Marry *you*?" Bea had to be asleep, or Claire would've heard her cackling.

"What, you don't think I'm good enough for that sassy-mouthed little harridan?"

"I think you'd have to ask Beatrix," Claire said, coughing a little. She hadn't laughed that hard in a long time. "I don't know if she wants to be anybody's wife. But who knows? She might make an exception for you. Though . . ."

"What is it?"

"Lately her tastes have been trending less toward trousers and more toward skirts."

"Oh," Miller said, and then: "*Oh.*"

"Hippopotamus or not, you'd better have a word with her about it before you set your heart on that harpy."

"Fair enough, fair enough." Miller clapped her on the shoulder. "Can I say something?"

His words had an uncanny echo of Beatrix that morning. This time, she said yes.

"I don't mean to make light of what your father did to you. The things the General made me believe, the things he did to my mother . . ." He trailed off. "They made me a hateful man, and for a very long time. Hell, maybe I still am hateful. But I think you're wrong. I think that anything you made that man do—whether you made him succeed, whether you made him happy—you did it out of sheer force of will. Not magic. And Claire?"

"Yes?" She was close to crying again, but for a different reason this time.

"That was more than that son of a bitch deserved."

They sat in silence.

"Thank you," Claire said finally. She wiped again at her face. "I . . . we both need to get some sleep."

In the morning, they alit from the train. Lizzie left the rest of them at the station; the *Star* had put her up in one of the hotels designated for press covering the weeklong event. They hadn't so much as nodded goodbye to her on the platform. There was no point in advertising their relationship, not if their plan was to work.

As Miller arranged for their luggage to be sent to their hotel, and Daphne and Beatrix bought pastries at the little café, Claire purchased a stack of papers at the newsstand. The *Philadelphia Herald*, the *New Columbian*, a free tourists' guide to visiting the King's Palace. There wasn't a copy of the *St. Cloud Star*, unfortunately. She would have liked to see the morning edition, to continue following the downward arc of Secretary Wallinger's fall from grace.

At the curb, Miller called for a hack while Claire and Beatrix waited alongside him. They still wore their mourning garb, and Daphne, half mourning. Miller was wearing his redcoat uniform; he looked like a Livmonian. It had seemed like a safe enough thing to be in New Columbia. To give the women more room, he swung himself up to sit with the driver.

As they rattled along, Daphne didn't try to hide her yawns. Beside her, Claire's head buzzed with exhaustion as she paged through the *Philadelphia Herald*'s coverage of the King's birthday week. She had that particular hollowed-out feeling, as though she were a loaf of bread that had been devoured from the inside, leaving only the crust behind.

And yet there was a relief in her this morning, too, that she hadn't expected. It had been cleansing to weep for the girl she once had been. No one had ever cried for her.

"You have the dossier?" Beatrix asked Claire.

"I have it."

"And you want to do this directly after we arrive?"

"I do," Claire said, enunciating from behind her thick black veil. It was hard to hear each other over the noise of the busy streets and the heavy beat of their cab horse's hooves. "The first event is tonight. Fireworks on the river."

"Which river?"

"The Delaware. The Schuylkill River has too convenient a view of the Blockley Almshouse." As they waited their turn at an intersection congested with soldiers and horses and cabs, Claire craned her head to read the street signs.

"The almshouse is about four blocks west of here. Hospital, orphanage—"

"And a madhouse," Daphne said darkly.

"And a madhouse." It took some effort for Claire to reorient herself, but she managed. "You can imagine that the King doesn't want his guests to look upon such . . . unfortunates. So he's taking his court to the Delaware. From what I've read, the truly influential will be watching alongside the King from the comfort of their own barges."

"They're buying barges for this event?" Daphne asked. "At what expense?"

"The King's. Apparently his secretary has sent out thirty invitations—"

"Because he's turning thirty," Beatrix said. "How original."

Claire rolled her eyes. "Thirty invitations. They were couriered to people's households a month ago. With that invitation, you're not only granted access to events, but to lodging at the palace, dinners in the ballroom, breakfasts on the balcony overlooking the Delaware, boats and carriages and dressmakers—here, there's a list in the paper. It's absurd. Tonight, his thirty households will pick up their barges at the King's marina. They'll be 'bedecked with flowers and stocked with champagne.'"

"And we'll be on one of them," Beatrix said, grinning. There was nothing she loved more than to be in charge of her own craft.

"I hope you brought your sailor hat," Claire said as their cab slowed to join the procession of carriages waiting to let off their passengers in front of the Fox Hotel.

As they idled, she took in a breath. After the blood scent of Monticello's stockyards, the smoke-choked streets around the mansion, breathing Philadelphia's air was a revelation. There was still the effluvia from the lined-up carriage horses, the fish smell of the rivers, the chemical stink of her veil, but in this moment she could smell, too, bread baking down the road, hot asphalt, the perfumed lobby of the hotel. The three girls waited quietly, breathing, until it was their carriage's turn.

"What now?" Beatrix asked.

"That depends," Claire said as Miller helped them down to the road. "Are you up to making threats, or should Daphne and I do it alone?"

"The two of you are perfectly terrifying, you'll be fine without me." Bea shot Miller a bright smile. He flushed. "And anyway, I want a bath."

"More importantly," Daphne said, looking askance at Beatrix, "I need to get a message to my cousin. Last I heard she was working as a gardener at the palace. I haven't seen her since I was a girl, so I don't know what good it might do. But on the off chance she knows a way to get at the King . . ."

"It's certainly good to have a contingency plan. Can you write it in a way that disguises our true intentions, in case the message is intercepted?"

"Of course I can. I'll go speak to the concierge now," Daphne said, and headed for the hotel.

Claire turned to Bea. "There will be baths for all of us, I promise."

"But first, blackmail," the other girl said cheerfully.

"Indeed," Claire said. "We have a timeline. I need you to come along and stand menacingly behind me."

"If you're truly going to be hiding in plain sight tonight, we need to find you a wig," Beatrix said. "I think I'd be of more use hunting you down a hairpiece than acting as your bodyguard."

"Will I do?" Miller asked as he paid the driver. "I can growl on command. And that crate of lightning rifles should already be upstairs in our suite. One of those would look good strapped to my back."

The driver looked down at Miller, startled. He snapped his reins, and the horse took off at speed.

"Fine," Claire said, watching the cloud of dust rise in the Philadelphia road. "I suppose I'll settle for the only one of you who has experience with a weapon."

TWENTY-THREE

"We are here to see Chester Barrington the Third," Captain Miller said to the man who answered the door.

The butler's livery was flea-bitten, his expression sour. "Mr. Barrington is not at home to visitors."

Claire stepped out from behind Miller in her full mourning garb. Silently she extended an envelope to the butler in one trembling hand.

"You can imagine the urgency of the circumstances that have led my sister, despite her recent and devastating loss, to venture into the public's unforgiving eye. She seeks Mr. Barrington's counsel," Miller said. Claire was impressed. They'd rehearsed this bit on the way over, and he was performing admirably. "Will you convey this note to your master?"

The butler sketched a bow and began to shut the door, but Miller stuck out a foot to block its path. "We will wait in your parlor."

Grimacing, the butler said, "As you wish," before scurrying away.

Though the Barrington manse was imposing from the outside, all cast-iron gates and ivy-covered brick, the inside gave the impression of a family fortune in slow decay. Running errands for her father, Claire had seen many genteel old houses that were comfortably shabby, filled with well-loved, worn-in furnishings that were tended with care.

The Barrington house was another matter. As she and Miller showed themselves to the parlor, she studied the gaudy, gilt-edged curtains that had already been nibbled upon by moths, the undusted mantelpieces pocked with the outlines of their recently removed ornaments. Sold, perhaps, to pay off debts. A house this size should have been bustling with activity, above and below, but all Claire could hear were the butler's quick footsteps above them, the hum of a quiet conversation.

"You really can't find good help these days," Miller said, flopping down onto a cane-backed chair. He swung his rifle around to his lap; he'd hidden it under his dress cape on the walk over to avoid the attention of passersby.

"Where did you find that lord-of-the-manor voice you used on the butler?" she asked him.

He smirked. "I've always done a good impression of my father."

Upstairs, the murmuring abruptly stopped. Now there was shouting instead.

"Excellent," Claire said, plucking off her gloves. "I see he's read our note."

"Any moment now. Ah, here we are," Miller said as the butler raced back into the parlor, sweat beaded on his forehead. Before the man could speak, Miller stood. "I imagine that Mr. Barrington will see us now. Will you show us to him?"

Chester Barrington III was a thin-faced, nervous man. His ginger mustache was enormous; it dwarfed his thin lips, his thin nose. If it weren't for his clothes, he would look like a starving prospector just back from Alta California. But he wore a lavender silk cravat under a cherry-red silk vest, into which he'd tucked a pocket watch the size of a dinner plate. Between that riot of colors and the skittish energy that animated his movements, looking directly at him was as difficult as squinting into the sun.

"What is the meaning of this?" Barrington demanded. He held up the clipping from the *St. Cloud Star* about Secretary Wallinger's downfall. "'You're next'? I have nothing to do with *showgirls*. And even if I did, I have no wife to scandalize! My dear friend King Augustus Washington will have something to say about these . . . these *threats*—"

Claire made a show of looking around his study, tilting her veiled head back and forth. "And yet you agreed to see us," she said, in a voice lower and raspier than her own. "I think we both know what you are afraid of."

Chester Barrington III pulled at his mustache. "I will have my—my butler go and fetch the King's guard—"

"Certainly. We'd be glad to tell the King's guard all we know."

Barrington looked as though he might vomit. "Tell me," he hissed. "Tell me what it is you think you know?"

"I know many things," she said. *Thank God for Lizzie's file.* "I know that you inherited significant debt. That the lumber company that your grandfather founded razed swaths of forest along the Canadian border until there was nothing left to cut down. What is a lumber mill without lumber? Bankrupt, I believe. And your father, instead of—God forbid—taking a position working for someone else, he took to drinking away the dregs of your family's money. Leaving *you* with a rotting old corpse of a mansion and no coin to maintain it. Which in and of itself is not a crime. I do have some sympathy for those who suffer from their fathers' sins."

"You *shrew*—" Barrington said, then snapped his mouth shut. In the corner, Miller was examining his lightning rifle, polishing it with one gloved hand.

"None of that is criminal, of course. It's only ill luck, and easily mended by living within one's means. But a man with your ambitions would never be content to do that. No, you weaseled your way into the King's inner circle. It took years, and every last social connection you had. But how else could you be sure you'd be granted a Crown contract to expand your lumber holdings? Oh, yes, the King tossed you that clerkship, had you tend to his social correspondence. It's meant to be a cushy job, a few hours a week, the kind of perk he hands to a friend. But it's an honor, not a profession, and it doesn't allow you enough money to live on. What you need is that land on the Canadian border. Land that the King has the power to grant you. And you've known, known in your *heart*, that once the King had finished rewarding his oldest friends, it would be your turn. Any day now, it would be your turn."

Barrington stared at her as though hypnotized.

"But days turned into months, didn't they? And months into years. And all this time, you've been forced to walk such a very fine line—wealthy enough to linger in the King's company, but not so flush that he would think you wouldn't need his help when he finally thought to give it. But you're clearly in a hard way. How *have* you maintained what little you have? Everyone knows you haven't any money."

"I have an idea," Miller said. In a fluid motion, he shouldered his rifle and aimed it at Barrington, who shrieked. "No, it's not quite right." Miller lowered the gun to adjust its sights. Before him, Barrington fell into a coughing fit, the result of gasping in too much air.

"Your idea?" Claire prompted.

"I think this little weasel's been abusing his access to the royal seal."

"*Has* he," Claire said, as though this was a surprise. Really, Lizzie's dossier on Chester Barrington III had been very thorough. "Tell me more."

"Oh, it's only a guess. But follow me here: Barrington, in his role as the King's social secretary, is given the stacks of letters and packages and presents that have made their way to the palace. Nothing political, of course. Nothing important. Barrington isn't an important man.

"No, what he's meant to handle are invitations to parties, casual correspondence from those too important to be ignored, and he's told to draft his replies in the King's own hand. We can't have the heir to the governorship of New Teshas think that the King is ignoring his invitations. It's Barrington's job to write a polite refusal. But what if that correspondence— especially the letters that only look like letters, that don't appear on first glance to have, say, *money* inside, or, I don't know . . . *jewelry*—"

Barrington went paper white.

"What if that correspondence is dropped on Barrington's desk willy-nilly? No one else keeping records. No one else keeping track. No one else *knows* that some woman in West Florida has sent the King a bribe of a hundred dollars in hopes that he'll entertain her beautiful, eligible daughter the next time she comes to Philadelphia—"

"Stop!" Barrington shouted. "Stop talking!"

"Really, all it would take would be a thank-you letter in the King's penmanship," Claire said, mercilessly, "adorned with the King's wax seal, and that hundred-dollar bill just *falling* into Barrington's pocket—"

"And all it would take on *our* parts would be to send a note to our favorite reporter at the *St. Cloud Star*, expressing our suspicions—Mr. John Mackenzie, as you can see, isn't afraid of exposing a powerful man—"

"What do you *want*?" he cried. "What do you want from me?"

Beneath her veil, Claire smiled.

Miller stood and shouldered his rifle. "Where should we begin?"

It took a laboriously long time, but soon enough they were in possession of one ostentatiously heavy invitation to the King's birthday fete, addressed to the Barrington household, as well as a timetable of events, hour by hour. Claire filed them away in her reticule.

"The King will notice if I am not there at his party," Barrington was saying. "He relies on me."

"Oh, the King will have more important things on his mind," Claire said. "Trust me. Now . . . we need one final item. Your personal copy of the King's seal."

"I don't keep it at the house," Barrington sneered.

"I think you're lying," Miller said. "And even if you aren't,

I might just kill you anyway. You're odious enough that I don't think too many will miss you."

"Fine . . . yes, fine." Barrington was trembling with rage as he lifted the blotter off his desk. Below was a folded piece of foolscap, and within that was a key. He fumbled open the drawer at his right hand and used the key to open a compartment within. With evident care, he removed a box and set it before him. He'd composed himself enough by now to be able to glare at them as he lifted the lid. "I don't see how you think you're going to get away with this."

"Who would you tell?" Claire asked him. "And what would you say? A widow and a man with an electrical rifle robbed you of the King's personal wax seal, which you just happened to keep in your desk at home?"

"Disgusting woman," Barrington said. The seal, when he produced it, was massive, clearly sized to prevent theft. Claire wondered how he'd secreted it out of the palace. "Here. I can't imagine what you think you will do with it."

"What I'll do with it? What *you* will do with it." Claire took a note from her reticule. "You are going to write me one more letter, in the King's hand. Do remember that I have a sample here." She unfolded it and held it before Barrington's eyes, to assure him; it was the careless note of welcome that the King had left her on the Royal Limited. "So I will know if you are playing us false. I imagine, by now, that your skills as a forger are quite exceptional, so let's have your very best, yes? Now, take my dictation."

Barrington sat. He thrust his pen into the inkwell, darkening his hands. Fuming, he cleaned them off with a rag and began again. "I will find you," he seethed, "I will find you, and when you least expect it I will . . . I will, ah, have you murdered, and—"

"Toothless little man," Miller muttered.

"I refuse to be treated in this way!" Barrington stood. "I'll—I'll call for my butler! Who will call for a guard! Who will—"

Miller rolled his eyes and fired his lightning rifle into the ceiling. Plaster rained down around them.

Barrington sat. His eyes welled with tears.

Claire brushed off her dress while she waited for him to get ahold of himself. "Are we ready now? Good. Write this: 'I, King Augustus Washington, being of sound mind and body . . .'"

It took Barrington four attempts to write the letter. By the end of his best copy, he'd finally stopped crying. He jabbed the seal into the hot wax at the letter's folded seam.

Before Barrington could tear it up, Miller snatched the letter from the desk. He held it level while the wax dried.

"And now, one final letter," Claire said. "Take my dictation. 'General Montgomery . . .'"

"What have you done?" he asked himself, scratching down her words. "What have you done?"

"You aren't asking the right question," Claire said to Barrington when he'd finished. "You should be asking, what *will* we do? Now, I can see that you're very tired, perhaps on the verge of a nervous collapse? I would recommend a short stay in a good sanatorium, but alas, I've had word that Adams Island is closed for the duration. But I do understand that there is a little rustic cabin in your family's name in the northern wilds of New Columbia. I might suggest that you take yourself there for the next month to look after your health."

"And if I refuse?" the man said, in a final show of bravado. "What will you do to me?"

Miller raised his eyebrows. Deliberately, he let a hand rest on the barrel of his rifle.

"Refuse," Claire said, "tell *anyone* of our visit, and John Mackenzie will have an article about you and your sins in the evening edition."

"It isn't what we'll do to you," Miller told him. "It's what the King will do, when he finds out how you've betrayed him."

At last Barrington deflated. "I will leave by the next train," he said. "Now, please—leave me to make my arrangements in peace."

Outside, Claire and Miller walked quickly, avoiding the main thoroughfares. His rifle was once again hidden under his cape. The Fox Hotel was another mile or so on foot, enough time for the two of them to finish developing their plan.

"When did *you* perfect that lord-of-the-manor voice?" Miller asked. "You make threats with the best of them."

"I've always done a good impression of my father," she said. "Now, there's only a few hours until the party on the Delaware. This is what I imagine we'll do. . . ."

Amid all the gaiety on the river, they were a grim procession.

Not outwardly, at least. The mourning veils that had served Claire and Beatrix so well were stowed away in their luggage. Women in mourning did not so much as call on their sisters at home for a visit, not when their grief so consumed them. They certainly did not outfit a barge in their house's colors and float it down the Delaware River, sipping champagne and shouting in glee at the fireworks display overhead.

"The wig looks nice on you," Beatrix said. She'd foregone her golden eyepatch; it attracted too much attention, even at a distance. But no one would come close enough to their craft to see her half-shut, clouded eye. "Always thought you should be born a redhead."

Daphne dared to dangle her fingers in the water; as the evening darkened, no one would be able to see her face. "It suits you."

"Does it, now?" Claire was hardly listening. Too much was on her mind.

Thirty households had been invited to sail tonight, thirty households all known to each other and to the King. In the prow of their ill-gotten barge, Captain Miller stood like a figurehead, resplendent in a brand-new summer suit of clothes. From a distance, she hoped he looked anonymously handsome, the scion of any favored New Columbian family. He was mere set dressing. Onlookers might glance at him, and move on. There was too much else to see: the river full of lilies and floating candles, and on the shore, a brass band playing the Sousa marches the King so loved. Common folk had gathered, too, to picnic and to gawk at the display of wealth that floated past them.

Many of the other barges kept pace with a partner as the King's favored guests chattered among themselves. But a few, like theirs, floated serenely at the edges of the celebration. They had taken care to stay at a distance; their oarsmen had clear instructions.

But still they were taking a risk tonight, drawing this close to the royal household before their real plan was put into motion. Claire had told the others that she thought it more dangerous *not* to claim the Barrington barge with their ill-gotten invitation; when the King summoned you, you came. You drew attention when you didn't, especially if you were a toady like Chester Barrington III.

But she would be lying if she didn't admit that tonight what she most wanted was to clap her eyes on the King. She wanted to see him for the flesh-and-blood man that he was, rather than the specter that had been dogging her steps for weeks. At Adams Island, when she'd watched Aislinn Kelly lie down in her hole in the ground, she'd thought of him; she'd thought of him while her husband's mansion burned; she'd thought of him in the berth of their train to New Columbia, its luxury a mere candle to the grandeur of the Royal Limited. She thought of him turning his back in the King's Box while the General's men dragged her out screaming. His cold arms around her, holding her baseball bat, teaching her something she already knew.

Beneath her dress, Claire had tied a drawstring bag at her waist, and she could feel the heavy reassurance of the invitation within. The forged letter beside it weighed far less. And still she would cut her own throat before she would let someone take it off her.

A part of her wanted someone to try.

Here we are, she thought as the King's oarsmen maneuvered the royal barge down the river. One by one, as though in a ballet, the other barges glided off toward the shoreline to allow the King a clear path. Miller turned his head, a silent question. *Should we move ours too?* At Claire's nod, he shouted an order to their pair of rowers. She told Beatrix and Daphne to get belowdecks; the King might recognize Beatrix from her stunt with the glider at the ball game, while their plans for tomorrow night hinged on Daphne remaining anonymous.

But Claire stayed where she was, turning a parasol over

her shoulder, the last lady visible on the Barrington barge as the King's boat drew nearer. She hadn't mentioned this to the others, this half idea that had grown in her since the afternoon, when she'd seen herself in the wig that Beatrix had bought her.

In normal times, Claire's hair was dark and curly, her skin as pale as paper, and she had generous hips. But with the weight she'd lost to Adams Island's meager portions, her cheekbones had grown pronounced; the inmates' twice-daily walks in the sun had left her face freckled and flushed. Already her reflection was a stranger to her. But today when she had tried on the wig and turned to the mirror, she'd tasted bile at the back of her throat.

For a moment—for only a moment—Aislinn Kelly's face had stared at her out of the looking glass. Her face as it once had been in all those newspaper stories from Claire's youth, before Adams Island had ravaged Aislinn's body and mind. When Claire made herself stop shivering, her own features reasserted themselves. But it was enough to plant the seed of an idea.

For their plan to succeed, they needed the King seeing ghosts wherever he turned.

Tonight, on the barge, Claire wore a dress in shimmering bronze. It had been Aislinn's preferred hue, setting off her coloring to stunning effect; though the photographs that Claire had seen of Aislinn had of course been black-and-white, Aislinn had caught the fancy of several society column illustrators, who had rendered her in full color. Claire remembered one drawing in particular—Aislinn all in starry copper, a parasol leaning against her shoulder as she laughed at something the King had said. An evening dress with an afternoon accessory. It had been daring, and for months the women of the First American Kingdom had mimicked her insouciance.

It wasn't in fashion anymore, but tonight, as the King's barge drew closer, Claire twirled her little lace umbrella. It would draw attention. Full evening had fallen, and she had no need to hide from the sun. She bit her lips hard to bring the color back into them, then turned her face to catch the light from the floating candles, posing as though for a portrait.

Eyes lowered, she waited as the King's boat made its procession nearer and nearer. There, his oarsmen; there, his personal secretary, a gaggle of girls all in white, laughing, the members of his guard all kitted out in Washington blue; there, the shortstop from his ball team puffing on a cigar as a servant handed around drinks. There—the King, broad shouldered in his suit, turning away from her to wave at the barges he'd just passed, at the well-wishers on the shore.

And then he faced forward again and went still.

The King had once asked Tesla if he could raise the dead. Tonight, Claire was the one with the power of resurrection.

She felt, more than saw, the way his eyes raked over her frame, her face. She didn't dare look at him dead-on for fear of dispelling the illusion. He took in the Barrington colors hung up and down the barge, and then he lifted a hand in welcome.

She waved lazily back—it was expected, after all—and then called, too loudly, "Chester, honey, I'm coming down for a drink!"

"Who is that?" she heard the King say. "Who does Barrington have up there on his boat—"

As she ducked belowdecks, flushed with success, she let herself look up one more time through the lace of her parasol. The King's face was impassive, as though he was holding himself still before the guillotine fell.

Your move, she thought.

But behind him, on his boat, what had she seen? A young man, standing tall and straight and slim in his sober suit—no. It couldn't have been him. Not Remy. There must be a million men just like that in Philadelphia, here to pay court to the King.

A million men, standing just as still and stunned as their monarch at the sight of her stretched out on a barge on the Delaware River, as though she was someone's long-lost love, here again somehow underneath the fireworks that chased each other through the night sky.

TWENTY-FOUR

"After that stunt you pulled," Miller said, "*this* was delivered to the Barrington household."

It wasn't yet eight in the morning, with an impossibly long day stretching out before them. Still, Miller had hammered on the girls' hotel room doors at dawn.

Daphne, bless her, arrived with the coffee service she'd ordered, and Beatrix behind her with a tray of pastries she'd taken from the kitchen. Miller didn't wait for them to eat—he tossed a letter down on the table, and waited for Claire to pick it up.

They clustered around to read.

Barrington—

I hope you will be accompanied by your new paramour at tonight's events. I'd like a word with her after the performance.

Come by my rooms. My guards will let you in.

It was unsigned, but the handwriting was unmistakable. It was the King's.

"Do you realize how much trouble we would be in," Miller was saying, "if I hadn't been there to intercept it?"

"Why were you there, anyway?" Claire's head felt full of cotton wool. She poured herself a cup of coffee, drank it down black, then poured another.

"To make certain that Barrington actually left! I realized it first thing this morning—all Barrington needed to do was come to tonight's events, and the King would know that someone was using a stolen invitation. Especially after he saw you last night. I needed to get into his house, make sure he was gone. Thank God he'd left behind a maid. She let me in through the kitchen, and I was questioning her when the King's messenger came knocking. I took the liberty of answering. Told him that Barrington was still dressing. Paid everyone else off to say the same to any more men that came from the palace."

"At this rate, we're going to empty the St. Cloud treasury, and this week," Beatrix said, tearing apart a pain au chocolat. "What funds do we have left?"

Daphne cast a surreptitious look at Bea's expensive French pastry, but said nothing.

"Does it matter?" Claire asked. "All that money was to be used at the Governor's discretion. It's meant for—for *orchestras*. Entertainments. Jugglers. We have enough money to keep us going for years. The only time Remy ever used it was to pay Nikola Tesla to make things explode." She winced, and took a sip of coffee to cover it. She had been resolutely telling herself that she had *not* seen Remy on the King's barge last night.

"Can we talk about something more important?" Daphne asked. "How about . . . the King is interested in taking lord's rights with Barrington's lady friend?"

"That surprises you?" Beatrix asked, popping a bite of croissant into her mouth.

"Well, no . . ."

"Of course he's doing that, and of course it's disgusting. But we need to remember that after tonight, he won't be in a position to do any of that again."

"And you do realize that this is the best possible turn of events," Claire added. "We have an open invitation to see the King tonight, if we need it."

"Fine," Daphne said. "I'm *thrilled* that the King is a rapist."

"Name a powerful man who isn't," Beatrix said.

Remy Duchamp, Claire thought, unbidden. "There's also the distinct possibility that, apart from the King's taste for redheads, he's concerned that Barrington has been harboring Aislinn Kelly, and wants to see with his own eyes. We'll only find out when we answer his invitation."

"When *we* answer it?" Miller asked her, and he sounded more exhausted than anything. "When *you* do, you mean.

He's not letting a soldier into his rooms with 'Aislinn Kelly.' And what do you plan to do when you get in there? I know you have that letter—but do you really think that you can stab Washington through the heart and leave that forgery on his corpse and watch as this country magically remakes itself?"

Claire said, "Our initial plan still stands. We'll see the spiritualist woman tonight." But she slipped the letter from the King into her bodice as Miller watched unhappily. "Has anyone—has anyone heard a rumor that Remy might be attending the party tonight?"

"Nothing about the Governor. I did hear that Tesla had come," Miller said, "lugging one of those generators of his in its own train car. But he would have found a way to tell us if he was here. And anyway, I heard all other kinds of malarkey, too. That the King brought in a pair of trained giraffes to do tricks for him. I don't buy any of it."

"Still," Claire said.

Beatrix chewed her lip. "If there's the slightest possibility he's here—"

"Yes, all right," Miller said. Unexpectedly, he grinned at Beatrix. "You and me, harpy. We'll go on the hunt for him tonight."

Beatrix winked at him.

"Thank you both," Claire said, and stood.

"You really think we'll succeed," Daphne said, worrying the tablecloth with her fingers. "That we can take down a king."

Across the room, in a pretty mahogany box, Claire's auburn wig was waiting for her. "I think," she said, "that we've already proven our ability to scare the King to death. Now we need to do it again, in front of an audience."

That night—the first true night of the King's birthday festivities—there was to be an illusionist's act in the echoing ballroom that served as the King's court. A stage was constructed, plush chairs and divans were set out, and the tall windows were muffled in curtains. All around the room, candles flickered away in the darkness.

The illusionist was a famous one, of course, best known for the part of his act when a dozen white doves came winging out from his top hat. He sawed women in half and plunged himself, chained, into tanks of water, all in the forgiving glow of candlelight. Claire could never remember his name. It wasn't important, really. Not to her.

Because the illusionist had an opening act: the well-known medium, Miss Alexandra.

The medium who had once visited her cousin in Lordview, just a few doors down from where Claire had lived with her father.

"My process is simple," Miss Alexandra was saying. Her dark hair was severely parted, her face creased with concentration lines. But she wore the simple white dress of a young girl, and in her hands, she turned over and over a long piece of cloth. "To be honest, I do prefer to work within a drawing room. I would always rather create a homey environment for any spirits that choose to visit."

"Of course," Claire murmured. Daphne nodded her head reverently.

In the crush of guests waiting to kiss the King's ring, the two of them had told the guards that they were the medium's assistants, and asked to be shown back to her dressing room. When Miss Alexandra opened the door, Daphne had pushed forward to take her hands. Her grandmother's spirit, Daphne said, had led them here. Couldn't Miss Alexandra share her expertise with a pair of budding spiritualists?

Everyone wanted to be adored. Claire knew it for a fact. She also knew, from the whispers around Lordview, that Miss Alexandra enjoyed her port wine, and when she'd held out the expensive bottle she'd brought, the medium had ushered them right in.

As she spoke, she eyed the wine, but made no move to open it. "The spirits are slower to come to me when I am onstage before a larger audience. True, some mediums thrive in such an environment, but I find that there are many distractions. Particularly tonight, when . . ." She trailed off.

From her reticule, Daphne produced a corkscrew. "May I be so bold?" she asked, reaching for the bottle. "This is a particularly fine vintage."

"I don't often imbibe before a performance," Miss Alexandra said hesitantly.

"Just a small glass," Claire said, "all around, if you don't mind us sharing the bottle. I have so many questions about what it is like to have the Sight."

Miss Alexandra sighed. "It is a burden," she said.

Claire lit upon a set of wineglasses on the sideboard, and fetched them. "How do you find your spiritual frequency when on so mighty a stage? And in front of the King, no less."

"I've heard he beheads performers who displease him," Daphne said.

Claire shot her a look. *Don't lay it on too thick,* she thought, but Miss Alexandra had already seized the bottle of port. She filled her glass to the brim.

"Bravery," the medium said. Her voice shook. "Bravery is the key." And she took a mighty swig of wine.

In the hour before the performance, as the King's nearest and dearest toadied up to him in the darkened ballroom, as Beatrix and Miller went off in search of Nikola Tesla, Claire and Daphne got Miss Alexandra rip-roaring drunk.

The medium was terrified. Though she'd risen in prominence in the years since Claire had last seen her, she'd never performed for royalty. Not even provincial royalty. "Alan—I'm sorry, you'll know him better as the Wondrous Ducrot— Alan and I were part of the same spiritualist community in northern New York. The Lily Dale Assembly. Our children played together. And after my husband died, and Alan's star began to rise, he would sometimes have me booked alongside him, to deliver spiritual messages to the audience in the hour before the show." With trembling hands, she refilled her glass. "I never imagined his star would rise *this* high."

"It is certainly a daunting proposition to perform for the King." Claire's auburn wig was itching her. She resisted the urge to scratch.

Miss Alexandra's eyes focused in on Claire's face. "Tell me," she said abruptly. "You and your friend, to have these invitations to his birthday fete—you must be intimates of the King."

"I wouldn't claim that *I'm* an intimate." Daphne smoothed her skirt.

"Yes, intimate is really too strong a word."

"Oh, hush," Daphne said, elbowing Claire. "You've had the man over to dinner."

"Oh, pssh."

"He taught you how to swing a baseball bat!"

"He loves my corn chowder. What can I say?"

The medium leaned forward. "So you know him well."

"Well, I don't advertise the fact, but yes. Gus—I'm sorry, King Augustus . . . to be honest, I think he's told me things he's never told a living soul."

It wasn't a lie.

Miss Alexandra took another swig from her wineglass. "What kinds of things has he told you?" she asked artlessly.

"Oh, well—"

Daphne swatted her on the arm. "You mustn't. Think of how upset your Gus would be if he knew you were off telling tales behind his back."

"The audience is about to find out all his secrets anyway," Claire protested. "Isn't that the point of calling in a medium? The spirits whisper things to them that no one was ever meant to know."

Claire had never believed in spiritualism. To her, it seemed too simple an escape. Séances promised both mystery and the reveal of the truth behind that mystery. But in her experience of the world, an unknown was only a trapdoor into the next. There weren't any answers to be had. Not easy ones, at least.

And she had heard the gossip, that spiritual mediums were in truth just excellent researchers. They demanded a list of their attendees beforehand and chose one or two prominent names—séances were expensive to attend, after all, and the wealthy attended in droves. Before the performance, the medium would read every bit she could about her chosen attendees in the papers. Then, at the séance, the medium would deliver a very specific message from the "spirits" to her selected personage. "Your grandmother Marianne misses you." "Your business deal with the railroad is about to fall through." It gave them cover, and credibility, and the rest of the messages that night could be vague ones about good fortune just around the corner, or the danger of a dark-mustachioed man.

To be sure, Claire didn't resent spiritualist practitioners. Women had to find some way to make money, after all. And she couldn't fault those who missed their loved ones, who would believe anything to hear their voices one last time.

Claire would have given anything to talk to her mother again.

In this moment, what Claire appreciated the most about Miss Alexandra was that she knew *exactly* what the woman wanted. And as the daughter of an abusive, mercurial man whose behavior she could never predict, she had always appreciated people with obvious motives.

"Yes," Miss Alexandra was saying as Daphne refilled her port glass. "All will become clear tonight. I was just hoping to . . . have a general sense of what may be revealed."

"Do you usually perform alone?" Daphne asked.

The medium looked uneasy. "At times I've had an assistant," she said, after a moment. "Someone to help me . . . manage the crowd."

And dim the gaslight at the most dramatic moment. When they aren't making eerie banging noises in the other room. "Of course," Claire said. "You don't have an assistant tonight?"

"I don't," the medium allowed.

Daphne toyed with her wineglass. "I've come to believe that I perhaps have some small psychic gift. I . . . hear things, sometimes. Sometimes I can look at someone and know that they are soon going to die."

Miss Alexandra ran a hand over the back of her neck. "That is a compelling gift," she said.

"Yes." Daphne gazed forlornly at the medium. "It is a heavy burden."

As the medium squirmed, Claire recorked the bottle of wine. "We ought to go take our seats," she said. "It's nearly time for you to begin."

Though she was tipsy, and afraid for her life, Miss Alexandra was no one's fool. "Sit," she said. "Daphne, is it? I take it that you would perhaps like to assist me in tonight's performance?"

Daphne widened her eyes. "Oh, it would be an honor—"

"Yes, of course it would be," the medium said, and pulled the bottle of port from Claire's hands. "And you, missy. You have some stories to tell me about the King, I think."

The girls exchanged a look.

Please, Aislinn, please. I hope you told me the truth.

Claire took a deep breath. "King Augustus really is a gentle man," she began. "A man who, more than anything, misses his older brother . . ."

Ten minutes later, Claire had said what she needed to say. While she'd talked, Miss Alexandra had methodically worked her way through the rest of the wine, growing more and more relaxed. She'd have an impressive revelation for the King's birthday after all.

Claire judged it time to leave when the medium, giddy, showed Daphne one of the tricks of her trade: how to forge messages from the spirits.

You wrote them with your feet.

"You do it under the tablecloth, where the audience can't see, and then, presto, you produce the letter. Most of us have very pretty foot writing, as it were. No, hold the pen a little higher, arch your foot. That's it!"

Daphne, toes pointed, was nearly biting her lip through with the effort not to laugh. Claire left them to it, and hoped, fervently, that the medium was sober enough to do what she needed them to do.

If all was going according to plan, this hour would find Beatrix off with Miller, sweet-talking a groundskeeper into showing them the tools of his trade. Tonight, the staff was giving tours. Rarely did the King allow visitors into the palace's famous gardens, but before tonight's performance, they were open for pleasure-seekers—the dogwood paths, the orchid houses, the lily pond with its lovely arching bridge that graced so many of the postcards tourists sent from Philadelphia.

All of it was open, really, except for the King's private rose garden.

And she was noticing it now, walking through the ballroom, head low under her wig—the roses were everywhere. Great pillars of them framed the breezeways, soft and fragrant, and they bracketed the sides of the illusionist's stage, all white and peach and red. Claire had the confused sense of a man standing onstage, wounded, bleeding.

A butler clapped his hands and gave a ten-minute warning. The serving maids, always invisible, lofted their trays of champagne flutes and lined up against the walls. Claire thought of Daphne's cousin, one of the gardeners; she hadn't responded to their message. Perhaps she'd never received it. Perhaps she rightly wanted nothing to do with the harebrained scheme of a cousin she'd hardly known.

The performance would soon begin. The King swept ostentatiously to his seat in the front row; he hadn't seen her, couldn't, through the swarm of toadies that surrounded him. As the would-be nobles drifted to their seats, all subtly jockeying to sit as close as possible to the front, Claire slipped through the throng toward the exit.

In the crush and sway of nobility, she didn't see any of her friends. Lizzie was here, somewhere, with Bill the photographer, ostensibly to write a society piece about the soiree. Really she needed to be close at hand for what was to come later. A pair of generators flanked the stage, humming, but Claire caught no glimpse of their inventor. Surely Beatrix and Miller would have found her if Tesla was here. She still couldn't imagine a reason he'd have to leave his laboratory for New Columbia, but then a man that wielded that much power couldn't afford to shun politics. The lightning rifle Miller now carried was proof of that. Had Tesla lost faith in the Duchamps? Was he planning on brokering his own deal with the King?

He should have talked to me, she thought, surveying the room. *The King might not be King very much longer.*

Claire had half expected to see Rosa Morgenstern, but then the King saw her as a nuisance, and one didn't just waltz into the palace uninvited the way one might, say, Wardenclyffe Tower.

And the General? She couldn't see him, but she could hear him. He spoke in the way of a man determined to be noticed, bluff and desperately loud, and the laughter that answered his statements was loud, too. Men performing for each other, performing for the room.

Tonight, for once, he wasn't the man she was most afraid of seeing.

Neither was the King.

At the door, a butler stood at attention. Claire drew a sealed note from her bodice with one gloved hand. "Would you see this delivered to General Montgomery, please, after the performance?" she asked, looking up through her dark eyelashes. "It's very private correspondence."

The butler, expertly trained, took the letter with no more than a nod.

The gaslight dimmed. It was her cue to go. She needed to be backstage before Miss Alexandra began her performance. What happened tonight depended on it.

And still she lingered. This was a needless risk she was

taking, the same risk Miller had chided her for this morning, and yet here she still stood. *Am I a worthy adversary,* she wondered, *or am I a girl who just can't help herself?*

Because here in this room, somewhere among the power brokers and the sycophants, Remy Duchamp was waiting. He had to be. Why else had he been on the King's barge last night?

And I have no idea what he's about to do.

At the door, she paused to glance back over her shoulder— and across the ballroom, she locked eyes with the King.

He half stood, stricken.

Claire took a breath—and then a hand caught her by the arm and pulled her off into the corridor.

TWENTY-FIVE

She was jerked around the corner, into an empty powder room. A hand was clapped hard over her mouth.

"Why are you here?" Remy Duchamp asked her, and he backed her up against the door to brace it closed. He was tall and lithe in a summer-weight suit, his eyes dark and fixed on hers.

Panting, she pulled his hand away at the wrist. "Saving my life," she spat. "But you knew that already. Why are *you* here?"

"Saving *my* life," Remy said.

"Saving your governorship, you mean."

"No. There isn't a way to have both, and you know it." He crowded her closer, until her shoulders were pushed back against the door. "You proved that yourself, when you set fire to the mansion. The people don't want me. This *country* does not want me. I think . . . maybe it never has. So I've come to Philadelphia to abdicate my position."

Claire shook her head tightly. "And then what do you think

will happen? That the King will just let you leave? What about the General? You could come back at any time, be a threat to his rule—it would be far easier just to kill you."

"Tesla had the same concerns," Remy said. "That is why he's traveled here with me. We will make an exchange: the King will have his court magician, Tesla will have a laboratory paid for by the Crown, and I will have my escape. My freedom."

She had never seen him like this. He looked lighter, freer, and he looked too like he was burning.

"But where will you go?" she asked.

"My cousins, they have a vineyard. In Provence." He took a loose strand of her auburn hair, twirled it in his fingers. "Lavender. Honey. A place to make a home. I could have my books sent over by freighter—"

"Your books."

"And your books, as well."

"I have nothing. You took me off a stage in the Fair with the clothes on my back. *My* books?"

"We would buy you books. I'll take you with me—"

"Like a package. You'd have me sent over by freighter?" A laugh caught in her throat. "Have you thought at all about what *I* want?"

"I could teach mathematics," he said. "We could open a school. You know calculus, history, we could teach in French and in English—"

"Remy, I don't speak *any* French—"

"Tant pis, je peux t'apprendre. Claire, I can teach you."

"A school."

"A school for girls. Your mother would approve."

"Don't tell me what my mother would have wanted," she snapped, but something in her was breaking. "What about our armies, on the western border of St. Cloud? What will happen to St. Cloud? You'll just hand us to the General?"

"I spoke with him last night on the King's barge," Remy said. "I told him I was leaving the country. He promised clemency. Even if he will not honor his promise, the King has agreed to keep me under the aegis of his protection until I sail for France tomorrow."

My God, if only he had spoken to me first. The note she had just delivered would contradict what Remy had done.

"Remy, I—tomorrow?" Claire squeezed her eyes shut. "Why on earth would you think I would go with you to France?"

"I thought about how you have freed me," he said, and he touched his forehead to hers. She could taste his breath, hot and sweet. "I thought that I have not been worthy of any task I have been set. Not tending to my province. Not tending to my people. And now—"

"And now what?"

"Did you see them, the Monticellans, cheering on that madman? What is it you think those people deserve?"

Claire had been trying to rid herself of the image since the night the mansion had burned. "I don't know," she said quietly.

"I think, perhaps, they deserve a madman. If that is what they want. And you and I deserve to be in a place that wants us."

"You want to run away with me."

"I think . . ." Remy's eyes clouded, wet, and then he blinked it away. "Yes. I think I see clearly, now."

Outside, she could hear the audience applauding. The performance had begun.

"Everything you just said is about you," she said. "You haven't answered my question."

He drew back a little to look at her. "What I am saying is that I know my own mind now, and I want to know yours. So tell me, Claire. What is it that you want?"

"You want to steal me away again," she whispered.

"I do," he said. "More than anything in the world."

Her arms crept up around his neck, and then she was on tiptoe, pulling him down to her. His mouth was soft, then insistent. His thumb came up to trace her jaw. Then he groaned low in his throat and pressed kisses to her neck, whispering something she couldn't quite hear, something like "mon coeur"—and that was when Claire pulled away.

"I wanted that," she said, flushed. "That was what I wanted."

What power did she hold over this man? What fascination? Was she the only thing he wanted that he thought he couldn't have?

Claire could touch him and touch him and touch him, but she could never make him better than he was.

She was powerless to change anyone other than herself.

"And you'll come," he was saying, disbelieving. "You'll come with me."

This man. This brilliant, starry-eyed, cowardly *man.*

"I wish I could," she said, and before he could stop her, she ducked under his arm and back out into the palace.

Standing behind the velvet curtains, she felt her heart in her throat.

Fields of lavender. Honeybees buzzing, hard at work. A knot of eager young women reciting their lessons on a veranda, gathering the lines of history to weave into a tapestry. A whole. A story that made sense.

And what on earth would she say to them about her part in it all?

If you follow my thread, you'll see where it ended.

I fled.

No. She could never forgive herself.

She could never sit in a lavender field thousands of miles away, knowing her home was ruled by such awful men.

For a minute, Claire buried her face in the curtain and let herself silently cry. Just until her pulse slowed.

On the stage, Daphne was calling on audience members as Miss Alexandra cast her wide net.

"I am sensing—a name that begins with a J. John? James? Has anyone here lost a loved one named James?"

Despite her despair, Claire had to stifle a laugh. The medium was beginning with the most common names in the country.

"Ah, yes—you, sir," Daphne said. "Please stand."

Miss Alexandra's voice, unctuous and urgent: "A spirit hovers over you. He wants me to tell you . . . yes, there's recently been a rift between you and a family member. A friend? A loved one. Some misunderstanding. Yes, this spirit—perhaps your grandfather? He wants you to make amends. . . ."

There was a smattering of applause, and the performance continued on. Really, it seemed an innocent entertainment. Miss Alexandra was careful to only give messages of unity and prosperity, to encourage her listeners to embrace their fellow men. There was no hint of drink in her voice. Claire was impressed.

She was impressed, too, by Daphne's sylphlike tone as she corralled the audience members. She called on raised hands, and Alexandra told their fortunes. "You are about to embark on a great journey," she told a woman, who responded drily, "Well, tomorrow I *am* traveling to Orleans to see my niece. . . ."

And then, ever so subtly, the medium began to build to her finale. The messages became clearer, more pointed. She was fishing for the well-known audience members now. The Governor of West Florida was told to beware a betrayal "like Cain and Abel"—the audience tittered, knowing he and his brother, the Governor of East Florida, had been at it for years. An oil tycoon's wife was told, by her "grandmother," not to spend all her money in one place.

Even the General was singled out. Daphne called on him in a voice so cool butter wouldn't melt in her mouth.

The medium told him that he was embattled, that he had been embattled for too long. That a woman's spirit hovered over him, imploring him to seek peace instead. "Thank you, ma'am," he boomed, "but I take my military advice from men," and the audience tittered.

Miss Alexandra paused. "You will see an end to this story soon," she said. Her voice was different, silvery and old. "Sooner than you may think. Those are all the messages I have for you, sir."

"You may sit," Daphne told the General.

"In a few moments, you will bear witness to the breath-taking illusions of the Wondrous Ducrot. But first I have some birthday tidings for the King."

"Who is hovering over me, Miss Alexandra?" the King called out gamely.

"Someone whose age you have now surpassed," she said. "Someone who loved you very much."

An uncomfortable silence settled over the room. Claire went very still.

The King coughed. "And what does he say?"

"A baseball team," Miss Alexandra said, and the crowd released a laugh. "A beautiful train."

"Yes," he said. "Of course."

"Two horses in the night. Two horses in the morning."

The room poised, as though on the head of a pin.

For Miss Alexandra, Claire had invented an innocent story about the King and littered it with true details. He and his brother planting roses, a recurring dream about a forbidden isle, a girl with red hair who had loved him, once, and the palominos they rode.

And now the medium recited those "visions" for the King in a voice distant and strange. "A vase of thorns. An island shrouded in mist. A girl taking tickets in New Teshas. So much digging. You in the rose garden, digging—"

"Enough," the King shouted. "Enough! Take this woman from the stage! Take her out of my sight! Guards!"

The scrape and clatter of chairs pushed back, men hustling. Running. A woman shrieked, once, and quick, hard footsteps went across the stage, someone's heels dragging against the floor—

I am so sorry, Miss Alexandra.

But she and Daphne had counted on this happening, and

with luck, Miller would be trailing the King's guards, ready for the next part of their plan to unfold.

"And now," the butler yelled, "the Wondrous Ducrot!"

The plan was never to kill the King. If you killed the King, you'd soon have another one. Someone else, someone worse, perhaps, someone determined to rip the country apart in his quest for power. Never mind that the King's nearest cousin was in Russia, that the one after him was three years old. Power abhorred a vacuum. It might require winning a war, but sooner or later, an ambitious man would be back on the throne of the First American Kingdom.

No, you couldn't kill the King. You had to kill the monarchy instead.

When Claire stole out into the rose garden, in the night, she was there to commit a murder.

This was the part of their plan that she couldn't control; it all depended on how well she knew the King. From what she'd seen of him at Wardenclyffe, in the King's Box, from what Aislinn Kelly had told her in the bowels of Adams Island. From what she knew of him now.

He couldn't come right to the garden. Not yet.

He had to go interrogate the medium first.

The guards had run inside when the commotion started, and Claire was able to slip immediately out and past the hothouses, the tulip beds, and around the corner of the palace to the little rose garden that the King wouldn't let anyone tend. She couldn't tell if the Wondrous Ducrot had taken the stage, but she could see through the giant windows into the ballroom that people were still milling around, and so she thought not. Questions, she knew, were being asked, questions about why the King had grown so upset at what the medium had said—he loved and missed his brother, surely, but that riding accident that had killed Ernest had happened years ago.

Was there something he was hiding? Why, the audience was asking, would he possibly be upset at the mention of an island in the mist?

The moon was nearly full, and under its light, the roses were limned in silver. Everywhere, these great wild profusions of roses, not tamed into rows or trained up trellises; these were flowers tended by an amateur, someone too hesitant, perhaps, to prune them back into pleasing shapes.

Or someone who wanted the bushes to conceal as much of the ground as possible.

A roving cloud covered the moon, and in the sudden shadow, Claire slunk low between a row of rosebushes and the brick wall of the palace, just outside the King's private quarters. The heavy door to his rooms was painted red. Always this door was guarded—why on earth wouldn't it be tonight?

But Beatrix and Miller had taken care of that.

From where she crouched, she could see the unconscious

guard, hands tied, tucked safely under a bush of pink damask roses. It was good that the night was warm, because he was only wearing his underclothes. They'd taken his uniform and his ring of keys, and left Claire a pair of shovels. And something else.

A pistol.

Quietly, as quietly as she could, Claire crept forward and took it in her hands, and then looked around for the Carolina roses.

The General would be here soon.

TWENTY-SIX

Claire heard the General before she saw him.

He walked like a man who had never hidden in his life, the heavy, swinging walk of a giant. Behind him, his cape twitched back and forth. The silver braid on his uniform gleamed.

He had her letter clutched in one hand, one of the two penned so expertly for her by Chester Barrington III—and his other hand on the gun in his holster.

> *General Montgomery,*
> *We must meet to discuss the terms of your stewardship of St. Cloud. Meet me before the final performance, in my private garden.*
> *A*

This was to be a friendly meeting with his liege. A meeting where the General would get everything he had ever wanted.

Why did he have his gun?

No matter. I can aim at him from here. Claire's hands twitched on her own pistol. She let the General pace as she worked up her nerve.

The plan had never been to kill the *King*.

Her gun must have belonged to the guard; she'd never held anything like it before. Miller had explained how to work the safety, check the chamber, how to aim, what to expect when the bullet was fired. "You feel it," he'd said, miming the kickback. "Especially if you've never felt it before." Now, in her hiding place, she tried to open the chamber to check on the bullets inside. She couldn't. Her hands were shaking too hard.

I am about to murder someone, she told herself. She couldn't quite believe it. *I will be forever a murderer.*

But she wasn't the only one rehearsing. The General was kicking his foot, looking at his pocket watch, worrying the ground a little with his toe. He was talking to himself.

"No, of course I didn't mean to do it," he was saying. "It was an accident—I came upon an intruder. No, no. Wrong. It was an accident—he thought I was an intruder, and you know the King, he's a bold man, bold with a gun, and he turned around and—but no, then how would the bullet end up in him? Bullets don't ricochet off brick, not really. Ha. Know that damn well. No, begin again. Get it right, they'll ask again and again. Remember, they love you in St. Cloud, they love you here. Again. I didn't mean to do it, it was an accident. . . ."

My God, Claire thought. *St. Cloud isn't enough for him. He's planning to kill the King.*

Why on earth should she be surprised? When had the General ever been satisfied with what he had? Remy Duchamp sailing off to Europe and leaving him the keys to the kingdom—that was too easy of a win. The General had a compulsion to take what he wanted by force.

Any scraps of regret fell away. From her hiding place under the bush, Claire lifted the pistol and cocked it.

The General whirled at the noise, gun up before him, aiming directly at her rosebush. "I hear you, you coward. Come out and face me like a man."

Claire didn't feel any fear. In fact she wanted to laugh at him, and so she did, a sneering laugh that he clearly couldn't place. It drove him to take a step back, his nostrils flaring in fear.

She laughed at him, long and hard, and then she fired three times at his chest.

Click. Click. Click.

There weren't any bullets in the gun.

Frantically she backed up against the brick wall, trying to fumble the chamber open. What had happened? Why would Miller leave her an empty pistol? The shovels were on the ground beside her, and she grabbed one, wild with fear, and below it were the bullets that Miller had left for her to load the gun with. How could she have made such a stupid mistake?

It was too late. The General was nearly upon her. He fired his gun once, twice, into the bushes, and the sound nearly deafened her, but somehow both of them missed. His gun was empty; he was reaching into a pouch on his belt to reload when Claire grabbed the shovel beside her. From the ground, she swung it up on a diagonal, hard, but he dodged. "You!" he hollered, fumbling to get his hands on her. "You little *bitch*, I had you locked away—"

Like a wildcat, Claire struggled, kicking and biting, and when she raked her nails across his face, the General lost his grip on her shoulders. His hands went into her hair instead, yanking hard, but her wig came off in his hands. She took his moment of confusion to swing the shovel again at his ankles, and the General fell hard to the ground.

She struggled to her feet, still holding the shovel as the General tried to pull something out of his boot.

A Derringer. A vest-sized pistol, the kind that could only hold a few shots.

"I've dreamed about doing this," he said, "every night since I met you," and he aimed the gun between her eyes.

In her head, Claire was watching herself die.

And then.

A sharpened hoe came down onto the General's face. Blood

sprayed up onto Claire's dress, onto her hands, her cheeks. The little pistol in his hands fired once on the impact, wildly, and his body jerked again, and then he was still.

Claire looked up. A grim-faced, dark-skinned woman in the King's livery looked back at her. She held the bloody hoe with gardening gloves. Behind her, a pair of empty-handed maids, and a third with something bundled in her arms.

All Claire could do was stare.

"My cousin Daphne sent me a letter," the gardener said softly. She eyed the General's body with some distaste. "I've never received such a letter. At first I thought it was a test, that someone was luring me into an act of treason. But then I read it again. And all she said was that there would be an evil man in the rose garden on the second night of the King's birthday celebration. She didn't say the King was the evil man. He is the only one who comes in these gardens, but she didn't say his name. So I knew it wasn't treason, not really."

Claire stood there stupidly, holding the shovel.

"I didn't know what little Daphne wanted me to do. But she was asking me, she knew I was a gardener. So I thought I'd maybe keep watch tonight with something sharp and see. Turns out there was something to be done."

"Thank you," Claire whispered, with tears in her eyes. "I don't know how to thank you."

"Looks like an important man, all that silver on his uniform," one of the maids said behind her.

"We could roll him up in a rug," the other said. "Stow him somewhere in our quarters. No one ever goes that way."

"They might, if a man like that goes missing."

"They'll look to the other military men first. Not the maids."

Daphne's cousin looked up at Claire. "Did you have any thoughts?" she asked, as gently as though she were asking a child what she would like for dessert.

"We need to bury him," Claire said hoarsely. "Under the Carolina roses. A shallow burial. We need to leave his hand above ground. Or a foot. Something people will notice."

The gardener looked back at one of the empty-handed maids. "Don't think you're needed, dear."

She didn't need to be told twice; she turned and headed back to the house. The third came up, and the bundle in her arms was a cloak and a dress. "I'll burn yours," she said. "Change into these."

"Thank you," Claire said again. "Let me dig first. Miss . . . what was your name?"

Daphne's cousin regarded her for a moment. "I didn't give it to you," she said finally.

"That's probably for the best," Claire admitted. "Ah, would you mind telling me which are the Carolina roses? I don't . . . I don't know flowers."

The three women took up shovels. Claire thrummed with a terror that made her movements quick and strong. When the hole was deep enough, two of them took the General's arms and the third his legs and together, they heaved his body in. Claire dumped a spray of loose dirt over his body. She left his right hand uncovered, the one with the signet ring.

If Aislinn's account was correct, they'd buried him on top of Prince Ernest Washington's corpse, right where the King had left it years ago. Ernest's corpse, with the King's stab wounds still visible against his rib cage.

"How can I thank you?" she asked the women, as she turned her old dress inside out so the blood wouldn't smear on the maid's uniform while she carried it.

"In her letter," the gardener said, "my cousin Daphne said you helped her escape a terrible place, at great risk to yourself." She eyed Claire. "I believe it. Tell no one you saw us."

"No one sees us anyway," the last maid said, and laughed. And before Claire could thank them again, the women disappeared back into the gardens.

Claire stood for a long moment in the night air, eyes closed, as the clouds chased each other across the moon. Then she walked over to the heavy red door that led to the King's private quarters and knocked three times.

It opened.

TWENTY-SEVEN

Miller ushered her inside the King's quarters. "You're shivering," he said, his hand on her back. "I take it you did what you needed to."

"It's done." Her voice still sounded strange to her. "There were some . . . complications."

"There always are."

"Are you alone?" she asked.

The rooms were dim, but she could see the glitter of Miller's eyes, the glint of the rifle on his back. "I am."

All at once, the lights around them flared impossibly bright. Claire's sight went dark red, then black, and she had to struggle not to shout.

When her vision finally cleared, she saw that Miller hadn't moved. He said, "I suppose I should tell you that you missed a conversation with an old friend of ours."

"My God, Miller," she said. "I thought Tesla was looking

for a new patron in the King. Why would he be helping us dethrone him?"

"Promised him what's left in the Duchamp coffers, enough that he won't ever be under anyone's thumb again. It's a better offer than being at the King's beck and call. This is the last political show he'll be a part of."

Claire rubbed her eyes. She was still seeing spots. "Was that Tesla's opening salvo?"

"Oh, no," Miller said with satisfaction. "He's been at this for a while."

"And the King?"

"Is where we need him to be."

She was unsteady on her feet—she reached out and found her hands on the back of a silk divan. With a shuddering sigh, she sat and hugged one of its pillows to her chest. "Tell me everything," she said, "while I try to gather myself."

The King had had his guards haul Daphne and Miss Alexandra off to be questioned, following hot on their heels, but after they bundled the women into a room, he had insisted that his men remain outside. He couldn't risk their hearing what the medium might know.

The King had murdered his older brother in order to inherit his throne. Any whisper that escaped his palace would soon turn into a deafening shout, a story plastered across every newspaper's front page. When he stepped into that room, he knew he had to silence the women inside it.

("I was there as soon as I could, but Miss Alexandra was . . . unwell." Miller paused. "Daphne said the King vowed to kill her family."

Claire's stomach twisted with guilt. "And Daphne?"

"You know her," he said. "She's made of iron. When I arrived—")

Miller wore the uniform he'd taken off the unconscious guard. The King's men tried to keep him from knocking, as they'd been instructed, but as they pulled him away he began to shout. "Your Majesty, there's some kind of disturbance. . . . There are horrible noises coming from your—your brother's old suite!"

The King's guards released him, unnerved, perhaps, by the way the lights in the corridor flickered. "Storm brewing?" one asked the other.

The hall went dark. The King flung open the door. Inside, Miller could hear Miss Alexandra weeping.

The King wasn't himself. He was sweating, pulling at the collar of his uniform. "Speak, man!"

"Your brother's rooms . . . we heard noises," Miller said. "Do you think it's an intruder?"

Behind the King, he heard Daphne cackling in the dark. "An intruder," she said, her voice low and dark as any medium's. "Yes, the ghosts are walking the palace tonight."

"Silence!" Sweat began to bead along the King's forehead.

Miss Alexandra's sobs crescendoed. "Don't kill them,

don't kill my brothers! Your Majesty, I meant you no harm—"

"Bad omens," Daphne said, an echo of the King's words from the ill-fated baseball game in Monticello. She and Claire had gone over and over them, getting them right. "Bad omens. All men must sit, or else we'll lose."

The lights again burst bright, and the King flung a hand over his face. "No," he said. "Avert—"

Daphne shoved back her chair. "Your brother is waiting."

The lights were humming, humming, humming.

"No," he said again. "Do you hear them? Do you hear the bees?" He clutched the doorframe. "Avert! Avert!"

"Pay the piper, Hiley," Daphne whispered.

"Ernie?" he asked brokenly. "Where's Ernie?"

Miller took a risk. "In his rooms," he'd said, and the King had paled even further and took off at a run into the palace's family quarters.

Growing up, after they'd left the nursery, Augustus and Ernest Washington had their suites next to each other. Each had a bedroom, a dressing room, and their own parlor, while their parents had their much larger suite in a separate hall. But after Ernest's death, the King had never taken up residence in the official monarch's quarters; he instead had kept the rooms of his adolescence, those that shared a wall with his brother.

And his brother's rooms had been shut up after his death, the furniture draped in cloth, the windows and mirrors covered. All was heavy with the smell of disuse, the kind of rooms into which a ghost could easily walk. After his brother's death, the King had ordered them sealed off; their exterior door, the one that, like his, led out to the pleasure gardens, had been boarded shut. In his grief, the King had been said to want to stopper up the past.

Tonight, Miller had held open the door to Ernest Washington's suite, and the King had rushed right in. Then Miller produced the ring of keys he'd taken from the guard and locked the King inside.

What the King didn't know was that Beatrix was waiting within. Unseen. She'd mewed herself up in one of the wardrobes, behind a hanging set of winter clothes, and she was busily whispering through the crack in the doors. "Hiley," she was whispering. "Hiley. Didn't you love your brother? Didn't you love him into the ground? You sit on a throne of lies. Tell the truth, Hiley. Tell them what you've done."

(Beatrix had a lightning rifle, just in case she was found. "Fingers crossed," she'd told Claire. "I have a five-page script to get through!")

"The King has left orders that he's not to be disturbed," Miller said, when one of the butlers came looking for the King to rejoin his celebrations. "He's paying respect to his brother, after that upsetting show with the spiritual medium. Tell the others."

Then he had come here, to the King's quarters, to wait for Claire.

"How long has he been inside?"

Miller pulled a face. "Awhile. I can hear him crying," he said, "but that's it. I know the second-best solution is for him to be packed off to an asylum—"

"Poetic justice," Claire said.

"—but the monarchy is still in place. And what then? The King's three-year-old cousin takes the throne, with the Governor of East Florida as his regent? The country will turn into a crocodile wrestling pit. We'll fall from the spit into the fire."

The lights convulsed again. She'd stopped startling when it happened, and if she'd grown used to it, the King couldn't be far behind.

"We don't have much time. He might be putting it all together, now—everything we're saying to him, he said to me first. And he knows . . ." She grimaced. "He knows I'm a worthy adversary."

"Then what do you propose we do?"

There was a humming coming from the bulbs above her head. It made her think of summer in Lordview, the flower beds their neighbors kept. The constant thrum of bees.

"Find our magician," she said. "Tell him we need noise."

"Little cat," Tesla was saying, a mess of wires in his hands. He wore rubber gloves, and his generator was at his feet on a small cart. "I did not think I would see you again."

"I didn't think I'd be alive, either."

"Not in that way." He frowned. "I rather thought you'd go to France."

"This is all darling, friends, but we only have a minute. The pacing inside has stopped." Miller had his ear to the door of Ernest Washington's suite.

"You say you need a hum," Tesla said, and bent to his generator. "After all the theatrics. Lightning, like the Norse gods, and rifles that shoot power, and now you say you want a *hum*—a hum, something you can make with your mouth—"

"A very loud hum," Miller said. "If that makes you feel better."

"The money will make me feel better." Tesla stood, clutching a pair of wires, one in each glove. Already they traded sparks.

Then a long arc of light.

Claire took a step back as the generator rattled and buzzed. Louder it hummed, against the marble floor. In the bursts of incandescent light, Tesla's face was oddly impassive. Was he disappointed in her? And for what?

They locked eyes, and Claire felt a surge of something she couldn't quite name.

I think this is the last time I'll see Nikola Tesla, she thought.

"He's weeping," Miller murmured, and took his ear from the door. He hammered on it with his fist. "Your Majesty, the hives! The hives from the garden! The bees!"

Tesla's generator began to smoke. Coughing, he waved

his hand to clear it, then thought better. He began wafting it under the door.

Just in time, Claire ducked around the corner and put her back to the wall. She willed her pulse to slow. Any moment now, the King would muscle down his fear. He would draw on his good sense. He would open his door to see this for the sham it was and prove himself a worthy adversary.

But a minute passed, and then another, and the door still didn't open.

Then she heard the edges of a low voice speaking inside Ernest Washington's rooms.

Miller's brow creased as he listened. "Yes, sir," he said. "Yes. Right away."

Claire took a breath. "What happened?" she mouthed.

"The King has called for his secretary," Miller said. "He says that his brother Ernest wants him to draft a statement."

TWENTY-EIGHT

The next day, it was splashed across the front page of the *St. Cloud Star*.

It was, of course, also in the *Philadelphia Herald*, and the *New Columbian*, and in every last newspaper that their great country boasted. In three-inch type, red ink: THE KING ABDICATES HIS THRONE. KING WASHINGTON: I KILLED THEM BOTH. The most salacious headlines Claire could ever have imagined the newsboys shouting on the corners.

When they'd gone to dig up Ernest's bones, under the Carolina roses in the King's rose garden, they'd found exactly what Claire had intended: General Montgomery's body directly above it, if off maybe two or three feet.

The King was denying that he'd had anything to do with the General's death, but on Montgomery's body, they'd found a note written in the King's own hand, asking to meet in the rose garden.

The King claimed forgery; of course he did. And few of the papers could explain why the King would admit to a years-old murder, a far more serious crime, while refusing to admit to one he'd likely be able to excuse. Surely the King had only acted in self-defense with the General. But the confession to Ernie's murder muddied the waters, made the King's story look even more suspect. Made the King himself look most unstable. The *New Columbian* was calling for the King to be sent to Adams Island to be evaluated.

But the *Star* was the one that everyone was buying, and they, at least, had gone in for some dignity in their headline: FRATRICIDE IN THE FIRST AMERICAN KINGDOM. And while the world had been remade while they'd slept, some things remained the same. The byline read John Mackenzie, not Lizzie Cochrane.

Who had something that the rest of the newspapers didn't.

A dossier of letters, a small sheaf of them, written over the course of a year between the King and one of his friends-turned-secretaries, Chester Barrington III. In a fit of conscience, Mackenzie's article read, Barrington had made these letters known to the *Star* after the chaos at the palace the night before. The King had been unstable for some time, his note to the paper had read: "See the enclosed correspondence for proof, sealed with the King's own seal."

(This was, of course, the forged correspondence that Barrington had provided to Claire and Miller when they'd come knocking.)

In the letters, the two men had been debating the merits of a democracy. The King confessed to being a student of history, a man who liked to pull at the threads of the story, as it were. How would his life be different if one small thing had changed? How would the lives of his citizens have changed? What if King George Washington, all those years ago, had resisted the pleas from his military to declare himself the country's monarch—what if he had stayed the course and committed to being their president instead?

Barrington had written back in a sprightly hand that, if the King were not the King, what he would be suggesting was treason. Why, how could a country hope to govern itself if the people voted their leaders into power? How could we trust the common man to make their own decisions? Surely they needed to be led. Surely they would choose poorly.

It was, Claire realized, the same argument Remy had made to her, that the people of St. Cloud deserved a ruler like the General. And perhaps that was the risk; perhaps, in a democracy, the people would choose the wrong leaders.

But even if they did, they would have the opportunity to choose again, only a few years later.

To choose better.

In the King's final letter to Barrington, he'd written that he'd come up with a plan. An election every five years. Term limits on the leadership of the country. He'd be able to ride the Royal Limited with his ball club, the beloved former monarch having forever signed away his powers to the new electorate. What did Barrington think?

"Barrington" hadn't replied. But the *St. Cloud Star*? They thought it a compelling idea.

The debate carried Claire through her next week, and beyond. She read about it each morning from her suite in the Fox Hotel; she debated Lizzie Cochrane over sandwiches at lunch, while Beatrix wired Rosa Morgenstern and asked her to meet at the palace with the heads of the Daughters of the American Crown, while Captain Miller sent missives back and forth to St. Cloud to understand the state of their finances and their military and their support, the state of their union. Tesla had decamped to parts unknown. In the chaos, he'd slipped out without saying goodbye to any of them. It was perhaps what they deserved for using him as they had.

Claire Duchamp, for her part, stayed out of it.

She awoke on the morning of the King's abdication and, after scanning the John Mackenzie articles with a tired smile, turned to the *New Columbian*. It took her a few minutes, but she found the thumbnail story about the luxury passenger ship leaving that day for Europe. She knew Remy would have taken one of its berths. Was he looking out the windows, dreaming of his new life?

A small voice inside her wondered, *Is he still thinking of me?*

She banished the thought. There was talk, now, all kinds of talk about who would govern not just St. Cloud, but the other provinces as well. Would the brothers of West and East Florida be expected to give up their fiefdoms just because their King had lost his mind? Certainly not, they wrote in their own editorials to their own province's newspapers, and the Governor of Nuevo Mexico, for his part, agreed with him. Charles Monroe of Livingston-Monroe was characteristically silent. It was said that he'd never quite gotten over the loss of his wife, though he'd at least released a statement that said that he didn't think immigrants had anything to do with her disappearance. Claire wondered who would decide Abigail Monroe's fate. She was still down in that dungeon.

They talked about the future, the five of them, Claire and Beatrix and Lizzie and Daphne and Miller, together in the messy sitting room of Claire's suite at the Fox Hotel.

"Power abhors a vacuum," Claire said, "and there isn't much time until a definite move will be made. Someone needs to make a bid for the highest seat of power. What are we calling it?"

"A presidency, I think," Beatrix said, nibbling a biscuit. "I still like prime minister better. It gives the sense that there are other ministers besides you, that you're just one voice of many."

Miller was sitting on the floor cross-legged, and Daphne was stretched out beside him. Claire had noticed, in the past few days, Miller's eyes catching more and more on Daphne's diminutive frame; it made sense. They'd spent so much time together in the last week, and they were both attractive and of an age. Her bravura performance as a spiritualist medium had perhaps been the thing to win him over. Miller loved a powerful woman—and Daphne was joking about taking her show on the road.

Beatrix found the whole thing delightful. Claire wasn't sure if it was her own desire to tie up loose ends, but she rather wondered, at times, about Beatrix and Lizzie, about the way they'd been looking at each other lately. She wanted her friends to be happy.

Maybe it was because she didn't know how to be happy herself.

"I think I'll be able to bring the Daughters of the American What-Have-You to heel," Beatrix was saying. "I've had some productive talks with Rosa Morgenstern. Sometimes I wonder what she would do if she were just . . . given an actual seat at the table. If she didn't have to kiss up to some man to have her voice heard."

Daphne snorted. "Do you honestly want to make her president just so you can find out?"

"God, no," Beatrix said. "But I think she'd be a pretty stupendous parliamentarian."

"Give it five years," Claire said. "Let's see if she reforms."

"Bea, you're talking about people like they're chess pieces." Lizzie laughed. "You can't just assign people roles. And anyway, what do *you* want to be doing?"

"Making things." Beatrix grinned at her. "I fully expect to be given some kind of ridiculous contract at the end of this. I can make gliders for the royal—er—the presidential fleet. For gobs of money. Wouldn't that be something? Live in a mansion with a big old workshop out back. One you can see from France! And . . ."

Beatrix was still talking, but Claire was lost again, looking down at her teacup, swirling the liquid around and around.

Miller tapped her toe to get her attention, and Claire startled. "You all right?"

"I'm having some trouble with all of this," she admitted.

"What trouble?" Daphne asked.

"I don't really know what I should be doing. I don't want to be some dinosaur, come lurching back in from the days of the monarchy. If we have any hope of setting up elections, of functioning like a real republic, I think all the remnants

of the old system need to be swept away. And besides . . ."
She laughed a little. "I'm eighteen years old, and I haven't
ever done anything but what other people want me to do.
These last few weeks aren't even the exception to that. I
never wanted . . . I never wanted to be a leader of men."

"Or women?" Beatrix asked, with an eyebrow raised.

"Or women, or anyone," Claire said. "I want . . ."

More than anything, in that moment, she wanted her
mother. She blinked away tears.

"You've had a hell of a run of it," Lizzie said gently. "I
imagine some rest would do you a world of good."

"Take a month," Daphne said. Beside her, Miller nodded.
"If you're really sure you don't want to be a part of this new
republic—"

"I want a new republic," Claire said, through her tears. "I
want to vote for my next president. I want everyone to have
their voices heard. But I don't want to be in charge. I want
you in charge," she said to Daphne, "and you, and you, and
even you, Miller—"

He snorted. "I'm just the brawn."

"Oh, stop. You know that isn't true." Claire rubbed her
eyes. "I just don't want to be the midwife, birthing this new
system into the world. I don't want to be the power behind
the throne. I don't want to be anyone's muse. I want . . ."

The fireplace crackled. Beatrix leaned back into the floral
sofa, kicking her feet up on the table, and Lizzie leaned over

to tweak her nose. Outside, the wind was rushing along the Philadelphia street, and Claire thought, for some reason, of Margarete, the sister that she'd always wanted, out there in Wardenclyffe Tower on the border between two provinces that might not exist this time next week, reading the letter she'd sent that deeded her Jeremiah Emerson's house in Lordview, now paid off in full. And she thought about her father, too, wherever he was, preaching his version of the world while the world around him remade itself. She thought about Nikola Tesla calling her his little cat, eating figs while he and Remy sorted out a superconductor problem. She thought, as she did all the time now, about Remy, her husband, who was quiet and good and not cowardly, in the end—he was a man strong enough to know when he wasn't fit for a job, to know when to step down and let the ones who wanted to lead do so. It had taken him too long, perhaps, but it had taken her a long time as well.

She thought about a house in Provence in a lavender field.

"I want to go to France," she said finally. "I think I left something there that I need to bring home."

EPILOGUE

They grew lavender, kept olive trees, tended the pines that bordered their property. It wasn't much, a few hectares—she was learning new ways to measure, here—but it bloomed with thyme and rosemary and the wild sweet garigue that somehow smelled like the sea. That morning, she was taking dried bundles of herbs down from where they hung in the rafters and crushing them with a mortar and pestle.

Beside her, Remy was trussing the chicken. "We should perhaps reconsider the midday meal."

"All together?" She tried out the words in French. They sounded like a cat's sneeze.

He smiled, but did not correct her pronunciation. His face was brown from the sun, and his fingers were busy with twine. She adored him this way, his collar open, his face unshadowed. "You know what I meant. We take an hour each day to cook for our students while they run like heathens in the yard."

It was true, the girls were chanting a song through the open window. It had a rhythm, a movement. She couldn't make out the words yet. But she was learning.

"Let them be hoydens." Claire passed him the mortar and pestle, and he scattered the herbs over a ramekin of butter, then worked it in with his hands. Before this summer, Remy had never made a meal for himself. And now, each day, the two of them cooked side by side. When it grew warm enough to brave the ocean, she planned a trip to teach him to swim.

"So many things I was not allowed to learn," he'd said to her. "How is it unmanly to not prepare your own dinner? I do not understand."

During the day, he taught botany, anatomy, the ongoing developments in electricity. Together they led a class for their three oldest students in calculus. She read to them poems by the Brownings and essays by John Ruskin and, when a bundle of newspapers made the monthlong journey to them from Lizzie Cochrane, she read to them of the revolution happening over in what was now simply called America. The girls thrilled to hear of the women in the highest positions of power. The first election would be held that fall.

But then Claire tucked the papers away. The girls went home. Remy had hired a gardener to show him how to work with the plants on their property, and she read novels on the divan while he buried his hands in the soil. In the beginning she'd thought sometimes of the General's shallow grave in the rose garden. Then days passed, and she thought of it less and less.

"A letter came for you," Remy said today, smearing the chicken all over with butter. "From Beatrix. She sent along schematics. She wants to fly across the ocean to see us."

"That must be a very big glider."

"I left it on your desk, if you want to reply. It's with . . ." He hesitated. "With the letter from your father."

It had come through the village mail, so at least he hadn't found their address. As long as she didn't open the envelope, she could believe that it might be an apology, and so she left it unread for days. Finally she'd poured herself a glass of wine, and Remy had read it to her.

It was a short note, stilted. Jeremiah Emerson wrote to ask if his daughter was well. He wrote that he did not know how she had given up so much power. And he wrote to ask for money, as he had lost what little he had. If she could touch the envelope with an ungloved hand, he would treasure it forever.

"Will you call the girls in to eat?" she asked Remy.

"I will," he said, and dropped a kiss on the top of her head. Then she took his collar with her herb-stained fingers and pulled him in again.

Claire watched him through the window. Tonight she would burn her father's letter in the fireplace. Then she would write Beatrix, asking her to please take a passenger ship for this first visit.

And tonight, Claire would have her dinner in the garden with her husband.

When she'd arrived at his door, bags in hand, the first thing he had done was to call in the village priest. They were married now in truth.

"Come join us," one of the girls was calling, and Claire washed her hands clean, and did.

AUTHOR'S NOTE

In sixth grade, I wrote a book report on Elizabeth Blackwell for my history class. When she applied to Geneva Medical College to study medicine, the faculty let their male students vote on whether a woman should be admitted to their ranks. As a joke, they voted yes. That was how the first woman successfully graduated from medical school: she had the bravery to stand up to an entire school of men who saw her as a mockery. When I read out that part of my book report in class, the boys snickered behind their hands.

At boarding school, I remember lying in my top bunk, reading novels by Sarah Waters and Margaret Atwood and A. S. Byatt. I was swept away by the ghosts and séances in their nineteenth-century stories; their women's prisons and "lady visitors"; the girls living with their "special friends," their love an open secret; the dramatizations of the racist and sexist "science" of phrenology. I loved reading about con artists and reformers and suffragettes. In college I read Sir Arthur Conan Doyle's *The History of Spiritualism*—if his name rings a bell, it's because he's the creator of everyone's favorite logician, Sherlock Holmes—where he professed his sincere belief in the ability to communicate with the dead. (Doyle's wife was a spiritual medium who once very much offended Harry Houdini by claiming she had received messages from his dead mother.)

In my doctoral program in English, studying Victorian and Edwardian literature, I was stunned by how many novels of that time dealt matter-of-factly with the horrors of the institutionalized woman. If you had inconvenient opinions, if you loved inconvenient people, if your existence made a man's life harder in any way, you could be committed to an asylum against your will. Game over. (If you haven't read Wilkie Collins's novel *The Woman in White*, which gleefully dissects this phenomenon, you should!) I read *Ten Days in a Mad-House*, the journalist Nellie Bly's exposé of the terrible conditions for patients on Blackwell's Island (no relation to the good doctor Elizabeth), which she discovered by going undercover as a "madwoman." That short book is ferociously smart and at times darkly funny, and in *Manifest*, Claire's struggles on Adams Island echo Bly's own. Bly's real name was Elizabeth Cochran; my Lizzie Cochrane is named in honor of her.

My First American Kingdom is a Frankenstein's monster, built from these ideas and images and from those in my imagination. As I researched this duology, I read piles of books: firsthand accounts and textbooks and almanacs and some very scandalous biographies—here's to you, Victoria

Woodhull. I read too much about Thomas Edison and Nikola Tesla's "current wars." (As my books probably make clear, I am very much Team Tesla.) Of course I read *The Devil in the White City* again. I spent long days, too, looking at beautiful World's Fair memorabilia in university libraries, and I dog-eared almost every page in my copy of *Chicago by Day and Night: The Pleasure Seeker's Guide to the Paris of America*, which serves as both a terrific introduction to the Fair and also, weirdly, the present-day stock market. Perpetua's dance hall in *Muse* was plucked from 1902, where it was called the Everleigh Club and where, in fact, a prince did sip champagne from a courtesan's shoe.

And I did things other than read. I played BioShock: Infinite for the third time and marveled anew at their World's Fair gone horribly wrong—I described it once as an Epcot Americana for the Damned. I spent a long night grilling the bartender in the Chicago Athletic Association—a beautiful World's Fair building that's now a hotel—about the CAA's history and about the ghosts she'd maybe seen there. In western New York, I visited the Lily Dale Assembly, a gated town full of psychics, and attended a service at their spiritualist church. During the message service, a medium told me that she saw the spirit of my grandmother watching over me. I cried as I drove away. I believed, and I didn't believe.

There were so many horrors in the nineteenth century, as there are now. So many voices that went ignored, experiences no one wanted to look at too closely. I think often about the difficult, decades-long friendship between Frederick Douglass and Susan B. Anthony as they fought for equal rights for Black men and white women, at times partners in that fight, at times adversaries. My (invented) Daughters of the American Crown are, I hope, a commentary on the perils of white feminism, of what happens when those women grab what they can from the patriarchal buffet, and damn everybody else. I think too about the fun I had writing zany séance scenes, when in fact so many historians attribute the nineteenth-century spiritualist craze back to the mass casualties of the Civil War, when nearly everyone had a dead loved one—or two, or three—who they were desperate to speak to again.

Even though there are many horrors in my alternate America, as a white woman writing this novel in 2020, I did not want to design an America from the ground up that had ever practiced slavery. I talked to many friends and editors and fellow writers about this decision and am still unsure if it was the right one. I did know from the beginning that I wanted to write an America that could put a Black woman in its highest seat of power.

As for Claire, once she leaves her father's house and the toxic stew of privilege, isolation, and abuse she grew up in, she begins to overcome her own myopic suffering enough to understand the suffering of others. I like to think of her teaching at a school in Provence, doing her best to make a space for other women to have their voices heard.

This began as an annotated bibliography; somehow, it grew into this author's note. For a full list of books I consulted and thought about while researching the Muse duology, please see my website, brittanycavallaro.com.

ACKNOWLEDGMENTS

Thank you so much to my wonderful editor, Ben Rosenthal, for your care, intelligence, and compassion as we worked on this book together. This was a difficult one, and it's not an exaggeration to say that it would not have been possible without you. Thank you so much, too, to Katherine Tegen, for making such a wonderful home for my novels, and to the team at KT Books and HarperCollins, especially Julia Johnson, Aubrey Churchward, Team Epic Reads, and everyone else who supported this project.

Thank you so much to my terrific agent, Taylor Haggerty, for your insight and kindnesses during an impossible few years. Thanks too to everyone on the team at Root Literary, especially Melanie Castillo. Kristin Dwyer, you are an angel. Thank you for your pep talks and tireless support.

Thank you to Emily Henry and Jeff Zentner, for everything. Emily Temple, Kit Williamson, Chloe Benjamin: thank you. Thank you to Joe Sacksteder, for the title and the friendship, and to Mika Perrine, and to everyone else at Interlochen. And thank you to my students, for reminding me each day with their enthusiasm and joy why I want to write books.

Thank you to my family, to Mira and Avery, to Ann Marie, to Daisy, and to everyone else who helped me make a home this last year. Thank you, endlessly, to Andrew. For once I am well and truly without words.